Have We MET?

Have We MET?

a novel

CAMILLE BAKER

LAKE UNION
PUBLISHING

Published by Lake Union Publishing, Seattle

www.apub.com

Amazon, the Amazon logo, and Lake Union Publishing are trademarks of Amazon.com, Inc., or its affiliates.

ISBN-13: 9781542029858
ISBN-10: 1542029856

Cover illustration by Tyler Mishá Barnett

Title treatment by Philip Pascuzzo

Printed in the United States of America

To Grandmother, voracious reader and keeper of the best stories. I love you endlessly.

CHAPTER ONE

Bessie is trying to kill me.

It's the only explanation as to why she's behaving like this. Two months ago, she handled the sixteen-hour drive from Houston up to Chicago like the champ she is. Well, *was?* Now I'm not so sure. Dashboard lights I've never seen before illuminate, and even as I'm pressing the gas pedal as far as it can go, Bessie decelerates. When I first see the flashing lights outside, I think it must be lightning interspersed with the heavy rain, but no. Bessie has decided to compromise my visibility, too, because those are my headlights wavering.

With angry cars beeping at me, oblivious or indifferent to my turmoil, I navigate my car to the right lane of the highway to take the next exit. If Bessie gives out on me altogether, the last place I need to be is on the side of this shoulder-less section of I-290. The access road is congested with people trying to beat the highway traffic, but they steer clear as my tires start hydroplaning. I turn at the first light and then again, off the busy street to find a safe place to stop. When I remove my foot from the accelerator to brake, Bessie shoots forward as if possessed, a warning symbol blinking on my dashboard. My steering wheel locks up and I swerve. An unpleasant popping noise sounds, immediately followed by a dip as I hit a deep pothole.

This brings Bessie to a halt. I put her in park, and the dashboard lights disappear. Scoffing at her audacity, I pull up my coat hood so I can run out and get a look at my tire, hoping a simple change to my spare will do.

"Damn," I curse under my breath, noting the wonky angle of my wheel. This won't be drivable, even if I am willing to risk whatever the hell else is going on with Bessie. I get back in the car, shivering. It's nearly forty degrees, which delusional meteorologists insist is mild for the end of February. The temperature is expected to drop overnight, creating icy roads. Not for the first time, I wonder if moving here during the winter was a subconscious self-punishment.

Taking a deep breath, I force myself to figure this out. I start with calling AAA to order my tow, ignoring the instinct to call my mom first. After a lengthy hold time, in which I cave and text my mom a preview of the situation, I get connected to an agent. She follows the normal checklist of questions before getting to the sending-help part.

"I'm seeing you're located off Harrison and Racine?"

I falter, the combination of those street names strikingly familiar, though I haven't been on this side of town since I moved. I glance around me, but it's too dark to see much, other than the few homes with porch lights. Guess I'll have to trust their GPS locator.

"That's right," I confirm.

"I'm dispatching a tow truck now. His estimated arrival time is two hours."

That means I won't get home until well after ten o'clock, per their policy requiring me to be here when the tow driver arrives. I glance at the grocery bags in my back seat. After my temp gig today, I picked up some things for the weekend. Things like wine, frozen fruit for my breakfast smoothies, and a half gallon of ice cream.

"Is it too late to change my answer on that first question? The one about if I'm in a safe place?"

"Yes," she says in a flat, unamused tone. "It'll be two hours, ma'am. It's a busy night."

The agent hangs up before I completely get out the words, "I understand."

I call my mom, intending to chat with her while I put the plastic-ware stashed in my glove compartment to good use and eat enough ice cream to ensure it won't melt over the edges of the container. I hear the jazz music in the background before her voice.

"Corinne, baby, what's up?"

"Where are you?" I ask instead of answering her question.

"At the jazz lounge with your auntie." She laughs away from the phone, and I hear my aunt's voice in the background. Just a few months ago, I lived in the same house with my mom, my aunt, my two young cousins, and my brother whenever he was home from school. Nice to know not much has changed since I left.

"Did you get my text?"

"No, hold on."

I wait for her to check her phone and put her ear back to the receiver. "Did you call—"

"Yep, they said it would take two hours to get someone here."

"Typical. Where are you?"

"Harrison and Racine. There's a storm, but I'm fine."

"That's near the West Side, where we used to live."

I knew it sounded familiar! Suddenly, I recall my mom making me recite directions to our neighborhood. If I needed to describe where our house was to a "responsible adult," I could. My heart squeezes as I realize that since it's where we used to live, it's where my best friend Joelle's parents still live, in the house they've owned for decades.

"It's near your cousin Tiwanda too. You should give her a call." The saxophone in the background starts a dazzling solo, and my mom and aunt both whoop into my ear. "Okay, Cori. Text me updates, baby."

I blink at my phone's screen when she hangs up. Postretirement Mom swings back and forth between modes like a pendulum. The first mode is *I got time on my hands. You mentioned you were considering changing vitamins? Here's ten pages of research I found.* The other mode is *Sorry, I'm busy living.* I'm here for both, to be honest. But right now, her being in the latter mode is not convenient for my situation at all.

I go to the contacts on my phone to find Tiwanda, the not-really-my-cousin Mom has been nagging me to connect with for weeks. She's a cousin of my cousin, so she counts, according to my mom. Instead, I find myself pulling up Joelle's contact info, which I'll probably never get around to deleting no matter how long she's been gone. I chew on the corner of my lip as I consider her home phone number. I had been planning on dialing it since I first moved back here. Reconnecting with Joelle's parents tops my to-do list, but I keep putting it off for reasons I don't care to confront.

I call the number, ignoring the reservations that have prevented me from reaching out for the past two months.

A high-pitched three-tone noise greets me. Their house phone is disconnected. I laugh to myself—a small, self-pitying noise. I couldn't contact them if I wanted to.

My phone flashes with a text from Mom. It's a screenshot of texts between her and Tiwanda. Looks like she had time for a little bit of the other retired-mom mode as well. Tiwanda sent her address but can't drive to get me because she's been drinking with the friends she has over. I'm slapped with the reminder of her text from two weeks ago telling me this get-together was happening—a belated "twenty-fine" birthday celebration. I promised to get back to her and never did. I plug her address in an app, and up pops a ten-minute walking route.

My umbrella is feeble—the kind that gets you more drenched with it than without. I'd have to take the ice cream, of course. And maybe bring the wine as a thank-you for taking me in. I spend a few minutes preparing myself: zipping up my coat, securing my hair inside the hood so my twist out isn't completely ruined, and consolidating all my items into one bag. I forgo the umbrella and get a move on.

Tiwanda's condo is a second-story unit on Washington Boulevard. Music greets me as I reach her floor. I add my boots to the others lined outside her door and knock, not bothering to worry about my appearance. After you spend a few minutes walking in the pouring rain, you tend to stop caring about a lot of things.

Tiwanda swings the door open with the gusto of someone immensely enjoying the party they're hosting.

"Cousin!" she yells as she throws her arms around me. "You're soaked!"

Before I can give her more than a look conveying my absolute exhaustion, she's pulling me in. There are at least ten people here. It's spacious enough for me to navigate without sprinkling anyone. Still, Tiwanda grandly extends her arm to clear the way. We veer into the kitchen to drop my grocery bag off.

"Corinne brought ice cream!" she announces to people I definitely did *not* bring ice cream for. Then she leads me to her room and pulls out a pair of sweatpants and a Bears T-shirt. I hang my clothes on a laundry rack in the corner. Tiwanda says she will throw them in the dryer later, when the noise it causes won't clash with the music playing in the living room. After changing, I check my phone. Nothing. AAA hasn't dispatched anyone yet. I text my mom that I'm safe at Tiwanda's—not that she cares much while being serenaded with smooth jazz. Then I rejoin the party in my marginally improved outfit.

Out in the living room, people lounge on the couch, eating my ice cream out of paper bowls. Four people have taken over the television and are playing an aggressive version of Mario Kart that includes pushing each other when they are ahead.

Tiwanda is laughing with an Asian woman sporting a flattering diagonal-bang cut. In lieu of disrupting them, I seek sustenance. The array of food in the kitchen has been well picked over, but there are enough wings, pizza, and veggies left to make a good plate.

"Here," a guy says as I wait for the microwave to finish reheating my food. He's holding out a shot of clear liquid to me. "It's your welcome gift."

"You're gonna have to be more specific," I say.

Tiwanda and Bangs Chick enter the kitchen. I think she'll be my ticket out of this until she says, "Pour one for us too!"

"I'm Elise," Bangs Chick says with a wave. She has delicate tattoos dotting her skin. *Fearless* is inked in thin script along her left collarbone, a tiny symbol peeks out from behind her ear, and a colorful flower flashes on her inner wrist as she greets me.

"Oh, right, she is," Tiwanda says, apparently realizing that even though she shouted my name to everyone in the apartment, I don't know any of theirs. She slides a container of limes closer to us while the guy focuses on not spilling the tequila.

"I'm happy you made it," Elise says. "Tee has been talking about her cousin who moved here for weeks. We started to think you were imaginary."

Tiwanda elbows Elise, more of a lean than a strike. "I wish it wasn't raining. More people would have shown up for you to meet."

I widen my eyes at the notion of considering this a poor showing. It's been a while since I've socialized. In fact, the last time I attended a gathering with mostly strangers, it was for a memorial service. So yeah, this group is the perfect size for easing back in.

"True," Elise says as she selects a lime wedge from the bowl. "Cory and Bebe Bri aren't here."

"That's not because of the rain," Tiwanda says with a side-eye to Elise.

"Okay, what are we toasting to?" our shot jester asks.

"To my cousin Corinne!" Tiwanda says, jostling her shot glass so that it comes perilously close to spilling.

"She exists!" Elise shouts.

I haven't had shots in a while and am surprised my body takes it well. It goes down smooth, and the lime takes the bite off. It's easy for the couple who come into the kitchen seconds later to convince us to do another round with them.

Tiwanda lovingly kicks some of her friends away from the small dining table and brings out a deck of UNO cards. The table is only meant for four, but we squeeze six of us there, making it difficult to hide your hand. Plus, Tiwanda sets up rules that include taking a drink whenever you lose a turn or draw cards. It's a mess, and no one really wins. UNO turns to Jenga turns to Bananagrams, each with drinking rules set up to get everyone very tipsy. For someone like me—who is both losing terribly in each game we've played so far and contending with a weakened tolerance—a nap right on the table is a definite possibility.

I simultaneously feel the loss of the social life I haven't had since Joelle moved from Houston and understand I haven't actually missed much in these past months. This would never happen in Houston. Here, no one painfully oblivious asks me of Joelle's whereabouts. Better, no one quietly acknowledges her absence without facing it head-on. Problem is, I can't decide which is preferable: the guilty relief of not having to reckon with it or the reassuring pressure of having people around who know that Joelle was once a vital part of me.

My phone vibrates on the table, a local phone number displayed on the screen.

"My car, yay!" I swipe my phone up and answer it.

"Tell them to tow it somewhere, and we'll get it in the morning," Tiwanda is saying for the third time, making it harder for me to hear the tow truck driver. The music isn't helping, and neither are the folks shouting at their video games.

I stand up to get away from the table, tripping over a rise in the area rug. I slip outside the sliding balcony door, where people have been going out to smoke intermittently. Thankfully, with the door closed it's quiet. The rain has slowed to a light pattering. In the distance, lightning traces the storm's path.

"Sorry, I'm here. Hello?"

"Ma'am, I'm at your car and—"

The door opens again, and out comes the noise with a new group of smokers. I find myself shushing them like I'm a kindergartner, but they don't hear me. I press my hand to block my free ear while I strain to listen with the other.

"Can you tow my car to the nearest place?" A more sober me would have had an exact destination in mind.

"We need you here, ma'am."

"I can be there in like five, ten minutes. Can you wait?"

I don't know what's happening behind me, but there's a surge of noise as the group begins laughing. I turn to ask them to be quiet for a second so I can discern what the driver is saying. But my movements are more fluid, less focused than usual. My arms swing, and my hand loosens just enough for my phone to slip out. Not to the balcony floor. Oh, no, that would be too easy. My phone flies over the railing, through the misty air, and down, down to the ground stories below.

CHAPTER TWO

I groan as I wake up, turning and kicking at the thin blanket tangled around my legs, nearly falling over the side of the firm bed. A bed much firmer than the one in my apartment—the one my mom insists is terrible for my back.

I scan the room and recognize my coat hanging in the corner, which helps to jog my memory. I'm still at Tiwanda's. Low voices sound from the other side of her closed bedroom door. Is the party still going on? I pop up out of bed so quickly, it makes my head spin and thump a warning.

"She's risen!" Elise says as I emerge from the hallway and into view of where she's lounging on the couch in pajamas. The space is much different from the cluttered mess I remember from the party. There's no trash lying around and no excess of people.

"Finally," Tiwanda says. She's leaning over the bar counter that separates the kitchen and the living room. "Do you want some Tylenol? A green smoothie?" She holds up the blender, an offering and an explanation of why I awoke abruptly.

"Both," I say. "How long have—" The clear plastic bag filled with rice on the counter makes me stop short. I hurry over to it. "Is that my phone in there?"

Hazy memories flood me, the most prominent of which is my phone flying over the balcony.

Elise joins me at the counter. "Good news is the screen wasn't broken. Bad news: I suspect the puddle broke its fall."

The sound I make is closer to that of a wounded animal than a human.

"My neighbor told me you were going down the back staircase outside. He was worried; it gets slippery out there when there's rain or ice. Anyway, I went down after you. Almost busted my ass for you, cuz."

"Me too," Elise sings. "I was the most sober one of the three of us. Figured I'd have a better chance finding your phone."

"Thanks," I say, poking the bag of rice with my finger. "What actually happened?"

"Well, I didn't really have to do much. When we got down there, you were sobbing over the puddle." Elise twists her lips to the side. I don't know if she's grimacing or trying not to laugh.

"Girl, I thought the lightning was going to get you before we could," Tiwanda says, shaking her head.

"How long has it been in there?" I ask.

"About ten hours. You should leave it for at least twenty-four hours, but forty-eight would be best," Elise advises. *As if,* I think.

"I don't have time for that. I need to check on my car, and I'm hoping to get called for a temp job next week." I break open the bag of rice to make sure none of the grains made their way into my ports. They're clear, so I press the power button and wait.

Tiwanda places two glasses of green smoothie on the bar surface. Elise takes one and slides into the seat beside me. The logo fills the screen—a good sign. But it lingers, taking forever to prompt for my passcode. I take the pills Tiwanda gives me and listen passively as she and Elise talk about all that happened last night and this morning. Apparently, six other people had to spend the night and were spread out between the guest room, the living room couch, and the inflatable bed Tiwanda keeps in her storage closet. The three of us shared Tiwanda's bed. I vaguely remember hitting what I thought was a large body-shaped pillow. Even the king-size mattress was a tight squeeze for us.

My phone's screen changes, and I jerk in my seat. It's now flashing the dead-battery symbol. *Shoot.*

"Can I borrow your charger?" I ask whoever responds first.

"You sure? There might still be water in there," Elise says. But she's already pushing herself off the stool and toward where her phone is plugged in beside the couch. She unplugs it and hands the charger over. As a precaution, I blow into the ports of my phone like it's a dusty Nintendo 64 cartridge.

"If you get electrocuted, the medical district is a few blocks down Taylor Street."

"We'll drive you there so you don't have to pay the ambulance fee," Tiwanda adds.

I scoff. "I'm not going to get electrocuted." *I think.* Tiwanda and Elise stare in dramatic anticipation as I plug it in. My phone vibrates the moment it's connected, the buzz making all of us jump.

Elise chuckles, her pitch rising a note from the shared nerves.

The charging screen goes away, and my phone powers on. Tiwanda leans across the kitchen counter to see better. The background picture of me and Joelle, taken a few Halloweens ago, fills the screen. Our outfits referencing popular memes of that year usually make me smile. But now, I tap the screen, willing my apps to populate and cover it. I don't want to answer any questions about Joelle. One day, I won't equate coping with avoiding bringing her up in regular conversations, but that day isn't today. My usual apps appear with a flash, then disappear and are replaced by a single option. Right in the middle of the screen.

"So it's working. That's good," Tiwanda says and returns to her side of the bar. She begins to rinse out the blender.

"I don't know, this is weird . . ." I swipe my screen a few times, and it appears to move, but the same app remains in the middle, no matter how many times I try. Its logo is a hot-pink icon with a white heart-shaped cutout. I lift the phone to my face to read the short name across the heart: MET. I don't recognize it. "Did anyone download an app on my phone?"

"Would that have occurred before or after you flung it into the puddle?" Tiwanda says offhand.

Elise takes the phone from my hand and adds, "Let me see," as she pushes the screen to open the app. "It's working." Her face scrunches up. "Fingerprint and face ID required," she reads off the screen. "Maybe it's a banking app?"

"I don't even have face recognition. Ugh, I can't afford a new phone right now." My mom is already paying my first four months' rent to slow the depletion of my savings. No telling how much my car is going to cost to get fixed. My phone makes a noise—the short, deep tone of denial.

"Access denied," Elise says, sliding the phone back to me.

Maybe I downloaded it and forgot. Or . . . "Maybe it's a virus that's installed to steal our biometrics. Fingerprint and facial recognition, in this case."

Tiwanda shoots me a look full of skepticism. "Your phone already has all that. Never mind the shitload of cameras that have seen your face."

She's right, of course. I sigh and press my finger to the scanner. It shouldn't work, because if I don't remember downloading the app, I sure as hell didn't take the time to set it up. Plus, the storage space remaining on my phone has been at warning level for a while. In last month's purge, I had to delete half my apps, including the science-and-technology-terms-in-ASL app featuring my brother as a model signer.

I feel the slight tremor of my fingerprint being accepted and then hear a shutter sound as my camera undoubtedly captures my image. I gape at it but don't have time to feel properly bewildered that this app accessed my camera without permission, because a moment later, the screen goes white. Across, in script font, a welcome message appears:

Welcome to Met, Corinne.

CHAPTER THREE

I press the home button to check on the rest of my phone, but this blasted app won't let me exit. Elise swats away my attempts.

"Let's see what it does," she says.

Tiwanda finishes washing the blender parts, sets them to dry, and then joins me and Elise on our side of the counter. She takes matters into her own hands and pushes the "Next" prompt that has popped up at the bottom of the screen. Nothing happens. She taps several more times.

"Elise told you to let it sit in the rice longer. We can go by the tech-repair shop after we make sure your car hasn't been scrapped."

I press "Next" myself, and it responds immediately.

Have you met your soul mate?

Elise, Tiwanda, and I exchange looks.

I scrunch up my nose. That answer would be a resounding *no*. I don't doubt the existence of soul mates. In fact, I had one. Mine came in the platonic form of my best friend, Joelle. Plus, I've heard stories that are qualifiable proof it's a thing that happens for some people. But a soul mate in the romantic form, brought to me by an app I never asked for? No.

The question slides to the top of the screen, making way for two options:

Don't Want to Know on the left. Reveal the Answer on the right.

"If I say I don't want to know, can I exit this thing?" My thumb hovers over the left.

Elise and Tiwanda loudly object at once.

"This is like that grade-school game with the folded paper," Tiwanda says. "Choose a number to find out who you'll marry. Or MASH."

"Ooh, I loved those," Elise says. "What is this app called? I'll download it and do it myself."

We wait for Elise to get her phone, pull up the app store, and search for Met. There are a few similar apps but none match the logo. It's not available. How did an app not in the app store get downloaded on my phone? Now I start to feel intrigued. I take a resigned breath and press Reveal the Answer.

The screen clears, and a timeline appears across it as if stretching into the distance. It's numbered from zero to twenty-seven—my age. Yet another thing I have to worry about when I check for identity theft. The black timeline is traced in glowing pink on a loop, as if waiting for the answer to be puzzled out. Tiwanda's and Elise's heads inch closer to the screen. Then it pings.

Yes.

There's silence for one, two, three seconds before I break. My sudden laughter causes both Elise and Tiwanda to jump back. Their bewildered expressions must mean they truly do think I'm off-balance, if showing up to a party soaking wet with a half gallon of ice cream didn't do the trick.

"Are . . . you happy?" Elise asks.

It takes two attempts before I successfully quell my laughter and follow-up giggles. "About what? This app is beyond dramatic. Can I delete it now?"

I press the home button, and this time, it allows me to exit. All my apps are back! I check twice to make sure, then pull up my phone log, where I see I've missed a few calls from my mom. I stand and drift farther into the living room to call her back.

She puts me on hold immediately upon answering. I listen to her background conversation, trying to glean details of her whereabouts as I await her attention. There are several people around her, so I know before she gets back on the phone this will be a short convo.

"Okay," she says, upbeat. "Tiwanda told me you dropped your phone in water?"

"Something like that. It's working now, but I still haven't figured out the car. AAA, uh, didn't work out."

"Ask Tiwanda if her aunt still works on cars. If not, she probably has a good place you can take it. Call AAA again. I've paid them too much over the years for them to not fix this."

That's right, my mom sponsors my AAA service. Which means it's probably not a good time to ask if she'd be willing to pay for the car repairs if the estimate comes out too high. I'll have to cross that bridge when I get to it.

"Text me how it goes, Cori. I have to get back."

"Back to what?" I start to ask, but she has already disconnected. Wow, is this the same mother who cried when I told her I was moving?

"Thanks for updating my mom," I tell Tiwanda.

"She called me last night after your phone kept going to voice mail. Surprised whatever I said was comprehensible." She shakes her head at the memory of her drunk self. For not being technically related, we sure could pass. Her brown skin tone is a touch darker than mine, and we have similar nose-cheekbone structure. As I marvel at how swift the solace of being around quasi-family is, Tiwanda slaps her palms together. "Okay. Your phone works; that only leaves your car."

"I'll call for the tow now, and we can get dressed and meet them there."

In the late-morning hours on a Saturday—after the previous night's storm made way for a deceivingly sunny, frosty day—the tow service is blessedly faster. It takes them only forty-five minutes to get there. The tow truck driver confirms I have a busted tire and speculates about an additional problem with the wheel or possibly the axle. Tiwanda's aunt recommends a shop. It isn't the closest to my apartment, but having someone vouch for it is worth the planning it'll take for me to either get a ride or catch a bus over there.

"We're getting lunch," Tiwanda declares. "This is way too much activity on a Saturday, partially hungover and with only a smoothie in my stomach."

We park outside Tiwanda's building and walk a few blocks in the frigid air to a diner trying very hard to maintain an old-school vibe. There are plenty of tables available, so we snag a booth near the windows.

"I should probably go home soon," Elise says after we order our food and hand over the menus to our waitress. "Maybe I'll swing by and check on Cory on the way."

My confusion must be easy to interpret, because Elise clarifies.

"Our friend is going through a breakup."

I realize they've been talking about this sporadically since I woke up, but I dismissed it because it didn't involve me. Not to mention I have other problems on my plate that would appreciate if I gave them a bit more attention. "My mom calls me Cori."

"Well, with the other Cory, you kind of entered a friend Civil War."

Tiwanda groans. "Having Brian around was cool, but Cory had us first. It's like the Union and Confederacy. There's not really a choice here."

Our food comes out, and we chat between mouthfuls. I tell Tiwanda and Elise all about the exciting world of temp work. Tiwanda works long hours as an auditor. Elise works in information technology. Their apparent stability piques my envy, but soon I learn Tiwanda is feeling overworked, and Elise is handing in her two-weeks' notice on Monday. She'll be doing freelance work while she gets back to her first love—theater. It's clear we're all giving adulting our best go.

My phone sounds from my purse. It takes me a moment to realize it's mine, because I keep my phone on silent. Before checking the reason for the chime, I verify the tiny volume-control switch on the side is still on my preferred mode. Strangely, it is, despite the insistent noise moments ago telling me otherwise. This is the second glitch I've noticed since I dug it out of the rice this morning. Maybe it's a side effect of the water damage.

I don't immediately recognize the notification banner. It's not a text message or call, or any one of my apps that usually bother me with alerts.

"Is it Met?" Elise asks right as I read and confirm it is. She scoots closer to me in the booth. I put my phone flat on the table so Tiwanda can see too. They're the reason I even entertained this app, so they are tethered with me now.

"It's asking me to rate it." I press one star as hard as I can without hurting myself.

Elise sucks in air through her teeth. "Harsh. What if it's right, though? This is like a cheat code for all the dating apps on my phone. You've already met your soul mate. How does it feel?"

"Useless," I say. "Do you know how many people I've *met* in my life?" I turn to her and stick out my hand. With a phony voice, I say, "Hi! I'm Corinne. And you are . . . ?"

"Uh, Elise?"

"Nice to *meet* you. See? Bam. A potential soul mate."

"Aw, that's so sweet."

I cast a harried glance to the heavens. "This app doesn't tell me shit."

As if listening, my phone chimes again. I wouldn't be surprised if it were recording me. It knew my age, fingerprint, and face, so at this point I'm putting nothing past it.

"Boost option," I read aloud.

"Now this sounds like a real app. Monetization, baby," Tiwanda says.

I open the app, curious to see how much it's charging for this supposed boost. There's no mention of cost. Instead, there's another question on the screen.

Send your soul mate? With two choices: No thanks, I'll pass or Yes, I'm ready for love.

The second option makes my head feel heavy on my shoulders. How do you know if you're ready for love? If I had to guess, I'd say no. I have too much to deal with in terms of earning a living and reckoning with the real reason I moved here.

"There's an info button," Elise observes. She starts to press it herself, then seems to remember the app won't respond to her. I open the short description.

Activating this boost will cause your path to cross with four people from your past. It's up to you to determine which is your romantic soul mate.

Elise and I look at each other. Tiwanda, struggling to read upside down, turns the phone.

"Well, hell," she says.

Elise starts to say something, but I shake my head and hold out my hand for Tiwanda to slide my phone back. There's no need for discussion. I know they won't let me leave this restaurant before getting me to use the boost, regardless of the inevitability of the whole app turning out to be an elaborate ruse.

I press the option claiming I'm ready for love, though I suspect that's the furthest thing from the truth.

CHAPTER FOUR

I get up early on Monday morning like the employed person I *temporarily* am. My car is still in the shop, waiting to be assessed for a cost quote. But I don't have time to worry about Bessie because I have a job!

My temp agency called yesterday evening, trying to fulfill a short-notice request. I'll be filling in as an assistant at Poehler's Investment Group for the week while the executive assistant is out for a family emergency. A full week of work! This is the longest offer I've gotten through the agency. I have an inkling if I perform well and get a positive review, they'll start to offer me longer jobs.

I decide to use a rideshare service to get to work this morning. I don't want to chance it with the Metra. I'll save that for getting home, in preparation for the rest of the week. In Houston, I drove everywhere. I like the idea of public transportation, but the logistics aren't convenient for me. Plus, the time in my car is when I decompress. I listen to music, podcasts, or books, and I zone out as much as one can while actively staying in their lane. Sometimes it takes a few seconds for my car to crank up, and my brakes squeak more often than not, but I can't wait until I have it back.

I shuffle around my apartment with haste despite having plenty of time. It's the same nervous energy that woke me up an hour before my alarm. I stuff my purse with a meal shake and a few snacks. If I don't find an affordable option for lunch in the area, this will have to hold me over until I get off. I go ahead and pull on my clothes—a variation of my favorite first-day outfit that always includes my peach-colored wrap top—then I summon my rideshare.

As soon as I'm dropped off downtown, I'm relieved to be early. It takes five minutes to figure out which elevator bank accesses the sixteenth floor. Poehler's is the sole company housed on this level. I press the doorbell and wait for someone to let me into the suite.

"Good morning," a chipper voice calls out from the speaker.

"Hi, I'm Corinne Evans, the temp."

"Great, come on in."

The lock on the door clicks to allow me entry. I wander only a few steps before the same woman is in front of me. She introduces herself as Sarah and shows me around the office, covering the important spots. My desk is toward the back of the suite in a spacious alcove across from my boss's office. Sarah points out the closest bathroom as well as a break room with free coffee, tea, and snacks.

"Jack should be in around nine. That gives you an hour to get settled. There's a paper on your desk that has your login info and the temp-email login. All emails that usually go to the assistant email are being forwarded to you. For anything that seems like a continuation of something Tim is working on, you can send an out-of-the-office email. New queries need to be noted and given verbally to Jack. Shoot me a message if you have any issues."

I get to work as the office starts to fill up with staff. Monday catch-up chatter follows them in. Most either ignore me or ask where Tim is. I'm tempted to post a sign, but I grit my teeth and repeat variations of the same few sentences as I send off another out-of-office email. For thirty dollars an hour, I'm willing to do this all day.

Jack, my boss and chief operating officer of the company, arrives and everyone takes it as an indicator to begin their work.

"Be in my office in ten minutes," he commands as he strides past me and into his office. *Okay then.*

After nine minutes, I rise from my chair, certain it will take me sixty seconds to walk the seven steps to Jack's office. I have the notes from his messages on my tablet. He didn't specify if now is the time for that, but I want to be ready.

I knock on his partially open door, and he waves a hand toward the chairs facing him across the desk. I sit with my back straight, the epitome of a competent temp worker.

Jack frowns down at the desk, where I've placed my tablet, a note-pad, and a pen. "We usually do this over coffee," he says.

"Oh, I don't drink coffee, but thank you," I say.

He stares at me for a beat. It becomes clear he's implying he would like a coffee, but I wasn't hired to be a mind reader. I want to get a positive review for this week, but it will go smoother if Jack realizes now I won't be able to predict his needs. My mom set high standards for communication growing up, mainly because of my Deaf brother. The longer I'm away from the home we built, the more I realize many groups don't have an effective system of communication in place, even when they speak the same language.

"I'll call for Sarah to bring me one, then," Jack says. He picks up the phone on his desk and quick-dials Sarah. "Morning, hon. D'you mind—yes."

That's all it takes. Sarah, apparently, *is* skilled in mind reading.

"If coffee is something Tim usually handles, I'd be happy to take it up. Just let me know how you like it."

"Sure," Jack says, but he seems immensely uncomfortable to ask for it. Why ask for what you want when the world trips over itself to offer it to you? "Er, do you have any temp experience?"

"Yes," I answer, choosing to leave out specifics unless prodded. So far, my experience consists of a two-day gig at the end of last week and nothing else. I suspect this job would have gone to another contractor if they weren't desperate to fill the request.

Jack, keeping true to form, does not seek more info. "Tim should be back next week. We'll do our best till then. He usually catches me up on what I've missed . . ."

I sigh internally. This very rich man did not adequately prepare himself to not have his hand held this week by his executive assistant. Wherever Tim is, he deserves a raise.

"I've checked the email and voice messages from over the weekend. I have notes."

"Oh, great. Go ahead." He nods and turns toward his computer, obviously intending to half listen to me as he tackles other work that requires his immediate attention.

I unlock my tablet and pull up the notes I typed, ready to show off the hustling I did in the last hour to get through all the messages in time. "Sky Wealth Group reached out via email—"

Jack stops me almost at once.

"Is that your personal tablet?"

"Yes?"

"You typed confidential, proprietary information into a personal device?"

Well, when he puts it like that, it doesn't sound like something I should show off anymore. "I planned to delete it afterwards."

"You will delete it at once." His gaze travels pointedly from me down to the tablet, which is tilted enough for him to see the screen and verify I've deleted it.

"We'll try this again tomorrow." He bobs his head toward the door, effectively dismissing me. I stand with wounded pride, but I'm relieved tomorrow is still a possibility.

Back at my desk, there's a new email from Sarah with a list of tasks to take on for today and tomorrow. It includes going around and following up with people, letting them know Tim is out but I'm available to help in the meantime. Also, Friday is the office celebration for all March birthdays. After the morning rush clears, I have to go to the bakery a few blocks down to place the order. Plus, there's a bunch of housekeeping items Tim has been postponing. I get the feeling his role has grown beyond that of a normal assistant, in ways I can't imagine. I make it my goal to ease his life a bit once he gets back next week. Sarah gives me Tim's personal email, which I only use to ask how he would prefer I organize his files. He responds an hour later with thanks.

At ten, I check in with Jack—who still wants nothing to do with me—before walking to the bakery. It's nice to get out of the office and into the streets of downtown. Since moving back to Chicago, I've only been downtown once, with my mom when I first moved. She spent most of that trip trying to take my mind off Joelle. We exhausted her list of local favorites and attended a tipsy painting night in Hyde Park to make decor for my bare apartment walls. After helping me get settled in my apartment and neighborhood, my mom insisted on having a touristy day. Driving us to Millennium Park was a terrifying game of Don't Hit the Pedestrian, but pounding the pavement is always a welcome rush.

Pastry Office is a small place with a great corner location. Inside, it's part café and part experimental pastries. People are spread throughout the seating area, hot beverages in one hand and cell phones in the other. There's a middle-aged Latina woman behind the counter, smiling in welcome.

"Hi. I'm here to place a cake order for Poehler's Investment Group."

"Ahh, it's that time. Where's Tim?"

"Out of the office for the week."

She nods. "Good, he needs a break. I always tell him, 'You work too much for the man!' You know?" She doesn't wait for me to confirm I know, but I do. That's part of the reason I'm struggling to find a job. I've been choosy this time with full-time jobs in a way I wasn't when I first graduated college. Then, the career counselor's advice was to cast a wide net. But now, I'm not settling for a job that won't satisfy me.

My brother says that's a privileged way of thinking. *Let Mom stop paying your rent, and we'll see how fast you find a job,* he'd told me. That brat. How dare he be younger than me but with such a clearer vision of life? Still, he's one of my favorite people. He promised to visit me after his semester at Rochester Institute of Technology ends in May.

"What can I get you, dear?" the baker asks.

"Tim doesn't have a usual order?"

"Nope, changes it up each time."

Ugh, of course he is considerate enough to be unique for each group of birthdays. I consult the list of employees born in March and the allergens to avoid. Then I do my best.

I walk slowly back to the office because it'll be another two hours before my lunch break. Jack has a meeting with the VP of Strategy that I'm required to attend and take *handwritten* notes. My lunch got pushed until after that. I'm waiting for the elevator when a trio of laughing men join me, enjoying their Monday in ways I didn't think possible. They ignore me, which is preferable. Until one ignores me so well, he disregards the space I'm taking up and backs into me, stepping on my foot that is already struggling in the booties I'm wearing. Yes, I know they aren't my most comfortable boots. But they're cute! And I expected to be sitting behind a desk most of the day, not walking to bakeries!

"My bad," the man says.

"Yes, excuse you," I agree.

He spares a look at me before turning back to his friends, then does a double take.

"Uh, do I know you?"

"No," I say. But it's not as an answer to his question. No, this can't be happening. Is the app already working? "I mean, maybe? You look familiar." In the way many generically good-looking men do. He has dark-brown hair in a neat, short cut that leaves more on the top than the sides. It contrasts with his rosy ivory skin nicely. His facial features are perfectly forgettable, except his nose—it's a long downslope line that brings an edge to his look.

The elevator opens, and we all lumber inside, the man's companions picking up their conversation. But he doesn't join in, still trying to riddle out how we know each other. Floor numbers fourteen and sixteen are pressed.

"Have you worked here long?" he asks me.

"Nope, first day."

"Huh. Are you from Ohio?"

"Texas."

The light bulb goes off for him, triggering a response in me too.

"UT," we say at the same time.

The elevator makes it to the fourteenth floor, where I expect them all to get off, but only his two friends leave. Guess we're going to sixteen together, then.

"Remind me your name again?" I ask him.

"Justin, and you're . . . Crystal?"

"Corinne."

"Ah, close."

"Not really." I laugh, but I mean it.

I remember Justin from several economics classes. If my memory serves me well, he frequently chatted with professors before and after class about whatever business-related books he was reading. I remember rolling my eyes and thinking, *Wow, this is what being passionate about money looks like.* Economics was only a source of enjoyment for me when it ceased to be about numbers and became more about its impact on real people.

He looks good now. Back then, he was your average undergrad—a little on the tall-and-scrawny side. But now, he's filled out and discovered the art of facial hair.

"You work at Poehler's now?" he asks as we step out of the elevator.

"No, I'm a temp. Here for the week." I flash my visitor badge, which specifies the dates it's valid.

He swipes us into the suite and holds the door for me.

"It's bonkers running into you. Not every day I see someone who understands the horror of Professor Marc's Intro to Accounting class."

"I still have nightmares about that class sometimes."

"Do you remember when he yelled at the kid reading a newspaper during lecture and kicked him out?"

"Are you serious? Anytime I see someone with a newspaper, in my head I yell, 'Newspaper? Are you frickin' kidding me with that?'" I give my best impression of our old professor's New Jersey accent.

We're laughing as we approach my desk. Sarah is there, placing something down—undoubtedly more work.

"Oh, perfect, the two people I needed to see. Justin, Jack wants to see the results from the focus group. He knows they're not all done yet, but he still wants to review it. Bring it to the meeting?" She poses it as a question, but the way she switches gears to me makes it obvious it isn't. Sarah and Tim must be the dream team, handling all these corporate men with ease.

"Jack assigned a laptop to you for the week. Something about preferring to take notes digitally? IT finished setting it up. You can pick it up from the fourteenth floor." She's off to handle her next fire, leaving me slightly in wonder that Jack would think to arrange this for me.

"You're Tim for the week?" Justin asks.

"Yeah, I . . . yeah." The urge to explain how I went from graduating with him over five years ago to doing odd jobs surges, but I push it down.

"All right, then, I'll see you in the meeting soon."

The meeting. With Jack and the vice president of Strategy. The VP of Strategy I was expecting to be a man in his midfifties, like Jack himself, but who instead is my fellow Longhorn. He's mildly hot, successful, and smiling at me like he can't believe his luck. Met is not responsible for this. Though . . . I didn't get offered this job until after I activated the boost. Could it have the power to cause a family emergency for poor Tim? No. I scoff at myself for being naive. This is impossible. And I refuse to allow a pesky app to take the credit for a mere coincidence. Still, it's not a bad idea to see what Justin is about. For curiosity's sake.

"Hey." I catch Justin's arm before he turns completely to walk away. "Would you want to get lunch today? Or coffee? I have a thirty-minute break."

Justin cocks an eyebrow up, a movement I couldn't imagine the younger version of him doing. He smiles, slow building and suggestive. I let go of his arm at once.

"To catch up," I add.

"Sure," he says as if we have a mutual understanding beyond the words exchanged. "And don't worry about time. I'll handle it."

CHAPTER FIVE

The meeting goes well, in that I am practically invisible as I type detailed notes for Jack. By the end of the meeting, I know exactly how important Justin's position is. He talks louder and with more bravado than necessary for the small audience of two, making me wonder if he's showing off. Or maybe this is who he's always been. The eager young man who showed up to class was only a sliver of him. There's a slew of facets yet to be discovered.

That's what makes the concept of soul mates unnerving. If Met were real, surely it would send me exes, or friends I had crushes on but never made a move. Someone I'm somewhat familiar with and have already begun chipping away the facades that keep you from truly knowing a person. Not someone I encountered once in the waiting room at the DMV. Justin and I had more contact than that, but still. I'm to believe an app orchestrated this? No way.

On the way out of Jack's office, Justin asks if we're still on for lunch. Of course, nothing has changed in the hour since we made the plans, but it seems Justin likes to make thinly veiled announcements.

Jack doesn't react to this information. Still, Justin says, "Oh, we're old college classmates."

Old? It's been five years, bro.

"That's nice. Got your notes, Corinne. Have a good lunch."

Is this Jack warming up to me? First the computer, then somewhat of a thank-you to the *appropriately scribed* meeting notes I emailed as the meeting came to a close. That was one of the tips Tim left in a temp-guide folder I found while organizing his files—Jack prefers notes delivered promptly. Check, me.

"Naturally, we have a lot to catch up on." Justin elaborates despite Jack's indifference. "You mind if Corinne takes an hour?"

Jack's face displays a series of minute movements—a squint, a glance at the time in the corner of his computer, then a slight wobble of his head. "Sure."

Justin looks pleased with himself as we finally make it out of the office. I, on the other hand, feel like I lost points with Jack. Justin swings by his office to grab his jacket and wallet while I grab my phone. Immediately, the Met notification chimes, continuing to bypass my silent setting.

Met Tip: Might be a good day to meet your match! With two heart emojis and a wink face at the end. I despise this app. Quickly, I swipe to dismiss it and fire off some texts to Tiwanda.

Someone from college works at my temp job!

I'm going to lunch with him. This is wild right? Can't be the app.

Justin comes back around the corner, and I pull on my jacket. As we wait for the elevator, my phone vibrates with Tiwanda's reply.

NO WAY

I'm not buying it, but I'm sure Elise will. Come to happy hour with us tonight!

She follows up with a link to the restaurant's address. It's close to my apartment. I can still follow my plan to take the train over there, then have Tiwanda drop me off at my place after.

Justin takes us to his favorite lunch spot, within walking distance of the office. It's a typical downtown bistro, overpriced but with a nice ambiance. I only tell an insistent Justin I'll pay for my own turkey wrap and soup once before I let him "win." I'm on a budget anyway.

"What was your major in undergrad again?" I ask as we're getting settled. The card they handed us with our order number is in the center of the table, on display for the food runner to easily find us.

"Finance, but the funny part is . . ." He leans forward for delivery of a punch line I'm sure not to find very funny at all. "The only job I've had that was your typical finance position was my internship before senior year."

"I know all about ditching your major," I say, momentarily forgetting to shield myself from questions about my job situation. I know it's ridiculous to buy into a system that defines some jobs as failures. In truth, every job needs to be done by someone. It's the system that's the failure—one that places the most respect in jobs that don't truly need to be done. Like, what is corporate strategy? I sat in an hour-long meeting, and it seems like an expensive way to pay for more marketing.

"Undergrad majors are a stepping-stone anyway. You can build a career off anything. It's just that some people choose boulders"—he inclines his head, indicating he's one of these people—"and others choose pebbles."

Our food arrives, saving me from doing something dumb, like asking him what majors constitute pebbles. It's suddenly clear Justin is the last person I should seek for a career-path discussion. I opt to make an abrupt convo change.

"What brought you to Chicago?" I ask him.

"Poehler's," he says. Attempt failed. "I was working for another financial company in Pittsburgh, doing market research and social media campaigns. Then a headhunter contacted me right when I started to feel I was worth more for the work I was doing. I had a wedding to pay for and was planning to ask for a raise when I got the email."

The spice from my chicken enchilada soup and the mention of a wedding cause me to cough midway through Justin's spiel. He obviously doesn't mind, since he continues uninterrupted. I take a gulp of water.

"You're married?" I ask as casually as one can manage that question, my eyes flicking toward the bare left hand resting on the table.

"Oh, yeah." He lifts his hand and twists it idly. "I don't believe in wedding bands. It sends the wrong message."

"Which is?"

"That I'm, like . . ." He takes a bite of his sandwich, chews as he fishes for the right word. "Unapproachable. Or something."

I laugh; I can't help myself. "The only people who wouldn't approach you because of a wedding ring are people who want to sleep with you, but not if you're married."

"Exactly." The saucy expression he directs my way makes me want to duck under the table. Yet an optimistic part of me counters I could be reading this wrong. Relationships exist in many forms. I brace myself to dig for clarity.

"Oh, so you're in an open relationship? Your wife has other partners too?"

"What?" He scrunches his face up, completely disgusted by that idea. "My wife is pregnant. Plus, she's not the type to need other men."

"But . . . you're the type to need other women?"

His cheeks grow a pleased pinkish hue as he grins and takes another bite of his oniony sandwich. Suddenly, I've lost my appetite.

CHAPTER SIX

I arrive at Tío Nico's happy hour exhausted, overdressed, and still slightly bewildered from lunch with Justin. After I forced down my wrap and slurped up my soup, I told him I needed to hurry back. I took only the regular half-hour lunch. There really wasn't a point sitting around chatting with Justin about how he's making lots of money and *wink wink* DTF.

I spot Elise at a high table in the bar area alone, picking at a large platter of nachos. Tiwanda texted me nearly twenty minutes ago when she arrived. I slide into a chair without drinks in front of it and dramatically slump onto the table.

"It's been a day, huh?" Elise asks. She lifts a hand, and seconds later the bartender is with us, offering me five-dollar frozen margaritas and wells. I order a frozen mango margarita with a chamoy rim, the only way to go after a day like the one I've had.

"How was your soul mate? No, wait until Tee comes back from the bathroom so you only have to tell us once."

"Yes, please." I probably only have enough energy to relay this story once tonight anyway.

"Hey," a low monotone voice says behind me. Elise jumps up.

"Cory!" she squeals as they hug.

Ah, the first and true Cory. We finally meet.

"Hey," he says again, toward me this time. His face—though handsome, with smooth chestnut-brown skin and a beard trimmed close to his jawline—is as plain as his voice. I suppress a laugh and return the lackluster greeting.

"Wow, it's been a rough one for both of you," Elise says, signaling the bartender again. Cory orders a raspberry tea.

"If I drink, I might go home and call Brian," he says.

"You will not." Tiwanda swoops in. She gives Cory an over-the-back hug and squeezes my shoulders before taking her seat. "Corinne, welcome to our seldomly occurring Monday-night happy hour."

"Whoop, whoop," Elise says.

"Whoo," Cory drones. He could have kept it, really. But for some reason his postbreakup slump has me smirking. Misery really does love company.

Tiwanda slaps Cory's arm with the back of her hand. "Ignore him. He's playing a role."

Cory sits up straight before asking, "And what role would that be?"

The bartender returns with my margarita and Cory's tea, so I'm well poised as this showdown unfolds in front of me. It's my happy place, being around people but not having to actively entertain. That was the luxury of being friends with Joelle. She genuinely loved talking to strangers and was skilled in keeping the conversation going. If I went to any social function with her, I knew I was in for a good time simply because I wouldn't have to try as hard.

Cory flips his attention to thank the bartender—the most emotion I've seen him express thus far—then he's back with Tiwanda, waiting for her response.

"The heartbroken one." Cory scowls and Tiwanda continues, "You've been telling me and Elise for weeks you wanted to break up with Brian."

Elise nods discreetly at me.

"Yeah, but I didn't."

"Why did he dump you?" I ask. Cory glares at me, and I smile as I gather a perfect nacho chip.

"No reason," he mumbles.

"No reason for breaking up?" I chortle. "Must mean there was no reason to be together in the first place."

He stares at me, and for once, it doesn't seem like my personal source of amusement. My smile slips off my face, and my chest constricts under his scrutiny. He breaks eye contact and lifts his glass without a word.

I exchange a look with Elise, who misinterprets it as a need to explain on my behalf.

"Don't mind Corinne. She's dealing with a weird love thing herself."

I shake my head.

"Are you kidding me?" Cory says. I know he's annoyed with me, that much is clear. But the anger in those four words makes me freeze. Tiwanda reacts similarly. I follow her gaze to the dining area of the restaurant where a cute guy is getting settled at a booth. He has light-brown skin and dark, wavy hair that's overgrown but clearly working for him. His companion has their back to us.

"I don't believe in this app, but every time I've seen a hot person today, I'm upset I haven't met them already." Not even Elise laughs at my attempted joke.

"You're not really heartbroken, but we can still get out of here," Tiwanda says, touching Cory's arm.

I still have over half of my mango margarita left, but I know it's a moot point when all three of them stand at once and begin pulling on jackets and gathering their things. Elise digs in her purse and pulls out a couple of twenties.

I take one quick lick of my chamoy rim and scurry after them toward the exit. I glance back at the attractive guy, who could only be Brian, now hovering awkwardly above his seat, looking in our direction.

We all climb in Tiwanda's car and sit in silence as we wait for it to warm up. I'm in the back seat with Elise, and Cory is riding shotgun. I can't see his face, as it's obscured by the dreadlocks hanging well past his shoulders, but I practically feel him brooding.

"I thought I'd have more time to ask, but can I have a ride home?" I say.

Tiwanda hiccups a laugh, and soon Elise and I are laughing at our predicament too. Cory doesn't join in.

"Yeah, I was designated driver tonight anyway," Tiwanda says. "Can we sit at your place for a bit?"

"Sure. No idea how I left my living room this morning, but I have wine."

She puts my address in the GPS and pulls off, the music the only sound in the car. I have the distinct inkling Cory would rather walk home than be dragged to another place, which is weird to assume since I don't know him well. But maybe I'm wrong with my assessment, because he doesn't make a peep of dissent during the trip to my apartment.

~

Elise and Tiwanda make themselves comfortable roaming around my living room and kitchen as I pick up the clutter I could only notice in the presence of company. Cory, more reticent than ever, picks a corner of the couch and plops down.

Soon, Elise has located the wineglasses and taken the mostly full bottle from the fridge. Tiwanda found a bag of popcorn in my pantry, and I hand her a bowl to pour it in. It's nice being the hostess for once. After my mom left, it's been two months of being here solo, unless you count the one time the technician came to fix my dishwasher. I miss the fullness of the Houston house and the apartment I shared with Joelle before that. The quiet emptiness of living alone is something I'm still adjusting to.

"Okay," Tiwanda says as I finally deem the place neat enough to settle down with them in the living room. I only have one couch and one lounge chair. Since I don't want to squeeze on the couch between Tiwanda and Cory, I sit on the area rug, placing my wineglass on the coffee table.

"How was your date?"

Elise bounces in the chair, skillfully keeping a steady hold on the stem of her glass.

"It wasn't a date; it was lunch," I clarify.

"Separate paying? Lack of flirting?" Cory asks, surprising me with his involvement. I falter, not wanting to reveal the answer.

"Aha, so it was a date." Elise grins over the rim of her glass.

"Whatever the classification," I say, "it was a disaster."

I recount the details of my lunch, how it consisted of Justin talking about himself for nearly thirty minutes and included a poorly veiled proposition to partake in his adultery. Tiwanda and Elise explain the Met app to Cory, who receives it with as much disdain as I feel.

"This guy could be your soul mate?" Cory asks, a phantom smile on his lips. This convo about the validity of an app seems to be what he needed to snap out of his sour mood.

"No. He's married and implies a willingness to cheat on his wife. This guy isn't my *soul mate*." I can't keep the contempt out of my voice.

"But," Elise says, holding up a finger, "he is one of the four people the app said it would send you."

Tiwanda is absentmindedly running the tip of her index finger around the lip of her glass, as if trying to riddle this out. "I still think this app is bogus, but if it wasn't . . . Married doesn't necessarily eliminate him. I've heard stories of teens falling in love but then separating. Forty years later, they reunite after they've both married and had children. They find out they were true soul mates and live the rest of their lives together."

That sounds . . . actually revolting. A quick glance at Elise and Cory confirms we're a split audience. Elise is all heart-eyes as she sips her wine.

"Maybe the app thinks you're perfect for an asshole." Cory shrugs, the epitome of nonchalance. "Someone has to be."

"No one has to be," I say. Contrary to popular belief, there *isn't* a match for everyone.

"Your soul mate loves you so much he'd cheat on his wife with you. And you, and you," he says, pointing to Tiwanda and Elise in turn.

"Well, I hope your soul mate knows what he's in for, since Brian clearly didn't."

I shouldn't have gone there. It's clear Tiwanda forced him out tonight to help get his mind off Brian. This must be the furthest thing from what she planned. First, the run-in at the restaurant, and now, this low dig. Elise presses her lips together, either trying to mask the tension she feels or to suppress a laugh. Often with her, it's both. Tiwanda stares pointedly at me. Cory, however, blows right past it as he adds a correction to my statement.

"Or she. Or they."

"Noted," I say.

"I got an idea!" Tiwanda jumps in. "How about we talk about something that's not soul mate or heartbreak related?"

"Please," Cory and I say in unison.

CHAPTER SEVEN

I only brush off Justin once before he understands I'm not interested in aiding his infidelity. Thankfully, Jack has no additional meetings with him for the week and plenty of work to keep me busy. After I complete Tim's files and send him a picture, he requests more of his areas reorganized. There are no more flubs with the delivery of Jack's morning messages, which I scribe on the company's laptop without cries of stolen proprietary information. When I leave the office on Friday with a foil-wrapped paper plate of birthday cake in tow, Jack thanks me for my hard work. Though I'm sure to get a positive review, my temp agency has no job for me next week.

Saturday morning, I finally get a call from the car mechanic. They might be trustworthy, but at the sacrifice of prompt service. The mechanic runs through a host of problems my car has, then focuses on the repairs I need to drive it. Thankfully, only one axle is damaged. They found nothing to explain the electrical malfunctions. Altogether their quote is $817, and they plan to have it ready for pickup early next week. That money is either coming out of my savings or what I earned from Poehler's. Regardless, the idea of that much dancing out of my account is not appealing.

I spend the rest of the morning unpacking a box that's been in the corner of my bedroom since I first moved here. My apartment is by no means settled. Mom did the best she could while she was here, and the bathroom and living room are testaments to her efforts. The bedroom was my responsibility, and the only thing I had the bandwidth to care about was having a comfortable bed to mope—I mean, sleep—in. Other than that, I found a used nightstand and dresser in good condition. Still, my room is bare and unwelcoming. I don't mind, though. It matches my mood. As I'm realizing I have nowhere to put my hair and skin care products from the box, my phone rings with a video call from my brother.

I pick up with haste. My brother and I text regularly, and I call him more often now that I'm not always employed. Since he's busy with school and other involvements, it's hard to catch him. We have resorted to sending videos back and forth just to see each other's faces.

"Hey." Lito waves, hanging off-screen a bit like he didn't expect me to answer. He's signing *"Hold on, hold on"* as he leans off camera, signing something to someone else with his free hand. Best multitasker I know.

"Okay, sorry," he tells me when I'm his focus again. He must be tired, because his signs run together. *"Mom tells me you got a job. Congrats."*

I swat away his praise. *"Mom doesn't understand temporary jobs. It was only for a week. I'm jobless again now. How's school?"*

Lito acts out hammering a nail but then pulls the hammer too far back and knocks himself out. He's "passed out" for a few seconds before he sits up straight again. *"It's stressful,"* he adds. He catches me up on how his internship interviews have been going, noting he should hear back from some soon for possible second interviews or job offers.

"We're both job searching now," I remark.

"Yeah, but only one of us is doing the 'searching' part."

I can't stand him sometimes. How do you search for a job when you don't know what you're looking for? For now, I can only focus on ways to generate income in the meantime and hope the right job comes searching for me.

"Have you seen Joelle's family yet?" Lito asks.

I shake my head. *"Remember when my car broke down? I ended up right next to where we used to live. I called them, but their house phone is disconnected."*

"Why didn't you stop by? You know people didn't always have phones to call ahead, right? Doorbells still work. Better if they flash."

"They don't know I moved here." I stutter over the signs composing my excuse. *"It's only been a few months since . . . They might not be ready for visitors."*

"You joking?" Lito laughs as if he's decided I am. *"How do you feel?"*

I sigh, remembering my disappointment when the automated voice droned, "The number you have dialed has been disconnected or is no longer in service."

"I want to see them. I miss Joelle, and they're the closest people to her. It might be like she's still here if I'm around them. But demanding they see me is selfish, right?"

"Corinne." He uses the sign for my name that he made up himself when he was four or five. It's simply spelling C-O-C-O, a quick closing and opening of the hand. When we were younger and he was learning speech, he called me Coco. Now, he rarely uses the nickname, but the sign name stuck.

"Wouldn't you think her family would feel the same way having you around? You should go by. Today."

And because, in general, my brother is wiser than me, I follow his advice. I'm hoping they haven't changed homes as I request a rideshare to the address where my parents, brother, and I lived over two decades ago. Lito was only a baby when we moved. I was halfway through the second grade and hesitant to leave my best friend.

Against all odds, we stayed in contact. I don't have much extended family left here except for some cousins and not-really-cousins like Tiwanda. But my mom liked to visit every few years for the friends she made here. Every time, Joelle and I would hang out as much as we could. Then when it was time to pick a college, we picked the same one.

Two friends decided at a young age they wanted to spend their lives in each other's company. No one expected it would be truncated.

On the ride over, I try to reconcile the current area with my memories. I didn't have the time or the visibility to do this the night of the storm. Now, I notice only a few things haven't changed. The Jewel-Osco grocery store we frequented has a parking lot teeming with shoppers. The regional bank across the street has been acquired twice over, and now a new logo is displayed.

My rideshare driver parks on the curb, and I consider asking him to stand by while I check to see if anyone is home, but I don't want to feel rushed. If I get no answer, I'll walk up the block to the corner store that's somehow still standing. Joelle and I used to beg one of our parents to walk us there so we could spend the few dollars we'd accumulated between us.

The house before me is my own—well, *was*. It was my family's home, as far as renting can allow. Joelle's family bought theirs. I remember Joelle telling me proudly one day as we were playing around, "I own this home, which makes me the powerful princess." I doubt this was on the paperwork, but it stuck with me. Half a year later, my mom sat me down and told me we were moving. She explained it was the best choice for our family, but still I felt powerless. Uprooted.

Our house has a different paint color that appears many years old. The shingles surrounding the windows are now a deep blue, while I remember them being brown. The door is a splash of pale yellow.

Instead of approaching my old stomping grounds, I walk two houses down. This house has undergone changes also, but it doesn't seem as foreign to me due to what Joelle filled me in on over the years through letters, emails, texts, and phone calls. "My mom decided to start a garden." "Daddy hired some guys to repaint the house today. One was cute."

The last time I was here, I was fourteen and with my family. My mom came to the city again while I was in college. By then, Joelle and I were together once more, dorm roommates with two other girls. Joelle even spent Thanksgiving holidays in Houston with my family, since it was a four-hour drive. Christmastime, she'd fly home. I never went home with her and didn't think much of it at the time. But now I'm wondering how I could let years pass without making time to see Joelle's family, beyond when they came to visit for Family Weekend or for graduation. And definitely not in the somber church where I saw them last.

I ring the doorbell.

The dog that acted as a backup alert system is long gone. For a while, there's nothing. I ring again and wait. If they're anything like me, the first bell lets them know someone's there—not necessarily an expectation for them to come to the door.

Now I hear movement from inside the house. There's a camera up in the corner that I notice right as the door opens. Joelle's dad, Mr. Walter, looks at me with an expression far from the shock I anticipated.

"My wife was expecting you," he says.

He ushers me in and gets me a glass of water as I wait in the living room. The furniture is a mix of modern and antique. Joelle's mom had always been a skilled interior decorator. This house, by all standards, was bare bones when she took it on, but they had such pride in it. I didn't understand it as a child, but now I think I might.

"Leyda's going to say you have to come back soon, when she's here," Mr. Walter says as he hands me my water, his cell phone in his other hand.

"I'm sorry for dropping by like this. I tried to call but it's disconnected?"

"We got rid of our landline. Only calls that came there were bill collectors and scam calls. JoJo used to call us on it if her cell phone was dead." He laughs ruefully. "It was the only number she memorized other than yours."

I nod and bring the glass of water to my lips.

"What brings you to town?" Mr. Walter asks.

"I moved here a little bit ago. I don't know why."

He gives me an impenetrable look that makes me reflect in the silence. After Joelle moved from Houston to go home and continue her cancer treatments, I moved back in with my mom. Following college graduation, way before Joelle got sick, she tried to convince me to do a few years in Chicago with her. She wanted to see how it could be with both of us there again. I didn't budge. I loved living in the same place as her, but we had more than proved proximity wasn't a requirement for our friendship. "You go," I told her. "I'll come visit."

But we both found jobs in Houston—me at a finance company and Joelle at a tech group that specialized in helping businesses build websites and apps. She didn't leave Texas until four years later, when the doctor estimated she had six months left before the newly discovered leukemia would overtake her body. Then she went to be with her family. I offered to go with her, even started getting my plans in order. But she told me not to come, not to upend my life. She'd go to a better hospital there, get some experimental treatments, get healthy, and come back. If her outlook changed, she'd tell me. But when I got the call that it was time for me to come to Chicago, it was from Ms. Leyda, not Joelle.

Mr. Walter finally speaks. "Well, I'm sure Jo would be happy you're home."

Would she be, though? Because I'm sensing some serious side-eye from the afterlife. I smile back at him anyway. For decades, Mr. Walter's aging process appeared stagnant from the outside, but it all seems to have caught up with him in the past year. He's bald, with a goatee that has turned gray. Deep wrinkles give the impression he's been frowning for a long time. Extra weight has even settled around his gut.

He asks me about work, and it's uncomfortable, discussing how I'm squandering my life. I'm searching for a purpose that Joelle had always instinctively known.

When I finally make a move to get going, I think we're both relieved. Mr. Walter gives me Ms. Leyda's cell number so we can arrange a better time for me to come back. Before I leave, he asks if I want to see Joelle's room.

"It's still . . ." I trail off. *There*, is what I was going to say, but of course the room is there. What I meant is, is it still intact? Does it still feel like her? Despite my unfinished question, he seems to understand and nods. He doesn't follow me up the stairs, trusting I remember the way.

Of course I do. Up the stairs, first room on the left. The walls are still painted robin's-egg blue, the color she chose for her thirteenth birthday. Her bed is against one wall, the headboard set beside the window. Her closet takes up most of the adjacent wall. But the other two are crowded with memorabilia—pictures of family and friends, posters of famous do-good humans, and abstract photographs Joelle shot herself. Back in high school, she had posters of musicians, actors, and models, but when she came home the summer after freshman year, she changed all that. I remember calling her one summer day after I'd finished my shift at the local movie theater.

"It's sad," she said, almost out of breath as she ripped each poster down. "Every day I wake up and see these faces on my wall. But who among them started a foundation to combat gun violence? Who created something that changed lives?"

She sent me a picture of her work once she was done, and now I stare at it in person for the first time. There's former NASA engineer Katherine Johnson and Joelle's hero, Mae Jemison. She has an entire section honoring the greats of Chicago, including Harold Washington, Ida B. Wells, and Michelle Obama. From the picture alone, I thought it was nice. But standing with every inch of my vision consumed by this collage of excellence, it's downright inspiring.

Yeah, Mr. Walter was right. This room is still Joelle. It's way too neat, and if I open the closet, I bet it would be empty. But she owns this space. She was the powerful princess of this house all those years ago, and she still is now.

CHAPTER EIGHT

I'll be honest—if I didn't have bills I can't afford to pay and an ever-present pressure to not take life for granted, I'd be perfectly content with staying in my semicozy apartment all day. Especially with this rainy Tuesday weather. The dropping temperatures have meteorologists warning it'll turn into snow overnight, their excitement evident in each clip my mom has sent me.

No problem here, I text back to her. I'm unemployed this week.

This morning, I accepted a job for Monday through Wednesday next week. I also succumbed to my mom's goading and applied for a substitute teaching job. The Chicago public school district is struggling to fill teacher absences and offering expedited processing and training. The promise of future work is the primary reason I've allowed myself the freedom to enjoy the time off, however forced it may be.

I stayed in bed to read an extra hour, received the call of my dreams—my car will be ready for pickup this afternoon—made breakfast instead of relying on my usual meal-replacement smoothies, and now I'm dressed in a pair of spandex shorts and matching sports bra. It's a workout outfit from two New Year's resolutions ago to exercise more. Or, more specifically, to do enough squats that a quarter could bounce off my ass, but I've never actually worn it to the gym. And now that I've moved to Chicago and am scrounging for temp work, I couldn't afford a gym membership if I wanted one.

My mom, in love or jest, sent me a care package consisting of a DVD player and ten of her old follow-along workout videos. She included a printout of an article about how endorphins can boost your mood. While I don't necessarily buy that working up a sweat with people from the nineties will carve a dent into the iceberg of my Joelle-related grief, I'm willing to try anything. I pick the bald-headed Black guy, who's currently making me punch, sway, kick, and twist my core in a rhythm that feels like a threat to beat the endorphins out of me.

About ten minutes in, I'm huffing. A sheen of sweat dampens my face. I'm considering pausing for water and to turn the heat down a notch when a heavy-handed knock sounds on my door. I freeze, happy for the break but annoyed at the interruption. Everyone in my six-unit apartment building should be at work. Someone knocking on my door likely means my neighbor directly below me decided to take the day off and is now taking offense to my stomping around, no matter how rhythmic.

I don't bother to pause the DVD as I make my way over to the door. I glance through the peephole but don't see the familiar figure of my neighbor. Upon closer look it's . . . the other Cory. That must mean Tiwanda and Elise are here too! As they left my apartment last week, I told them they were welcome back anytime. But shouldn't they be working?

I open the door and lean out a bit to get a wider view. No Tiwanda or Elise, just Cory. Cory with a self-assured smile on his face and his locs pulled back into a band at his neck. He's wearing a maroon pair of scrubs underneath his open coat. I swear, true Chicagoans don't have the cold receptors I do. A laptop bag hangs from his shoulder.

"Uh?" I say by way of greeting.

"Hey. I had a gap in my schedule and thought I could work here for a bit?"

"Uh," I repeat before remembering there are better words in the English language at my disposal. "I'm sorry, did I miss a text from you?"

"I don't have your number or else I would have called ahead. But I remember you mentioning you didn't have a job scheduled for this week . . . and took a chance you might be home."

I didn't think he was listening when I told Tiwanda and Elise that. He seemed to tune in and out of the conversation, undoubtedly between thoughts of his ex. That he can recall my schedule is surprising. The veil of moodiness draped over him that night has disappeared. The change makes me want to accept his company even in my current state of disarray. Still, I can't help pushing his buttons.

"So you got the bright idea to 'take a chance' but didn't think to ask Tiwanda for my phone number?"

"I *did* think of that. Right around the time I remembered you lived over here. But Tiwanda probably wouldn't have seen my text until after I got here. Plus, she would've given me the third degree. *'Why do you need it? What do you want?'* Then she'd have to ask you if it's okay to give out your number." He waves a hand as if this elongated spiel explains anything.

"Sounds about right," I say.

"The process would have taken maybe a half hour, by my estimates. I was only seven minutes down the way."

"Might be a long process, but it's in place for a reason."

He rolls his eyes at me. *Rolls his eyes.* The audacity! I planned on letting him in anyway, but now I can't relent so easily.

"If I'm not welcome, you had the option to not answer the door. Or answer the door and tell me to fuck off."

I laugh, high pitched and haughty. "Oh, wow, in that case . . ." I clear my throat. "Fuck off. Did I do that right?"

And then I shut the door in his face.

"Do it the proper way or don't bother," I shout through the door.

My workout DVD is on controlled high kicks now. I focus all the combative energy I have from the interaction with Cory into my movements. Part of me wants to look out the window to see if he's left the building, but that's merely curiosity. I couldn't care less if he chose to leave.

Ten minutes later, as the exercise routine shifts to a combination involving squats and my thighs are screaming after only three, my phone buzzes from the kitchen island. I hobble over to check it. It's a message from Tiwanda.

Okay to give Cory your number?

Huh. He didn't give up. I text back that it's okay. Then I wait for anything to happen. Maybe he left but asked Tiwanda anyway for future purposes. But then my phone's screen comes to life with a call from an unknown local number.

"Hi, this is Cori," I answer, pleasant as a plum. I always introduce myself as Corinne. Only a select few call me Cori, which is why I was fine when Tiwanda and Elise told me the name was taken. But now? I'm feeling petty enough to lay claim to the name. He chuckles just once, enough to let me know he picked up on my intent.

"Can I come in now?"

"I'm sorry, who's speaking?"

He sighs. "Hey, this is Cory—*Courtland*. I'm in your area and have two hours before my next client. Mind if I do some work at your apartment?"

As he speaks, I move toward the door. I can hear him on the other side.

"Right now? I don't know if I'm decent," I say, proving why I never became an actress.

"Yes," Cory says, monotone. I can picture how his face probably looks right now—blank yet annoyed.

"Sorry, me and my apartment are not available." I hang up the phone.

When I open the door, Cory is still looking down at his phone with his mouth agape. "Come in, dork."

He mumbles his thanks and shuffles in but not very far. He takes off his shoes and peers around my apartment like he's never been here before. A few things have changed—my coffee table is pushed against the far wall, the lounge chair is now in the corner, and the couch is pushed back a few feet. I needed space for my moves.

"Tae Bo?" Cory says. "What are you, fifty?"

"One day, if I'm lucky. You can sit at the counter, I guess." I point over to the kitchen island and a couple of stools. No way I want him sitting on the couch with me squatting, praying my knees don't give out on me. "Do you want water or anything?"

He looks at me like he doesn't trust my offer.

"Nah, I'm good."

"All right. Well, help yourself if you change your mind."

The stools face away from me, which is great. I should be almost done with this workout, and then I can carry on with my productive day off. Thankfully, they're done with the squat combo and are doing more upper-body stuff—core twists and punches. I'm feeling so good about it, I'm entertaining delusions of doing another ten-minute workout video. That is, until Cory decides to shatter my groove.

"You're doing that wrong," he says.

"What?" I ask on an exhale, glancing over my shoulder.

He doesn't answer, but I track his movement as the stool scrapes against the wooden floor and his socked feet land with a soft thud. He stands in front of me to the left, looking over my stance with a slight shake of his head.

"Your core should be burning right now," he says.

"It is," I huff. "What are you, an Instagram personal trainer?" I follow a bunch of those accounts, mostly to visualize my fitness goals rather than act on them.

49

"Physical therapist." He steps closer to me. "Don't turn your hips so much."

I scoff and try to do as he says, but now I can tell I'm doing it wrong. My core isn't engaged at all, as I'm mostly moving my shoulders.

"No," he says and reaches out to hold my hips. "Now, try what you were doing before."

I do, only this time my hips are locked in place by his steady hands. To compensate, I'm clenching my abs and twisting along to the rhythm Billy Blanks has set, and, *oh yeah*, I can feel the burn now.

"Okay, that's enough," I say, slowing to a halt.

"Push through," Cory encourages. But it sounds less like an encouragement and more like a demand, albeit a soft-spoken one. Suddenly, I'm very aware that some of his fingers are against the damp skin of my midsection, and some are pressing into the upper part of my ass. I *don't* dislike it. When he was moping over Brian a week ago, I thought he was good-looking in a bland way. But now that the postbreakup cloud has lifted, he's . . . decidedly *fine*.

I keep going until the end of the set, knowing I'll feel sore for days. My abs are on fire, Billy Blanks is cheering me on in between counting the reps, and Cory is holding me in place. I'm panting and probably have a crazed look in my eyes, but I don't allow myself to quit. Finally, the countdown for the final rep expires and my on-screen workout companions start stepping in place, getting ready for a cooldown.

I lift my arms above my head and bend back to stretch out the burn. Cory drops his hands from my waist but doesn't step away immediately. I meet his gaze. At first, I think there's a laugh hiding in there, like he's about to mock me for how much I struggled through that seemingly easy exercise. But all he says is, "Good." Then he goes back to the kitchen island.

I do the cooldown, checking over my shoulder a few times to see if Cory is being nosy again. But he's not. He's taken his computer out of his bag and is typing. Once the cooldown is done, I excuse myself to go to the shower, where I try really hard not to think about the places Cory's hands were and the places I wish they could be.

No, *no. Stop right there.* Cory is not for me. A contrary part of my brain recalls his comment: *"Or she. Or they."* He's a man with range—so what? I have approximately 2.5 potential friends here, and I can't go risking .5 of them because an extremely vapid part of me is wondering what it'd be like to sit on his face.

Once I'm out of the shower and dressed for a quick trot to the Metra station, I go back to the front of my apartment. One of my rules for unemployed days is to cut expenses as much as possible, which means no rideshare to the car mechanic when I can get there by train. It's considerably cheaper. I have about ten minutes to get out of here if I want to make it to the station in time.

Cory is sitting on the couch now, his laptop on the coffee table. I pause. He's returned my living room arrangement to its preworkout state. I can't decide if I want to thank him or get upset that he moved shit around of his own accord, so I don't say anything. Instead, I grab a shake from the fridge and settle in the lounge chair. It's turned slightly to face the couch when I normally have it facing the television. At this angle, though, it's perfect for scrutinizing Cory.

He has wireless earbuds in and is focused on whatever he's typing. I'm sure he sees me peripherally but is choosing not to engage in conversation. Fine by me. There's nothing like a man that can be quiet. Plus, it gives me a chance to observe him uninterrupted. I'm happy to find I can take stock of the intensity of his concentration, the obstinate set of his jawline, and his thick eyebrows in a detached sort of way. Yes, I'm undoubtedly attracted, but not to the point of questioning the capabilities of his mouth anymore. I'm in complete control. What happened before was a result of the exercise endorphins, surely. I smile in contentment.

Cory's eyes flick over to mine, then down, lingering on my upturned lips. He gets back to his work, typing out a few more words and what sounds like the finality of a period, then leans back into the couch. His hand reaches up to tap one of the earbuds, and the tinny voice coming from them silences. Still, he says nothing, but the invitation is clear.

I get up to grab my coat and boots out of the closet, then double-check my purse for my wallet. I'm apt to subconsciously forget to transfer it from bag to bag when I know I shouldn't be spending money. Though I don't want to spend this much on my car, it's an unavoidable expense at this point.

Cory starts to gather his stuff too.

"I'm not kicking you out," I say. "I have to pick up my car, but you can stay here as long as you need. Turn the bottom lock on your way out."

He stops, his head jerking back a tiny bit. "You slammed the door in my face for not calling beforehand, but you'd let me stay here alone?"

I squint at him with a derisive shake of my head. "Exactly. You've been properly vetted now. And I'm a Texan. Hospitality is kind of our thing."

"Is it? And see, I thought it was aggressive open-carry gun laws and football."

"It's that too," I say with a wink. "But seriously, don't leave on my account. You might be more productive without distraction."

He stares at me like there's hidden meaning in my words.

"Or leave. Whatever you want, Courtland."

He scowls, and it's better than the reaction I'd hoped for.

"You said you were going to pick up your car?"

I hum an affirmative.

"How are you getting there?"

"A train, which I'm going to miss if I don't get out of here. Are you staying or not?"

He checks the time on his watch, his bottom lip caught between his teeth as he works something out in his head. "I can give you a ride."

Dammit. There goes my restraint on errant thoughts.

~

Cory's SUV has a neat front seat, but one glance in the back exposes a rolled yoga mat, a set of weights, and some stretch bands in various colors. And that's only the stuff I can see from the passenger seat.

"It's not messy—it's my office," Cory says as he maneuvers the car away from the curb, following the prompts to the auto shop's address plugged into the GPS system.

"Explains why you needed to seize my apartment today," I joke.

"Still, thanks a lot. I live in South Loop, and driving home during rush hour would be a waste of time. I use Tee's place a lot. Elise's, not so much since she lives more north than I usually go. I used to use Brian's apartment. Not too far from here."

I try my best not to react to the mention of Brian. Makes sense he'd act impulsively in this area and seek out a replacement location. But oddly, his voice seems free of resentment.

"How is that going? Is your heart unbroken now?" I say it casually, eyes trained out of the raindrop-speckled window instead of on him.

He sighs and says, "Don't mention it to Tee, but she may have been right."

I can't help the gleeful smile that overtakes my face as I turn to him. "Really? How do you not know if you were in love?"

"I don't know . . ." He shakes his head and takes his attention off the road a moment to look at me. "We'd been saying the words for most of the year we were together. Guess I started to believe it."

I nod absently, recalling the one time I considered myself to be romantically in love, during undergrad junior year. To Joelle's chagrin, it took a while for me to realize that while my feelings might be true, it wasn't the kind of love I wanted to receive. I could understand Cory's predicament because I'm not sure I'd be able to recognize the love I want when I've never experienced it firsthand.

"You were really planning on breaking up with him?" I ask.

"Tee makes it sound worse than it is. I didn't have a concrete date or anything. I was just considering. And if I did it wouldn't have been until . . ."

"Until?" I prompt him.

"Until after I closed my client's case with the evening appointments on his side of town."

"Wow."

"It was only a consideration," he says defensively.

"Wow," I emphasize, then laugh. "No wonder Brian dumped you. Good job, Brian."

"So I've heard." He's grinning at the road ahead of us. *Not heartbroken* is a really good look on him. His off-centered gloom from last week inspired an impulse to incite. But this side of him stirs up a different reaction altogether.

"If you're a physical therapist, shouldn't you be in an office or gym somewhere?"

"I started there, but now I'm working as the full-time traveling physical therapist for my company."

"So you go to people's homes?"

"Most of my work is in the South or West Side, meeting people where they can. Either because their injuries make it difficult for them to travel or simply because they prefer home service."

Aha, now I see why he was comfortable approaching a near-stranger's door.

"Why do you need to borrow apartments to work? Isn't your work with patients?"

"Yes, but it comes with tons of paperwork. I have to approve invoices from our contractors for Accounting since I handle scheduling too. Coffee shops are too busy. Libraries could work, but they're uncontrolled. Also, I'm working on getting an article published in a journal."

Most of that he rattled off with disinterest, except the end. The slight lilt to his voice gives me the impression he's motivated by the journal. Though it's not the explicit communication I tend to seek, I trust that I'm right about this. What is it with this guy that makes me feel like I can understand him in subtle ways? Ways I've only mastered with my family, Joelle, and a handful of other close friends?

"What's the article about?" I ask.

He basically quotes the abstract of his article, but the passion he has for it is clear. It's all about providing access to physical therapy for those who need it the most. It ties together the research he's gathered—surveys of adults with physical disabilities on if their needs are being met and a study of his own patients' access. Then it goes further to propose changes on how to address the issues.

"That's really cool," I say. "It sounds like something my brother would be interested in. He's studying biotechnology and plans to tie it in to health care. His goal is basically the same thing: access."

"Yeah," he says, sounding pleased that little old me approves of his article. "What kind of job are you waiting for?" he asks.

My face scrunches up. "What do you mean?"

"You're temping now. I assume you're waiting for the right position to come along."

"I am. I don't know what, but something."

"You'll-know-when-you-find-it type of thing?"

I bobble my head a bit, noncommittal. "The only thing I've found so far are jobs I'm not a match for."

"That's a step forward. Trust me."

We pull up to the shop. I scan the cars out front, but Bessie isn't among them yet. I unbuckle my seat belt, rezip my jacket, then fluff up my scarf a bit more for the ten steps it'll take me to be in the warmth again. Cory regards me with a smirk but doesn't take the opportunity to tease me for my sensitivity to the cold. He's kind. It took me a while to grasp that with the initial traded jabs I'd instigated, but I see it now. A more peaceful dynamic can exist between us, which I might even enjoy more than getting a rise out of him.

"Feel free to use my apartment whenever you need." I open the car door. Before I heft myself up and out into the cold, I turn back to him and hold up an index finger. "Just text me first."

CHAPTER NINE

Bessie drives as smooth as ever on the way home, so I stop at a nearby grocery store to replenish a few of my commonly used items. With a near-empty stomach, I end up picking up junk food I would do better without. Even on a tight budget, I spring for brownie mix. In my head, I make a case for it: it's cheap, I have all the other ingredients it takes to make it already, and it's a comfort food.

At my prime, I made a batch of brownies biweekly in the postgrad apartment Joelle and I shared. Full-time work quickly began to stress me out, and though I generally didn't turn to baking as a pick-me-up, Joelle convinced me to try. We baked them together. First it was a simple box mix; then we leveled up to making brownies from scratch. When she initially began her chemo treatments, we made a batch with her medical marijuana.

Like much happening in my life, I revert to my most basic level of abilities and choose a rich chocolate mix.

Once I make it home, I realize I'm too tired to both cook a full meal and make my brownies, so I settle for making a quick turkey–grilled cheese for dinner. So much for endorphins and exercise giving me more energy. I play music from my television and make quick work of combining the brownie mix with the eggs, vegetable oil, and water. Then I grease up the square pan, pour half the mix in, and crush Oreo cookies over the layer. I cover it with the other half and pop it in the preheated oven.

With a plop onto the couch, I wait for the excitement of the promise of brownies in my near future to wash over me. Only it never comes. All I feel is the glaring emptiness of who this process is missing. Suddenly, it's obvious the brownies weren't the main reason the ritual used to bring me comfort.

Now I've gone and moved myself away from my family to a place where I only have a few distant connections, no career, and a permanent chill rattling my bones. I hate this. What the hell was I thinking when I made this decision? Everything I imagined I would find here I could have searched for within a week's time. When I inevitably fell short, I could've hopped on my return flight home. The exit from this inadequately considered move will be much longer.

The music becomes too raucous and cheery. I turn it off and go to my room, feeling the heaviness of my failure in every step. I've been taking so many wrong turns in my life. What might I have done differently if I knew I wouldn't have Joelle for long? For one, I'd try to not rely on her to the point of becoming codependent. Not spend so much of our time after graduation working, resulting in me being too tired to go out on weekends. Arrange group travel trips and threaten our friends against their flake-out tendencies. And most of all, I'd pick up on the fucking signs that she was sick earlier. Especially since I was the person around her most!

I held on to denial like a coveted grudge, starting with the initial diagnosis. It was stage three, but surely they could stop it? I confused hope with denial all the way until the end. Maybe even past it. Every truly happy moment I've had since, no matter how fleeting, has been because I've tricked my brain into imagining she's still here with me but just in another room. Or out of town, visiting family. Running late from work, perhaps.

I curl up on my bed, the pressure in my head building until I let the tears leak from my eyes freely. The warmth of them feels like scalding-hot shame.

"I'm sorry," I say aloud, voice trembling. It's a messy knot of things encompassed in my apology. I can't begin to unravel it, so I don't try. Each bit of release I give makes way for more, drawing from a seemingly endless pit. When a sob racks the depths of my chest, I attempt deep breathing. It takes effort to maintain a consistent rhythm. I hug myself, tears escaping at a much slower pace now. Both me and my tear ducts appear to be drained. Eventually, I doze off into a relieving slumber.

The smell of burnt chocolate wakes me up. I remember my brownies immediately and run to the kitchen. It's a little hazy, but not enough smoke to trigger the fire alarm. Leave it to me to ruin the most basic of baked goods. I cut the oven off and take the pan out, then crack open the windows in the kitchen and living room. The brownies are burnt to a crisp. Not even the middle survived. I wipe at my face, too exhausted to feel any lower than I already am. I don't bother to check my reflection before I grab my keys, slide on some shoes by the door, and leave to return to the store for more brownie mix.

CHAPTER TEN

Knock, knock.
(Who's there?)
Met.
(Met who?)
Not you! Can't send your next Met match if you don't get out there!

I'm woken up from my nap with this series of Met notifications. I swipe to clear them, noting location tracking as another problematic aspect of this app. Met isn't listed in the app permissions section on my phone. I've checked multiple times. I close my eyes to the surprise midafternoon sun, hoping for a few more minutes of rest. When my phone chimes again, I open a single eye to read it.

Resist and dismiss, smh. Don't make Met send them to your home!

An unexpected laugh escapes me from this follow-up notification because it's something my mom would say if I continually ignored her calls. I sit up on the couch and push my blanket to the side. The last few days of my off week elapsed with as little movement as possible. Since

I got my car back two days ago, I haven't used it. I've been stuck in a rut of no motivation, made worse by having to deal with my monthly cramps. So I sleep or watch television. Then I think about how much time I've wasted and feel worse.

Joelle isn't the first death of a close loved one I've experienced, but it's the first where I've felt this confused at how to handle it, how to move forward. She'd been at peace with her impending death and helped me accept it too. There were goals she had yet to accomplish, but in the grand scheme of things, she was satisfied with what she had done and the people she loved.

Every day since she died, I've tried to lead my life with the light Joelle had. Some days, I feel like I don't come close.

But today is the first day all week the sun has made an appearance. I might have wasted the first half of the day, but it's not too late to turn it around. I start by eating my first complete meal in days, because apparently my body doesn't have much energy when I don't nourish it. Then I go through the emails I've ignored. The only important one is for my Chicago Public Schools application. I fill out the background-check form required of substitute teachers. One task down for today—success.

I'm scuttling around, straightening up the accumulated mess while barely paying attention to the show streaming on my television, when my tablet starts ringing with a video call. I drop a handful of clothes in a pile near the hall entrance and go to where my tablet is plugged in. There are two boxes on the screen labeled "Lito" and "Momma Llama." It instantly puts a smile on my face as I slide to answer and prop it up to free my hands for use.

"Hey," I wave. *"Both of you at the same time? Why am I so lucky?"*

"You never returned my call from two days ago," Mom signs.

"And I texted you twice," Lito adds. *"About my interview in Chicago next week."*

Oh. I hadn't gotten around to the returning-correspondence part of my bounce-back day. I wince. *"Sorry. I forgot."*

Lito purses his lips and turns his head to look at me out of the corner of his eye. *"Come on, Cori. We know it was Joelle's birthday."*

Of course they would remember. She was as much a part of my family as she was her own. When she became my chosen sister, she inherited my family, and I hers. My mom alternated calling our cell phones whenever she wanted to check in on us. Lito bonded with her over their shared interest in technology advancement. They had a relationship that stood on its own.

"It's the first one without her. It sucks," Lito signs.

I nod.

"You all right now?" Mom asks.

I tilt my head from left to right. *"Getting there. Lito, when is your interview? Do I need to pick you up?"*

"Nope, the program is arranging everything. It's a tight schedule. I probably won't have time to see you."

Well, what was the point of teasing me, then? Seeing Lito earlier than originally planned could be just what I need to break me out of this funk. I briefly consider showing up at the airport just to see him in passing, then think better of it. If he didn't get offered the internship after me pulling a stunt like that, both of my parents would blame it on me.

"Don't pout. We came with good news," Mom tells me. Her gaze moves from the camera lens to somewhere below it. *"Lito?"*

He makes a playful face at her intro before signing, *"Mom is crashing my trip to visit you."*

"I'm your mother. I can't crash anything of yours if I'm the reason you're here to experience it."

"True," I sign, siding with my mom mostly because I'm excited to have them both here at the same time. *"When are you coming?"*

"My last final is May twelfth. Then I need time to wrap up things here. I'm tracking ticket prices." Lito places his hand over his heart. *"Look how happy she is."*

He's teasing me, but my cheeks haven't had this much action in days. When I was younger, I never felt homesick. I'd go to weekend camps or stay with a relative through the summer and be perfectly fine. During college, though I was only a few hours away, I mostly confined my trips home to the major holidays. Then I started my career in Houston and got used to having family around. I appreciated them more as an adult after being around people who didn't get me as intrinsically as family does.

Mom asks Lito more about his summer-internship search, and he goes through the list of places he's applied to along with a short pro-and-con list for each. He's focusing on research programs. I've gotten most of this information from my last conversation with him, so I watch passively as my mom expresses enthusiasm for each possibility. When he's done, Mom shifts to me.

"And Cori, how's the sub process going?"

I let out a shallow sigh and lazily sign, *"I submitted the background-check form. I should be able to get into one of the trainings next weekend. Then I can start accepting jobs."*

"Great. You never know—this might be your calling."

"Doubt it," I sign slyly, morphing it with the movement of pushing my hair out of my face. Only Lito catches it and snorts out a laugh.

My mom taught fifth grade for five years before moving into administration. When she retired as a beloved principal to an elementary school, the fourth and fifth grade classes put on a short production about her career in homage. I've attended enough school events with her preretirement to know working full-time in a school wouldn't be a good match for me. However, adding substitute teaching as a revenue stream is irresistible. There's an abundance of jobs available daily, hence the desperate call for new hires.

The arrival of a text is signaled with a vibration from my phone on the couch and a banner pop-up on my tablet. My two most popular contacts are on this video chat with me, so I'm momentarily confused by the unsaved local number until I open the message.

Okay to use my new South Side office?

When I swipe back to the video call, I still have a smile on my face that Lito immediately questions.

"I know you're not grinning like that because of substitute teaching."

"One moment," I tell them as I scurry off to reply on my phone.

Whoa, your nameplate isn't on the door yet. But I'm home so come on by.

ETA 9 minutes, Cory replies. I go ahead and save his number in my phone as The Other Cory.

When I walk back into view of the camera, my mom freezes her hand movement for a second to give me a suspicious look but continues telling us about her plans for the weekend.

Soon, there's a buzzing from my intercom.

"Who's at your door?" Mom's hands move in sharp accusation. Then she tells Lito, *"I heard the doorbell alert sound."*

I quickly press the mute button on my tablet. *"I'll be back,"* I tell them and disappear before they can question me.

I press the talk button on the intercom. "How did you get up without being buzzed in last time?"

"Door wasn't closed all the way. Gotta tell my officemates to make sure they are pulling it enough for the lock to latch."

"You should know I'm rolling my eyes right now."

"I felt it."

I buzz him in, unlock the door, and listen to him jog up the stairs until he appears on my floor. It's dark-gray scrubs and a navy-blue rain jacket today, his laptop bag hanging on his shoulder.

"Make yourself comfortable." I leave him to go back to the kitchen island as he takes off his shoes.

"Who was it?" Mom asks as soon as I'm back on camera. My tablet is angled away from my door and living room, shielding Cory from view.

"No one." She peers at me, bending her face closer to the lens. *"My friend."*

"You have friends already?" Lito asks at the same time Mom finger spells something.

"Wait, you can't sign at the same time. What am I supposed to do, split my eyes?"

"That's what I do," Lito signs. I don't doubt it. His peripheral skills are unmatched.

"What did you say, Momma?" I ask her, and make sure I'm looking at the box with her face to catch it this time.

"Is it Tiwanda?"

"No, but it is one of her best friends."

"See! I told you to reach out to her earlier."

I nod, though I have a case for timing. My mom only knows planning and action. Whenever I point out the validity of lying in wait, she likens me to my father. Not in a complimentary way. Thinking of my dad, my wires must get crossed with Mom's, because she tells us, *"I spoke with your father yesterday. He had a lot of questions about you two."*

"He emailed me," Lito says with a roll of his eyes, undoubtedly annoyed that this is the best way for them to communicate since Dad let his signing skills go to shit. Also, Dad finds joy in addressing emails to Lito's student account.

I get the feeling of being watched more than I should in a video call. Cory hasn't settled on the couch yet. He's looking my way, and for a moment, I worry he knows sign language and is eavesdropping.

"Sorry," he says when he realizes he's staring. He turns away from me as he takes a seat on the right side of the couch.

"I'll call him soon," I sign, trying to ignore the hostility from the box containing Lito's face. My dad is a lousy texter, so to really know what's going on in his life, I have to get him on the phone. He tries to see me and Lito once every year, but only I reciprocate the effort. I don't fault Lito for not wanting to go through a video remote interpreter to chat with Dad on the phone. Neither do I hound him for not wanting to spend holidays with Dad's very nonsigning household, though I always selfishly want him there to have my back. *"I have to go, but tell me when you buy your flights."*

We say our goodbyes and hang up. I close the cover over my tablet with a snap, then go to turn the television off.

"I can move this into my room," I say to Cory.

"Why?"

I wave my hand in a flourish in his direction. "So you can work?"

He laughs lightly. "I can work fine with you out here. It's a shared office space." He winks at me.

I take my tablet and the remote and curl up in the lounge chair. Cory opens his laptop and puts his first earbud in on the side away from me. As he lifts his phone to undoubtedly start his music, I interrupt his process.

"I thought you didn't like being around people while working."

"Did I say that?"

I frown, search my memory. "Pretty much."

Cory shakes his head. "It's the visual noise that's the problem. When there's too much going on in the environment, I can't focus. One person"—he tilts his head toward me—"is fine. Even one person watching TV and questioning me."

"Okay, fine. Get back to your work. I won't bother you. Much."

He grins as he plays his music and begins typing away on his laptop, never inserting his second earbud.

CHAPTER ELEVEN

Lito hasn't texted me since his flight landed last night. No updates about the dinner event the research program planned for the group of interviewees or how the interview itself is going. I know he said it wasn't likely he'd have time to see me in such a tight time frame, but the least he could do is give me a play by play. Finally, as it approaches two o'clock and I'm considering circling the research center in hopes of spotting him, he texts me.

> Interview ended early 1 hour. Wanna grab lunch before my flight?

I hop up from the couch before typing a response. On the way to throw on clothes, I text him, suggesting a café near the airport for us to meet.

I make it there before him and order for both of us. We aren't picky eaters, so I get two appetizing lunch options with the plan of giving him first dibs. I also tack on drinks, chips, and a couple of cookies. In the hours past the lunch rush, I have my pick of tables.

Lito makes it before our food arrives. Since I've had one eye on the door, I spot him first. He casts a look around the scarce crowd until he finally finds me. I jump up and meet him halfway to wrap him in a hug. It's been four years since he surpassed my height. He's a couple of inches shy of six feet and only three inches taller than me now, but I still dramatically pounce on him like he's a giant.

He laughs and drops his duffel bag to catch me before letting me back down.

"Sorry," I sign. *"Don't want to wrinkle your nice outfit."*

He's wearing a navy-blue suit, but the jacket is gone—I assume stashed away in his carry-on. The button-up he chose is light blue with gray pinstripes. His hair is shaved at the sides and back, leaving a curly fro only at the top of his head. As he gets settled at our table, I snap a picture of him to send to Mom and Dad. He pauses to pose for a few, then puts his backpack in the empty third chair at our table and his duffel on the floor, nestled between the chair and the graffiti art–covered wall.

"Well?" I ask. *"Are you going to come spend the summer with me?"*

He grins. *"I'd have to get offered the internship first, and even then it'd be my third pick."*

I frown. *"Me living here should have some impact."*

He bounces his head from side to side as he considers this. *"You're right. It's my fourth pick."*

I kick him under the table, which makes him laugh harder, but he still gives me the consolation prize of bumping it up to second pick. My name is called for our food order, so I excuse myself to run and get it. Lito chooses the jerk-chicken wrap, which leaves me with the chicken-melt sandwich. While we eat, he gives me the rundown on how his interview went.

He arrived yesterday evening, and the program arranged for all interviewees to have dinner, along with current interns and recently hired research assistants. They got to chat and ask questions related to internships and their careers. He had two interpreters there, who mostly interpreted the conversations happening directly with him. When they managed to relay bits of relevant side chats, it was oftentimes too late for him to jump in.

For the actual interview, he had a different interpreter who was assigned well in advance. Lito was able to send the interpreting agency background information about the job and a video of the signs he uses for high-frequency jargon. Then he met with the interpreter an hour before the actual interview, where they were able to chat with each other and prep a little more. When it was time for the interview, they both felt comfortable with each other, and he thought it went smoothly.

"How did the job itself sound?" I ask.

"It's strictly research, which I wanted. I'd help with two projects. Their facilities are top notch."

I nod, knowing it's often the people who make the job. Lito not mentioning any doesn't bode well for my chances of having him here for the summer. My own college-internship experience was at a small company in Corpus Christi, Texas. Joelle had accepted an internship in Austin. I was the only intern in Budgeting, and they did nothing to connect me with the other interns scattered around other departments. Halfway through the summer, the intern from HR reached out to ask if any of us wanted to join them for a sand volleyball tournament. I joined for the human contact, despite not being able to play ball-related sports to save my life. Once we gathered enough skilled players, they relegated me to scorekeeping.

A message comes through my phone. I hold it up for Lito to read what our dad sent.

Looking sharp, son!

"Those pictures were for Dad?"

"I knew he'd be the most excited. Look, he sent a GIF."

Lito shakes his head, then pulls open his bag of chips. He puts a few in his mouth, avoiding eye contact with me.

I wave at him to get his attention, though he's actively ignoring me. *"Hey, hey. Carlito,"* I sign, spelling out his full name, extending my arm with each letter so that with the ending *O*, my hand is right in front of his face. He was named after Dad's favorite movie, after all.

"I'm annoyed," he says after swatting my hand away. *"He struggles through conversations in person, but he's always posting me on social media I don't even have. If I'm not on there, who is he posting for?"*

I twist my lips as his point lands. It's easy to understand his perspective. When I told Lito I was going to spend last Christmas with Dad and his long-term girlfriend, Monique, he declined coming with me. Ever since he's been of age to decide where he wanted to go for the holidays, he's chosen against spending it with Dad. When I'm there, it's hard not to scrutinize how Dad interacts with Monique and her two children. He might not have remarried, but they are a family unit. And since everyone in his household can hear, they communicate in spoken English. It's like Dad dropped all efforts to learn sign language when he started his new family in a state separate from us. Right before their divorce when I was eight, I remember us all learning together. Dad was better than Mom at practicing with me. But after the divorce, while Mom resolutely took lessons and hired a couple of Deaf educators and advocates in the Houston area to come interact with Lito to teach him the language from native signers and surround him with role models, Dad took a load off his shoulders. I can see how that would feel like shirking responsibility for Lito.

"When I call Dad, he asks about you before letting me get out the reason I'm calling in the first place. I'm sure Mom gets similar treatment. He posts you because he's proud. And he's also probably bragging to Monique's family since they never really liked him anyway. That's why they never married. He wants to show them all he has a more accomplished son than any of their children."

Lito's eyebrows raise in swaggering agreement to the last statement.

"Tell him I said thanks," he signs in relenting swoops.

"Text him yourself."

"Now you're asking too much." He swipes a cookie from the table and puts it in the front part of his backpack. *"You feeling better since Joelle's birthday?"*

My head sways, noncommittal, as I recall the double-batch-of-brownies night. That's one convenience of living alone—having the option not to disclose my kitchen blunders. If I was back in the Houston house, I surely would've heard, "Corinne almost burnt down the house," a couple of times. Since that night, today has been the biggest high. Hopefully, the effect Lito has on my mood will hold well after he's left on his flight.

We clean off our table, then carry his bags to my car, parked a few blocks away. On our drive to the airport, Lito complains about how underwhelming the parts of the city he saw were and how he expects to see more when he visits at the end of his semester. If he's offered and accepts this internship, he'd be able to come for the planned visit with Mom and just stay to start his internship soon after. Even if they provide housing for interns, I'd still see him often. Though not much has recently, I dare to hope this works out in my favor.

CHAPTER TWELVE

The last week of March wraps around me like an embrace and squeezes a little harder each day. I work three days of the five, a relief after a week of no work. On Tuesday, when Cory texts if he can use my apartment, I'm at a conference, working as an extra pair of hired hands. They had me manning the registration table at first, and now I'm running around, doing whatever tasks the organizers ask of me. As I left my apartment this morning, I briefly considered leaving my key under the mat for Cory but thought better of it. During my brief break, while all the attendees are occupied with their catered box lunches, I follow up with him.

> *Me:* What replacement office did you find?
> *The Other Cory:* The library ☹️ it's children's story time and a woman at the next table over is clipping her toenails.
> *Me:* Sounds promising! If you want to break your lease, I totally understand.

While staring at the three dots as Cory types his reply, my phone alerts me to a call from my mother. I ignore it as a reflex, then cringe because I can feel her scowl from Houston. I quickly compose a text explaining I'm working, then slip my phone away as the organizer approaches me.

No doubt Mom is calling about my substitute teacher–training day, which I scheduled for Saturday. Last we talked about it, I said it would be either this weekend or next. I already committed to going out Friday night with Elise and crew for her last-day-of-work celebration. Following that up with an early morning of how-to-babysit-children training isn't appealing . . . at all. But my mom pestered me enough that I emailed my HR representative to sign up for this Saturday. I haven't updated her yet, hence the calls.

I also woke up this morning with a confirmation email that my rent has been paid. My mom was a few days early, probably as an exclamation point to this being her last agreed-upon month of covering my rent. The pressure of having thirty days until I take an $899 hit to my savings account is weighing on me. Unsolicited, Tiwanda made me a spreadsheet that will help make sure I accept enough gigs to break even each month. She has spectacular timing, because I didn't mention my finances were gearing to change.

Due to traffic, it's nearly six when I get home. I grab the mail before heading up to my apartment. Since I've started working more and getting out, I'm realizing how much of a solace it is to come here. Even with my minimal design effort, it's starting to feel like home base. I should do something about the decorations. No matter how temporary this move might turn out to be, the comfort would be worth it.

Among the short stack of mail I place on my kitchen island, the landlord has left a small brown envelope with the key copies promised at move-in. There are two sets. I slide them onto the palm of my hand and stare at them, remembering the time I locked myself out of the apartment in Houston. Joelle had an important team meeting that day, so I drove all the way across town to Mom's house to get her spare set.

Sighing, I replace them in the envelope. One set can go to Tiwanda. She is my sort-of-cousin, after all.

~

Cory's South Loop apartment is the designated meeting point for Elise's Friday-night liberation celebration. It's fascinating to finally get a tour of his space. The living room has a dark-green accent wall, and through-out the apartment, traces of the color resonate—the leaf pattern on a throw pillow, his bathroom shower curtain, the blanket hanging off the back of his couch, a thriving plant near the window. His bookshelf is a mix of fiction titles, nonfiction sociological topics, and texts pertaining to physical therapy.

While Cory is in his bedroom getting ready, Tiwanda and I sip an end-of-the-week glass of wine, chatting about the crossover of family we share and catching each other up on our weeks.

"Any job-search leads?" she asks.

I shake my head. "I'm borderline ready to give my mom free rein to start sending me vacancies."

Tiwanda widens her eyes. "Ever since I mentioned my work strug-gles to her, she sends me at least one posting a week. She'll be forward-ing you positions like lead financial analyst."

"Chief financial officer, more like it."

"President of the presidents."

I raise my glass. "The queen of falling up."

Soon, Elise arrives dressed in a fire engine–red high-collar lace top, and Cory is out of his bedroom. Before we leave, we take celebratory shots of tequila from a bottle Cory gifted to Elise.

"Oh." I fish around in my purse, then locate the brown envelope with my extra sets of keys and drop it on the coffee table. "I finally got spares and figured at least one of you should have a copy. For emergen-cies and stuff."

Tiwanda snatches up the envelope and shakes out a set. "Perfect. I'll keep it at my apartment."

Neither Elise nor Cory makes a move to take the second one, which is fine. I could give the second set to my mom. If anything happens and Tiwanda is MIA, she can overnight them to me. Of course, then I wouldn't be able to get them, with my mailbox key locked inside my apartment. All right, maybe I'll leave them in my car's glove compartment, then.

"I always lose keys." Elise shakes her head. "That's the reason my condo has a keypad."

"A key for Elise is a key for the entire city of Chicago." Tiwanda gives Elise a look as if she's speaking from experience. "You spend the most time over there anyway, Cory. You take it."

Finally, I look up at Cory, an act I'd been blatantly avoiding all this time. He's staring at me in a way that asks for permission. I give him an insouciant shrug, as if I didn't bring the second copy with him in mind. He slides the envelope toward himself and pockets it, a barely concealed smirk on his face.

"Don't think this means you can pop up all willy-nilly."

"Mhmm." He takes a swig from his bottle of water around a grin.

We summon a rideshare to a nearby bar. Even with Elise in four-inch heels, Tiwanda is the tallest, and her curvy frame deserves to be not only worshipped but also yielded to. She gets the front seat while the rest of us squeeze into the back, with Elise in the middle.

"How are you okay with not knowing what we're doing?" Cory asks.

Elise levels him with an exasperated glare. "I like surprises; you know that. Now, stop worrying. We'll get more information soon."

It takes two suspiciously chosen hip-hop songs to get to the bar. Per the instructions of Elise's ex–work husband, we wait on the sidewalk outside. I'm grateful for my decision to wear my fluffiest coat, damn the inconvenience of finding a place to store it wherever we land. Work husband, Samang, meets us outside with a few other friends Elise greets enthusiastically. Before I can meet everyone, he calls us to attention.

"We'll have time for that later," he says as he steps between me and a woman named Anne's outstretched hands. He pauses as he takes count of our group. "Where's Vivienne and Jae?"

"Here!" The couple speed walks up to us, arms linked. They start to greet everyone with hugs, but Samang shuts it down.

"Too late for that. I hereby welcome you all to Elise's Amazing Race to Liberation!"

Elise bounces up and down on her toes. Tiwanda grins indulgently. Cory is hard to read. Either he's apathetic about this ordeal or hyperassessing the situation behind his blank face. I'm queasy with preperformance jitters.

Samang explains the rules. It's basically *The Amazing Race: South Chicago* edition. He and the friends who decided the four locations aren't participating but will meet us at the final spot. Each place represents somewhere Elise couldn't meet up with friends due to work obligations.

"Elise, you arrange the teams."

A malevolent grin creeps up Elise's face as she turns to weigh her options. The participants are us four, plus the latecomers, Vivienne and Jae. She steeples her fingers together as she paces the sidewalk in front of us, oblivious to the people doing the Cha Cha Slide to get around our large group.

"You all have strengths and weaknesses I must consider."

There's a ruffle of angst among us five as Elise employs her dramatics. My arms are folded to trap heat. No need to puff out my chest like Cory, since I have no chance at being chosen as Elise's partner. I'm too much of a wild card. It's nice of her to include me in this celebration at all. I stand by as she decides how to pair us.

"For my teammate, I choose . . . Tiwanda!"

Tiwanda hisses, "Yes!" and shoves Cory in the shoulder. Already a sore winner. Her premature celebration makes me want to beat them to the finish line with whoever I have as partner. Elise surveys the four of us left, faced with a decision on whether to split up Vivienne and Jae.

"I fully intend on winning, but I do want some competition. Viv and Jae, you two can stay together. Cories"—there's a laugh dancing in the neon light reflected in Elise's eyes—"try to make it to the final stop before midnight."

Upon getting the envelope with our first clue from Samang, Cory and I huddle together away from our competition. He rips it open and reads it aloud.

"Work can be taxing. Though you cannot enter at this hour, find your next clue under an extinct friend with lots of power."

Cory lifts the paper closer to his face and mutters the words again under his breath. "What isn't open at this hour?"

It's past eight o'clock—plenty of places are closed. My streak of competitiveness fizzles as I realize the odds of winning are stacked in Elise's favor. Tiwanda is on her phone halfway down the block, ordering their rideshare by the looks of it. How am I supposed to riddle out the places she couldn't visit? Also, the shots we took at Cory's apartment are starting to hit me. The insides of my cheeks tingle with awareness, and I'm no longer as concerned about the windchill.

"Can we stop to get food?" I ask.

Cory must be at risk of whiplash by how fast he snaps his head toward me. He's wearing a navy-blue skullcap that manages to stay on despite the sharp movement.

"There'll be food at the last stop. Don't play with me, Corinne. I will carry you on my back if I need to."

The thought of him carrying me is so appealing, I'm unable to respond. Instead, I mumble nonsense about how there isn't a prize at the end of this and snatch the paper away from him to read the clue myself. Only then do I notice the partial underline of _taxing_. *Closed. Extinct.*

"Get us a rideshare to the Field Museum," I tell Cory.

He wastes no time prodding the thought process that led me here. Down the way, Vivienne and Jae slide into the back seat of a car. Tiwanda and Elise are still here, and the wind carries Tiwanda's voice cursing that her ordered rideshare driver canceled the trip. Cory shows me his phone screen estimating three minutes for our car to arrive. When it pulls up before Tiwanda and Elise's, we hightail it and wave goodbye with our middle fingers.

"We're one hundred percent going to the right place?" Cory asks once we're strapped into our seats and away from the risk of being overheard.

"*Taxing* makes me think taxidermy. That's at the Field Museum. Carl Cotton did a lot of the exhibits there. He's this badass Black man from the South Side and a World War II vet. My mom wants to go see his work and sent me lots of articles in preparation."

"I've been," our driver says. "Amazing. Highly recommended, but isn't it closed?"

"We're not going inside. The dinosaur statue." It dawns on Cory. "I knew there was a good reason for wanting you on my team."

"Bullshit." I call him on his lie, clearly recalling his sour face when Elise picked Tiwanda over him. He laughs, not bothering to deny it.

"Stuffing dead animals, though . . ." He shivers like he's swallowed a tablespoon of cough syrup. "On the obligatory elementary school field trip there, I ended up running out of the room and losing my class after a friend scared me."

I reach over and pat his shoulder. "Trust me, that's probably more common than you think. About a third of my class wasn't feeling it."

"It's a bit creepy," our driver agrees. "But, if you can get past that, worth it."

"It's about preserving life. That's all any of us try to do, in various ways."

Cory's attention on me is a weighted blanket. I haven't tried one of those myself to know if it's comforting or suffocating. Our driver gets us as close as he can to our mark. Cory bribes him to wait for us with the promise of a hefty tip. We get out and jog up the concrete steps and around a small garden, then tackle another set of steps before our Brachiosaurus looms ahead of us.

Three envelopes are hidden between the metacarpals, where a passerby wouldn't be likely to spot them. Vivienne and Jae must have gone to the wrong location, because they should have beat us here to pick up their clue by now. We hurry back to our car before opening the envelope.

Cory shines his phone's flashlight down on the paper.

"*Time to raise the steak. Planned to go to lunch in 1946, Elise stayed behind with a bug to fix.* What the hell kind of clue is this?"

"A biased one. Has to be a restaurant, maybe founded in 1946?" I lean into him, the refreshing scent momentarily stunning me. It's an evocative mixture of smoky vanilla and mint notes. I forcefully exhale the smell of him from my nostrils.

As Cory unlocks his phone to pull up a search engine, our driver says, "It's gotta be Ricobene's, right? Best steak sandwich in all of Chicago." I'm not familiar with the restaurant, but Cory slaps his hand on his forehead.

"I'm trippin'. That was my dad's favorite spot." He puts the destination in the rideshare app for our driver to accept the altered route.

Outside the restaurant, a chalkboard sign displays instructions: Elise's Amazing Race: See Cashier. My mouth waters the moment we step into Ricobene's. The line to place to-go orders is five people deep, and most dine-in tables are occupied. As Cory tries to jump the line, I get in at the end and stare at a young child at a table with their family, lifting a two-hands-required slice of pizza to their mouth.

"He won't give it to me. Says we have to wait our turn." Cory huffs. "I swear, if he lets Elise get hers before—what are you staring at?"

I shake my head to snap out of my daze in the nick of time. I'd begun having visions of sliding into the empty chair and asking to be adopted into the family for a slice of pizza.

"Mom?" Cory must have the same idea. "Hold our place." He leaves me and doesn't approach the table with my coveted pizza but instead one in the corner of the restaurant. There, a middle-aged Black woman shares a table with a man whose back is toward me. As Cory approaches, her face lights up but quickly dims as she casts a glance at her dinner date. She rises to hug her son and gestures to the man. The cacophony of conversations makes it impossible to decipher their specific words, but it's obvious an introduction is happening. The man rises, too, and he and Cory shake hands. It's incredible how Cory's demeanor changes as he grips the stranger's hand. He goes from his usual easygoing self to someone stiff shouldered and watchful.

"Next!" The cashier calls out aggressively. I scamper up to him.

"Do you have the envelopes?"

His eyes scan the line behind me. "Depends on who's asking."

"Elise," I say as convincing as a toddler learning to fib.

This kid can't be older than eighteen, but he skeptically eyes me up and down with all the power bestowed in him by being keeper of the envelopes.

"I was told Elise is Asian and wearing red. You don't look Asian, and I don't see any red."

This race truly is set up in Elise's favor. She's the person of honor, but what's the point of having us play along if the winner has already been decided? Viv and Jae are Asian, so on the off chance one of them has red on underneath their jackets, they can easily get this kid to hand over the next clue. We can't go down without a fight.

I gasp and hold up a hand to my chest. "Are you calling me Black?" I say in an unnecessarily loud voice, making three syllables of the word *Black*. The awareness of the people nearest us shifts to a tangible focus.

"N-no," the boy stutters. He reaches under the register and pulls out an envelope. I snatch it away.

"Because that would be correct. Sorry, I really needed this envelope." I glance at Cory. The three of them are now seated at the table, Cory leaning back like he has all the time in the world. *Oh boy.* "Can you also put in an order of whatever sandwich people get here, to go?"

I grab a vacated table near the door to wait on Cory and my food, keeping a lookout for the competition. When Tiwanda and Elise enter, I hop up.

"Ugh! I can't believe we went to the wrong place," I complain.

"Nice try but I'm the actress in this friend group," Elise says. She starts to bypass the line and walk up to the cashier. I block her with my body like we're playing man-on-man defense. It ultimately fails when Tiwanda grabs me by the shoulders and pulls me out of the way. When Elise reaches the counter, Cashier Boy takes one look at me struggling to rid myself of Tiwanda's grip and hands over the envelope while directing a shit-eating grin my way.

"Is that Miss Lorraine?" Tiwanda sets me free to hustle over to Cory and his mom. She gives her a quick hug and cackles past me as she and Elise leave us in their dust.

Thankfully, seeing Tiwanda reminds Cory of our quest. He pushes his chair back in sync with my order number being called. On my way to pick up my bag, I hand off the clue to him. I had no luck figuring it out myself.

The wall between Elise and her dreams has fallen. We see dragons in her future.

"It's Chinatown," Cory says when I'm back beside him. "Let's get out of here."

We leave, but our rideshare is long gone. Cory orders another one that estimates a five-minute arrival time. Instead of going back inside, we pass the wait on the sidewalk. Cory broods silently with his secret thoughts, and I try not to drip red sauce on my coat while eating my sandwich. Apparently, Cashier Boy ordered a breaded steak sandwich for me. It's so delicious, I forgive him for being an accomplice in this rigged race. Vivienne and Jae arrive after a few minutes. We hardly react beyond sharing a resigned sigh.

Cory laughs out of the blue. "At least you got your food."

"I'm counting it as a win." I lift it to him in offering. He shakes his head. "Go on, rip off a piece from the other end."

He obliges. His eyes close and his chin lifts a couple of inches as he chews. "Definitely a win." When he finishes his piece, he glances back at the restaurant, and the fog settles over him again.

"Seeing your mom was a loss, I'm guessing?"

"That's always a win. Unfortunately, the prize was meeting the man she's been dating for six months?" He hitches the end into a question, still doubting this information he's stumbled upon. I don't know what else could boost his mood, so I offer him more steak sandwich.

Our new rideshare arrives before Vivienne and Jae emerge from the restaurant. The next trip is quicker than the time we waited for our car to show up. We clamber out of the back seat, and the driver takes off before we think to ask her to wait. Both of us are off our game.

The lamplit gold-and-green wall before us is breathtaking. Nine dancing dragons in gold, blue, and red are raised from the surface. There are hundreds of smaller dragons adorning the wall too. It's surrounded by a spike-topped black fence. As I scan the perimeter for a white envelope, my eyes catch on an unbelievable sight: Tiwanda and Elise. They must be struggling to find the clue!

Cory and I split up to circle the structure and meet on the other side of the fence, fruitless.

"There's no place else it could be," Cory assures me. We both turn at Elise's voice cheering on Tiwanda, who has hopped over the fence and is running toward the wall. Only then do I notice the flash of white at the base. Cory springs into action, hoisting himself over the fence in one fluid motion. With her head start and speed, Tiwanda still reaches it first and is halfway back to Elise when Cory picks up our envelope. Tiwanda hands over the clue to Elise as she struggles to climb the fence again without hurting herself. Cory gains ground, hopping the fence adeptly to rejoin me on the other side.

As we rip open our clue, Tiwanda, having managed to clear the fence, and Elise, who read the clue while Tiwanda struggled, are jogging down the street. We follow on instinct as we read the final clue: *Swan song.*

"There's a karaoke bar right up the street," Cory says as he picks up speed, knowing where we're headed. We dodge people on the sidewalk as best we can, shouting out hurried apologies as they curse us. Tiwanda might be too far up to catch, but Elise is struggling to keep up in her heels. Tiwanda reaches the door and holds it open, yelling at Elise like a fervent basketball mom. As we pass Elise only three strides away from the entrance, I feel no remorse ripping this victory from her. But Tiwanda closes the door to deny us. The four of us push and pull and jostle each other until we stumble inside in a knot. Samang awaits inside the door and, because his loyalties lie with his work wife, promptly declares Elise and Tiwanda the victors.

CHAPTER THIRTEEN

The karaoke bar is crowded, but Elise's friends have snagged several tables in the public lounge. Onstage, a man is singing a K-Pop number. After easily accepting her unrightful victory, Elise makes a beeline to select a song, dragging Cory along with her. Tiwanda goes to the bar to get us drinks. A chime, loud enough to be heard above the crooning, comes from my coat pocket. I glance at the blessedly unfamiliar faces around me before reaching for my phone.

A duet with Met, perhaps? Or maybe with your soul mate?

I clear my screen, though I throw a few more cautious looks around the bar to make absolutely sure there's no one here I recognize. I'm in the clear, so I settle back into my seat beside Samang and Anne, alternating tuning in to their conversation and the performance.

Ever since college, I can't seem to escape karaoke bars. While I merely tolerated singing in bars, the friends I kept loved it. They got me behind the mic by picking songs from groups like Destiny's Child or fun duets. "The Boy is Mine" by Brandy and Monica was a favorite of mine and Joelle's. Knowing that customary performance isn't in store for tonight urges me to attempt an early escape, but I can think of nothing Joelle would bemoan more.

Tiwanda returns, balancing four glasses in her hands. She hands me a tequila sunrise. I sip on it and reel my mind back to the present. The guy onstage wraps up his song, and the emcee announces Elise singing "Freedom" by Beyoncé—a fitting choice.

"How is it her turn already?" I wonder aloud.

"She knows the emcee. She'll perform as often as she wants here," Tiwanda says.

Elise starts the song, and it's clear she's no amateur. There aren't many people on the dance floor in front of the stage, making it easy to spot Cory hyping her up. Tiwanda stands and grabs my arm to go up. Several of Elise's other friends follow, including Vivienne and Jae, who make it just in time. By the end of the song, a dozen more people are on their feet. No wonder she has a fast pass to the stage.

She goes back up three more times throughout the night, her picks varying from Broadway to pop songs. Cory gets up and sings an R & B throwback, and I am roped into performing "No Scrubs" with Tiwanda and Elise. Eventually, great song choices lead to the dance floor filling up. With the alcohol in my system, I have no choice but to join in. It's either move to the rhythm or fall asleep in our booth.

We dance as a group. At one point, Elise and Tiwanda start dancing on Cory, one on each side. I laugh at the sight, and I'm grateful I've been adopted by this group. In my decision to move here, I never imagined it would bring real friends. I didn't think I had the persistence required to recruit friends and create a group. That may be true, but I do have a not-really-my-cousin who has some amazing people in her corner.

I move behind Cory since there's no way—even tipsy—I would grind against the front of him while he's in the middle of a Ti-lise sandwich. First, I dance with my front pressed against his back. It's nothing sexy, if not a little awkward. My body still overreacts to the contact, my breasts brushing his muscular back and his butt firm against my lower abdomen. An unwarranted spark of heat in my chest has me turning around to hide the confusion playing out on my face. There's barely any contact between us now as I bounce to the beat. I'm still part of this clustered dance and able to keep my sanity.

Then I sense the absence of Cory, though Elise and Tiwanda are still going hard beside me. As I turn to make sure he's still there, familiar hands rest on my waist. I stiffen and forget how to move naturally. He leans into me, angling his chin in the crook of my neck. Tiwanda and Elise sing along to the song with more fervor and shift so they're partially dancing on Cory, partially on me. With Cory's hips setting a rhythm, I remember how to dance again. I lean my upper body away from him so I'm not distracted by how his breath tickles the skin along my jaw and wind into him, teasing him as much as possible. When I feel him match my intensity, rolling his hips in time to counter mine, I fear my plan is backfiring.

I spin out of his grip and cause our group to shuffle. They might be inebriated enough not to notice. When the song ends, I excuse myself to the bar to get another glass of water and bring a couple of extras back to the table. Elise is sitting on the booth side, swaying to the music with Samang and eating a pot sticker from our appetizer platter. Tiwanda and Cory are still among the crowd on the dance floor while a man with neon-blue hair is onstage crushing a song in Mandarin.

"It was getting hot out there," Elise says.

I nod in agreement, sliding the glass of water across the table.

"I mean you and Cory. Cory squared, if you will."

"I won't."

Elise laughs. "Met app said you've met your soul mate. It didn't specify when. A decade before it showed up, or days. Wait—" The alcohol must clear for a second, because she seems to realize she's not following the logical process of elimination. "When did you and Cory meet?"

"After," I say immediately. It's a thought I've had more than I care to admit, since the app is nothing more than a pop-up virus. "He wasn't at Tiwanda's party, remember?"

"Oh yeah." She waves this info away as inconsequential. "Doesn't mean you can't get some."

"Get some? You need to *get some* water in your system and stop trying to pimp me out."

Elise guffaws. "Fine. You're right. Let's wait and see who Met sends you."

I start to rebuke this, tell her Met is all pesky notifications and no bite, but her gaze has shifted to Tiwanda and Cory making their way back. This is outside the scope of topics I can deal with at my current level of intoxication. I mentally cut myself off any more drinking, my early morning with substitute-teaching training in mind. It's only when Elise demands she's buying the next round, since both her groups of friends have been treating her all night, that I notice Cory has tapered off his drinking too. I try to think back to the last time I saw him taking a shot or drink, but that, too, is above my abilities. I'm left to ponder, in my tipsiness, if our flirty dancing was a result of mutual alcohol-inspired loss of inhibitions or something I should follow up on.

~

After finishing the seven-hour training, I am granted access to start accepting substitute teaching gigs. Fortunately, I can put that nightmare off for three more weeks because my temp agency offered me another job. A nicely paying one, at that. It's an assistant position at Jones & Jackson Law Offices. I work a dreadfully early shift—7:00 a.m. to 3:30 p.m.—but underemployed bitches who need to pay their own rent for the first time don't get to complain.

In only a few days' time, I get into the rhythm of the J & J work environment. There are usually three assistants, and two of them are out, thus the hiring of me. Vicki, the only full-time assistant here while the others are away, always arrives at seven on the dot. I learned that lesson when I showed up fifteen minutes early on Monday, circling the building in vain while trying to find an unlocked set of doors. On Tuesday, no such rookie mistakes are made.

The office staff—consisting of two partners, six associates, three case managers, and a shared scheduler—usually arrive between eight and nine. My role is primarily answering the phone since Vicki hates that duty. J & J has a great computer database of information, which I reference for most calls to give clients answers. If it's something I can't find out myself, I refer to Vicki if she's available or take a detailed note to follow up. Easy enough on the surface, but after lunch, the call volume increases. By the final hour, I can barely go five minutes without the phone ringing. Either that or two people call at the same time. Vicki is good about picking up a line in those situations. She behaves like the voice-trigger technology of Siri and Alexa, except her launch phrase is whenever I say, "May I put you on a brief hold?"

By afternoon the office is in high spirits. There's a regular client visiting whom everyone loves, as well as one remaining new-client consultation. I, however, have an unhappy client in my ear compromising my bliss. I'm half listening to her recount the specifics of her case for the second time when the Jones half of Jones & Jackson comes out of her office at three fifteen. My purse is packed, desk neat; I'm ready for an on-time departure.

"Has my three o'clock called?" the partner asks Vicki. Vicki looks at me, and I shake my head.

"Nothing. Want me to give him a ring?" Vicki asks.

Ms. Jones waves off the offer. "No need. I'll give him a bit more time. I'm free till four. I'll be working in my office. If he shows, give me a ping."

"Sure thing." Once Ms. Jones walks back to her office, Vicki adds, "If he gets here before I'm out. Otherwise, he can deal."

I snicker. Vicki is a hard worker but a woman who sets her limits and abides by them. I suspect it might be the only way to last in a fast-paced job like this.

"Did you get that?" the woman in my earpiece screeches.

"What was that last part again?"

"Three-six-two!"

It's her case number for the tenth time. "Mrs. Williams, I think the best course of action would be setting up a call with your case manager." Not the attorney but the person who knows the most about her case.

"I don't want the case manager; I want my lawyer! That's who I paid for. Such a rip-off."

I inhale and sit at attention, gearing up to give this one last attempt at nudging the call along the appropriate chain of command. "Your case manager is highly knowledgeable, and if they can't resolve your issue, they'll tag in your lawyer. They work hand in hand that way. Think of the case manager as an extension of your lawyer. A fifth limb."

"Ah," Mrs. Williams said, sounding as if this explanation finally broke through to her. "Let me guess—goes by the name *Johnson*?"

I choke on my own saliva as the doorbell rings. On the speaker, a voice announces, "I have an appointment for a consultation." Never mind the appointment was scheduled for nearly a half hour ago. Vicki throws me a look that reflects my thoughts as she presses the button to unlock the door. Time is ticking, and I need to wrap up this call if I want to leave with Vicki. I go off script.

"If the, er, Johnson you have in mind is both capable and hard-working, then sure."

From the corner of my eye I detect Vicki and the new client's attention on me. I really should've waited to continue this analogy when they were distracted and speaking to each other. Or not at all. I start to mouth a silent *"sorry"* to them, but then I actually look at the new client, and my mouth gets stuck on the *O*.

"Holy shit," I mutter.

"Excuse me?" Mrs. Williams says in my ear.

Vicki gawks at me, and the man comes to an abrupt halt as his eyes squint.

"Corinne!" He shouts louder than necessary in a space of this size. He always was one for theatrics. I hold up a finger and force myself to close this phone conversation, though I'm freaking out. Because, dammit, is this proof Met is legit? That's silly—*no*. Met is simply taking credit for coincidences.

"My apologies. Something in the office distracted me. You were saying?"

Mrs. Williams sighs. "Fine. Give me the willy, then."

"Sure thing, I'll get you right over." I follow the transferring instructions carefully, like I haven't been doing it off book all day. Once it's successfully handed off to the case manager, I turn my attention to Tony, my ex–high school sweetheart.

CHAPTER FOURTEEN

High school sweetheart might be a stretch. We only dated for seven months of junior year. At the time, it felt like an important chunk of my life.

"Tony." I stand because his height makes me crane my neck if seated.

"Anthony now, actually."

He doesn't look terribly different than he did in high school. Just sharper and with clearer brown skin, like an aging software could have guessed it correctly. In high school he had braids, but those are long gone. Now he sports a forgettable fade, with a hairline less so. He must have stopped trying to give himself edge-ups.

"Why are you here?" It's three questions in one. I'm not certain which one I mean. He goes with the most obvious one.

"Some big corp is trying to use my image to sell something." He placidly lifts a hand. "You know how they do when you start taking off."

I nod gravely. Tony—no, Anthony—has been "taking off" since high school. He was in all the school plays because, let's face it, he was hot and talented. The theater director was thrilled he graced them with his presence instead of going the sports route. All the while, he scoured the internet for auditions, sending in tapes without an agent. He had few callbacks. Not a lot of teenagers can withstand that much rejection, but *Anthony* obviously did.

"You work here? Are you a lawyer?" he asks, despite the fact my standing here with him and not being behind an office door should clue him in.

"I'm here temporarily." Across the way, Vicki stands up, crisp as usual.

"The lawyer will be right out for you," Vicki says to Anthony. "See you tomorrow," she directs to me, leaving me to the ghost of my past.

"It's actually time for me to go too," I say. "But good seeing you."

"Are you kidding? I didn't know you lived here. Are you on Instagram?"

Yes. "Not really."

The partner comes from her office then. "Mr. Acres?"

Anthony turns and smiles in acknowledgment, extending a hand as she approaches. I furrow my eyebrows because the Tony I knew had a last name of Smith.

He turns back to me for a second. "Hey, here." He reaches into the inside of his blazer pocket and pulls out a business card. "Text me and we can hang out. If you scan the QR code, it'll link you to my portfolio." He waggles his brows at me and is off, explaining our high school ties to the partner on the way back to her office.

A thumbnail photo of him in a navy-blue sweater and a penetrating smolder tracks me from the card. ANTHONY ACRES. ACTOR. MODEL. TALENT. On the back, the left side lists details as if he's an article of clothing to be purchased online. "Black/African American. 6′3″. 205 lbs. Theater and television experience." On the right, there's his contact information and the QR code. I've never seen a card with this much information packed in such a tiny space. Impressive.

I open my group text with Tiwanda and Elise as I leave the office, attaching a picture of Anthony's business card with the update. When I park outside my apartment building, I have two texts waiting for me.

Both messages are from Elise. Tiwanda must still be busy at work. Elise, unemployed and happy, sends:

> *Elise:* KisMET.
> *Elise:* A high school ex? Yikes, but at least he's hot. What was he like?
> *Me:* We didn't get to talk much.

I head inside.

I wonder if being with Anthony now would feel how being with Tony did all those years ago. It was kind of like lying out in the sun without sunglasses or sunscreen. Tony was the only boyfriend I had in high school. To say I was unprepared would be an understatement.

Not the relationship stuff. We were pretty good on that, considering our age. We texted often, hung out on weekends. I supported him at his plays, he supported me at dance-squad competitions. But I never took to being the girlfriend of someone with status.

I was neither popular nor ostracized, just under the radar. It's what tends to happen when your best friend, the person you're most connected to, is nine hundred miles away. The group of friends I hung out with never moved beyond school walls. Tony was well known and widely liked. The theater crew he hung out with most often and the athletes he sat with during classes were his early fans.

Our relationship ended in the summer, when Tony, a year older than me, went off to college in New York. It was a compromise with his parents, who wanted him to get a college education, when he was focused on choosing where to really get his career going. I wonder how he ended up in Chicago.

My phone buzzes again. Elise.

It's a good thing you got his digits. 😉

My thoughts exactly, but I don't rush to reach out to Anthony. Following this first week of working at Jones & Jackson, I want to spend a weekend at my apartment, job searching online and then inevitably getting distracted by looking at Pinterest for room decoration ideas. Plus, I'm feeling uneasy about this situation. It was one thing when I thought Met was a harmless joke, no worse than the other apps that harvested my personal data. But now it's getting too weird. Running into someone I know in a random city once is a coincidence. Twice . . . Is an app I never asked for pulling strings to send me the love of my life?

When I delay texting Anthony over the weekend, I get a notification Monday morning at work.

Met Tip: Rise and grind (on somebody). That could be you, but you playin.

Who does Met think they are? I cackle under my breath despite its brazenness. It still captures Vicki's attention, but she doesn't question me. With each additional notification from this app, I'm starting to feel like I'm carrying a wisecracking friend around with me in my purse. Desperation, thy name is Corinne. It's equally as low as falling for emails sent out by fashion brands that try to capture sales by speaking the language of their target market.

Worries of being pathetic enough to accept comfort from Met in lieu of Joelle are paused when I get a call from her mom. My telepathy skills are going wild. Miss Leyda notifies me she's finally back in town and has free time. We arrange for me to visit tomorrow.

Once I leave J & J the following day, I drive straight to her neighborhood. Every time I've driven past the exit, I'm reminded that my parents once took this route daily to bring me home. And I recall more recently, when Bessie went into a tizzy and inadvertently dropped me back into my old stomping grounds.

Ms. Leyda opens the door and pulls me into a hug immediately. I sink into her, this human who, by some miracle, carried Joelle, raised her into the person who became a sister of mine by choice. Which is as powerful as—if not more than—the bonds that tie us together by chance.

We go into the kitchen, where she's preparing dinner—lasagna from a box for tonight and a pot roast she'll slow cook overnight for tomorrow. It's achingly familiar. She always invited me and Joelle to join her, but Joelle had other things on her list to conquer and dragged me along for the ride. This time, however, I offer to help. She puts me on vegetable-chopping duty.

Ms. Leyda invites me to stay for dinner, but I decline since I have chili cooking in my slow cooker at home. It's my grandmother's recipe. I called Auntie Renee to get it, though, because a conversation with Mom about chili would turn into a conversation with Mom about career options. To avoid that, I accepted Auntie Renee's chili antics. She's the most protective of that recipe and making sure it's done right.

"I'm happy you made it here," Ms. Leyda says.

"Sorry it took so long; I've been working a lot, which is good in a way but—"

"I don't mean *here* here. I mean Chicago."

I frown. This move wasn't premeditated. There was about a month's turnaround between deciding to move and packing up my car to drive across the country. I'm lucky to have a mom who is retired and typically down to shake shit up. Though she prefers having a put-shit-back-in-order plan in action sooner rather than later.

"Joelle said you'd be coming," Ms. Leyda adds when she notices my hesitation.

"She—" I falter. "She did?" I didn't talk about moving to Joelle, not beyond moving to help take care of her. She knew I would be in the way and not much help at all. Not everyone is strong enough to watch a loved one whittle away. Ms. Leyda was. More notable, she has the strength to persist in this world without her only child.

"Yep. She wasn't worried about you. But she knew you'd be around, looking."

"Looking for what?" My hand has stilled on the knife I was wielding to chop the carrots. I can't safely chop anything right now without risking injury.

Ms. Leyda takes her time answering. "Us, I suppose. A connection to Joelle. Answers. The same thing I'm looking for."

I swallow. It's the only response I can give to the statement that clearly summarizes what I couldn't when asked why I moved suddenly. "Change," is what I'd tell them. "Something different." Those who know me well knew Chicago was Joelle's hometown and guessed it had something to do with that. But this is the best verbalization of it I've heard.

"What have you done to find it?" I ask.

She smiles, and I'm surprised it's identical to Joelle's. "I travel. I stay gone, really. Walter hates it." She purses her lips as if those words are a bitter piece of hard candy. "It may cost us our marriage. Or maybe he'll finally come with me. I don't know. He's warming up to the idea."

"Where do you go?"

"Wherever is cheapest at the time. Sometimes it's a weekend trip to the spa with my girls. Once there was a flight deal, round trip to Dublin. Some places Joelle has been, some she's seeing only now, with me." She raises her hand and rests it over her heart.

Now that is a boss way to handle it. All I'm doing is hopping from job to job and wandering aimlessly through a city Joelle and I used to call home.

My phone vibrates in my back pocket. I dry my hands on a towel before checking it.

The Other Cory: You at the office? I got a few hours.

It's a routine text for a Tuesday. My workday at J & J ends early enough for me to be home about the time Cory has a break between South Side appointments. Last week, he worked diligently on his laptop as he ate five packs of the organic fruit snacks I keep in the cabinet. I sat in the living room with him, scouring the internet for job inspiration while sucking on Twizzlers to calm my nerves. I consider my options for a moment before responding.

Not there yet. Feel free to let yourself in.

I might not have admitted it, but this was why I'd given him the second set of spares. Why not allow him to use them? Before I put my phone away, I send one more message.

Stir my chili for me.

Might as well put him to work. Ms. Leyda has begun humming an upbeat tune as she moves around her cooking station. She looks . . . balanced. Her copper-toned skin is radiant in the late-afternoon sun. She's wearing her hair pulled up in a high, curly ponytail. It exposes her shoulders, which sway a tiny bit as she cooks.

"I don't know if the things I'm trying are helping," I admit.

She pauses her cooking and turns to face me fully, observing me closely from head to toe. Does she see imbalance in me? Joelle and I were on opposite sides of a scale, steadying one another. Rather than add new people to replace her, which would be impossible, I must figure out how to divide myself and find that equilibrium within.

Ms. Leyda gives me a small smile. "It's not a grand reveal. Her face doesn't take the form of clouds hanging low in the sky over the Dublin hillside. It's peace. That's all. Quiet. Quiet*ing*."

As we continue to cook, our conversation flows between childhood memories in this house, all wrapped up in the warm spirit of Joelle, and a discussion of more current events. We touch on my struggle with wanting a job to feel secure versus wanting to find a job I enjoy. She tells me about the places she's been and the trips she's hoping to take this year. She invites me to tag along whenever I'm up for it. When I get my bank account right, I might.

Before I leave, Ms. Leyda tells me to hold on. She goes upstairs, and from the sound of her footsteps, I can guess which room she stops in. She comes back holding a large brown envelope. It has my name on it in Joelle's neat handwriting. Me and my other college roommates used to make fun of how neatly she wrote her chemistry lab reports in those grid lines. It was as neat as a computer font. Here on the envelope, it's less precise than usual but still miles better than most handwriting. I take the envelope from Ms. Leyda and trace my index finger over the lettering.

"JoJo wanted me to give you this." I open my mouth to ask when, but she beats me. "She told me not to mail it. Only when you came for it in person. That girl got up to so much after she moved back home, despite everything. I can't count how many projects she started. It's a strange thing, bearing witness to someone on a mission, knowing their time is running out. Even stranger when it's your own daughter."

I huff out a shaky laugh in danger of morphing into sobs without a moment's notice. Ms. Leyda rests a hand on my shoulder.

"You can open it when you get home, for privacy."

She hugs me tight, and I promise to stop by often, whenever she's in town. I make it four blocks before I pull over to the side of the street, right in front of a No Parking sign. I keep my foot on the brake and my car in drive, technically following the rules.

I slide out the contents on my lap. There are papers of various sizes. Flyers. A few buttons. The necklace I sent Joelle for her sixteenth birthday. By college, she'd stopped wearing it but kept it hanging on her lamp switch. On top of everything is a note. It's concise, which makes sense. Joelle might have left us too soon, but I never once felt she left with anything unsaid between us.

Cori,

I knew you'd get here. And I was right, wasn't I? This is the place for you. I've been collecting some things you might like. Some of it is random but made me wish you were here. Think of it as a welcome home gift.

Love you, sister, always.
Jo

~

I enter my apartment building and climb the stairs in a daze. It's hard to wrap my head around the items Joelle left for me. She didn't leave an instruction manual, no notes explaining why she put them aside for me. Essentially, she left a puzzle. One without a solution in mind.

Distracted by my thoughts, I jump and yelp a bit when I open my apartment door. Cory is still here, sitting in his spot on my couch, looking up at me with a cautiously curious expression.

"Did someone steal your phone and reply to my text?" he asks.

"I thought you might be gone by now." My heart throbs as it settles from the spike in adrenaline.

Cory assesses me, his gaze dropping to the envelope clutched against my chest. "Are you all right?" His voice is low, concerned.

"Yeah, fine. The chili smells great. You should have some. I have to make the noodles real quick." I'm rambling, but maybe he won't notice. I move past him and into the kitchen to stir the chili, though it looks like it's been handled recently. It's chunky and thick—exactly how I like it. I replace the lid and move down the hallway to put the envelope in my room, but Cory speaks before I get far.

"I'm about to head out. I have a client at six."

I look at the clock on the microwave. It's nearing five thirty.

Cory smiles. "They're close, that's why I come here. It's an after-work appointment, and they usually spend the first ten minutes apologizing for running late and changing out of their work clothes anyway."

"Oh. Okay." Sometimes I forget that this is an arrangement of convenience. Though we've become friends, Cory doesn't come over just to visit me or keep an eye on my chili.

"But I did basically cook that chili. My stirring skills brought it all together," he says.

I roll my eyes. "Boy. You weren't up at six this morning on the phone with my aunt as she insisted I show her every time I added an ingredient. Salt included. 'Don't be heavy handed, Cori. Two shakes of chili powder—one! Two!'"

Cory laughs. "Still, if I wouldn't have come today, it could have boiled over. The apartment could be on fire right now."

"It was on the lowest setting."

He ignores me. "My point—I'll only be with my client for an hour. I plan to collect my share of chili, proportionate to the labor I've put in, afterwards?" His matter-of-fact, businesslike delivery shrivels up at the end as he turns it into a question. I stare at him in mock admonishment. Then I shake my head, not bothering to hide the smile he's put there.

"I'll see you later for dinner, loser."

CHAPTER FIFTEEN

By the time Cory returns, I have everything set up on the island. I only bought the toppings I use since this was a planned feast for one. He'll have to make do. There are the elbow noodles I boiled soon after he left. Next, I have two types of cheese. Usually I get a few pinches out of the bag, but since I'm having company, I put each in a small bowl. The toppings lineup is finished off with oyster crackers, sour cream, and chopped chives.

He knocks on the door, not abusing his key-holder power. When I hold the door open for him to enter, he accidentally brushes against me as he gets his shoes off, reminding me of the moment we shared in the karaoke bar. Instead of his ever-present laptop bag, he has a reusable grocery store bag with him. He puts his phone and car keys on the coffee table and goes to the kitchen, ogling my display.

"Wow." He rubs his hands together. "We did a good job."

I purposely bump into him on my way to get bowls from the cabinet. He laughs it off.

"What you got there?" I ask, nodding toward his bag. He holds it out to me and trades it for his bowl.

"Since we both know my actual contributions to this dinner are minimal, I thought I'd compensate by bringing dessert."

His unexpected thoughtfulness shoots an annoying thrill through me, like I'm unboxing a birthday present. There's a container of strawberries, a half loaf of pound cake, a tub of whipped cream, and a couple of pints of ice cream.

"I hope you like strawberry shortcake. It was the simplest thing I could think of. My dad used to whip it up whenever he was in charge of dessert. If you don't, I got ice cream too. A chocolatey and fruity option, like frozen yogurt."

He raises his eyebrows, awaiting a response. I could have cut him off at the mention of strawberry shortcake, which I love but never indulge myself enough to buy. But hearing him—one of the most self-assured people I've ever met—seek my approval makes me tongue-tied.

"Yeah, it's great," I manage to get out as I put the dessert ingredients in the fridge and freezer. I turn to face him. "This is cool of you. Thanks."

The uncertainty clears, and he looks down at his bowl.

"It's a fair trade."

We serve ourselves generous helpings of chili. I should get less to save room for dessert, but I don't. I'll just have to stuff myself until I'm borderline sick. Cory is a chili purist, opting for minimal toppings—a light spattering of cheese, a tiny dollop of sour cream, and exactly four chives. I, on the other hand, am extra about everything.

We sit at the kitchen island, side by side on the barstools. He pulls half his locs up into a messy bun. I try moving my barstool a bit before sitting, giving us more space. It's a good thing I do because after taking his first bite, Cory lets out a low moan that has me leaning toward him before I catch myself and straighten.

"Told you," I say, trying it for myself and agreeing. I realize I never sent an update to Auntie Renee, so I snap some pictures and a video of me taking a bite. I send them to the group chat with her and Mom before really digging in. We're quiet at first, both focused on crafting perfectly balanced spoonfuls.

My phone buzzes as I'm clearing the last of my bowl.

Auntie Renee: It's perfect. I can tell all the way from here.
Momma Llama: Whose arm is that next to you?

I check the pictures again. No Cory there. But then there's the video. It's not much of him. It's a fraction of his arm, well defined in the long-sleeve Under Armour shirt underneath his scrubs. My mom's a snoop.

"Did she approve?" Cory asks. He's tilting his bowl and scraping the sides. I force myself to look away before he puts the spoon in his mouth.

"Do you want more?"

"Yes. But no, I'll start getting dessert ready."

He gets up and rinses out his bowl and spoon. "Clean or dirty?" he asks. The question is clearly about the state of the dishes in the dishwasher, but that doesn't stop my mind from jumping to a fantasy of using it in the bedroom.

"Dirty," I blurt. No, that isn't right. I ran the dishwasher last night. Oh, hell. "I mean, clean. You can leave those in the sink."

He shoots me a quizzical look but continues with the prep work, starting with washing the strawberries. I finish my chili slowly, enjoying the sight of him moving around the kitchen. When he comes over for work, he's married to his side of the couch. The restraint he shows with the room he allows himself to use is such a contradiction to the man who boldly showed up at my door unannounced.

I point him to where he can find my cutting board. The knives are easy enough to locate beside the stove. He cuts the strawberries into quarters on the counter near the sink. I finish eating and go rinse my bowl. For the duration of this task, we stand beside each other, the picture of domesticity. I hurry away and start to open the pound cake.

"Unh-unh," Cory says. "This is on me."

"You helped me," I protest. "Marginally."

He grins. "Fine. You can fluff up the whipped cream."

It's quick work. After he's done with the strawberries, Cory gets the pound cake sliced and warms it in the microwave for a few seconds. Then we put it all together and resume our positions at the island.

I hum a little and bob my head. "This makes me so happy," I admit.

Cory's contented smile tells me he feels the same. It must be the nostalgia of having his childhood dessert.

"You feel better?" he asks.

"What do you mean?" I look over at him while licking whipped cream off my spoon. He sharply averts his gaze.

"You were upset when you first got here." He says this without an ounce of doubt.

"Oh. Well, in that aspect, I don't feel better. But this"—I raise a spoonful up in the air—"helps me not think about it."

"Hmm."

I ignore his judgy hum for one bite, two . . . *Ugh.*

"What?" I ask.

"Sorry. I'm trying to stop giving unsolicited advice. My sister says not everyone enjoys being on the receiving end of it."

"Is that right?" I jest.

He leans over, bumping his arm into mine. Freshman year of college, Joelle and I waitressed in a restaurant near campus. We used to make fun of couples who came in and sat on the same side of the booth with no one on the other side. Suddenly, I understand the perks of such an arrangement.

"Consider your advice officially solicited." I swivel in my seat to face him and pretend to fortify myself. "Give me what you got."

He swallows the cake in his mouth and takes a sip of water before starting.

"My work supposedly focuses on the body, right?"

"I'm sensing this is a leading question."

He ignores my jab and answers his own question. "It does, but the mind is connected of course. The brain sends pain signals, yes?"

"No."

"What?"

"Sorry, reflex. Please continue."

"Right. But my studies didn't include the mind, though it's an integral part of this. I see a therapist, which helps both in life and work. It made me think about facing emotional pain and physical pain. And how the strategies for both might be connected."

"Maybe you can write a journal article about that too." He shoots me a look until I add, "I'd want to read it."

"I'll send you some things I've read on it. The point is, in physical therapy you don't have the luxury of compartmentalizing your pain. It's all connected. You can try to numb the pain with medicine, or if your right knee hurts, maybe depend on the left leg instead. But sooner or later, you gotta face the injury and take measures to permanently repair it. The longer you wait, the more of a toll it takes on your body's other functions."

"Like emotional pain and compartmentalizing with that."

"Precisely," he says. He's visibly buzzing from this topic.

"Say I agree. How can you, a physical therapist, help me with an emotional injury?"

He purses his lips, resisting a smile, and raises his palms upward before softly clasping them together. "Maybe I can't as a physical therapist. But as a friend, I can listen. If you're ready."

Uneasiness at being vulnerable gnaws at me as I return his earnest stare. Strangely, I think I am ready. I don't want to talk with my mom about it yet, and definitely not Lito. He idolized Joelle as a kid, and once he became a teen, that transformed to unwavering respect. It helped that Joelle took it upon herself to learn sign language with me despite our distance. Once she was in Texas for college and spending

Thanksgiving and long weekends with my family, she was more than prepared for our mode of communication.

I eat the last bite of cake and set the dish in the sink. Then I go and grab the envelope from my bedroom. Cory's watching me intently as I sit on the couch and dump everything in the envelope onto the coffee table.

As I sift through the contents, in better lighting than earlier in my car, I hear him get up from the kitchen island. He takes his dish to the sink and pads over to me. He sits on his side of the couch, waiting.

"I went to see my friend's mom today. She gave me this—things my friend left for me before she died."

Cory nods; I see it peripherally since I can't bring myself to look at him as I talk. If I do, I'd get too caught up in trying to analyze what he's thinking. I don't understand what my malfunction is. I'm constantly trying to read him despite the evidence that it's not a skill of mine.

"Tiwanda mentioned that," he says gently. The words nudge me along.

"Apparently, Jo expected I'd move here."

"That's her name?"

I nod. "Joelle. She collected a bunch of random stuff and . . ." I wave my hand toward the coffee table. Cory stares down at the pile, his mouth slightly parted and eyes narrowed.

After a moment he asks, "The things she left were upsetting?"

"They're confusing. I didn't expect anything from Jo, but when her mom gave me this, I expected—I guess I thought it would be clearer."

"Can I?" he asks, leaning forward. I nod and he picks up a flyer. It's for an event that was held before I moved here. With a touch gentle enough for handling artifacts, he looks through the rest of the items. He lifts some things to get a better view, but he leaves most of them on the table. It's clear he's not trying to riddle this out or pretend he has the solution—he's simply getting a feel of the things Joelle left me. He leans back into the couch and turns to me.

"There are no answers here?"

I shake my head. "Just a whole lot of questions."

He tilts his head, a wry smile on his face.

"Unsolicited-advice alert," I warn him.

"Excuse me, I'm still operating under the previously solicited advice. It's not really advice, though . . . Questions can be good. Ask my therapist. He wields them like daggers."

Cory's phone chimes on the coffee table. He reaches across me to silence it.

"You can get that. I'm not paying you for this session."

"It's my reminder to start getting ready for bed."

I peer at him. "That actually seems quite normal for you." I stand. "I'll pack you some leftovers."

When Cory is gone, I clean up the kitchen and sit on the couch before Joelle's mementos. For the first time, I try to see it as a gift and not as the answers for my fragmented life. I collect the buttons and take them to my room to pin them on my corkboard. There's one referencing a movie we both loved, one in support of Black Lives Matter, another for women in STEM. The last one I didn't notice before. It says MET, and my heart drops into my stomach. It couldn't be . . . until I recall her family's trip to the Met museum. I laugh to myself as the tingles on my skin fade. Just a coincidence. As random as everything else in this envelope.

CHAPTER SIXTEEN

It takes three texts from Elise and another Met Tip nudge before I contact Anthony. Between my steady work schedule at J & J and the package from Joelle, I've been a bit distracted. We make plans to get together Friday night since I already blocked out Saturday and Sunday. Tiwanda and Elise promised to help me shop for used bedroom furniture and make cheap DIY decorations. Once the chore of reaching out and finding matching availabilities is done, I'm excited to catch up with Anthony. It's not often I get the opportunity to travel down memory lane with someone from high school.

On Fridays, J & J's reception area closes at noon. I use my extra time to meet Elise for a kickboxing class with discount passes set to expire soon. It's a couple of weeks into April, and since the frigid weather seems to be receding for good, outings aren't such an endeavor.

"See, these are the kind of things I can do now that I'm not stuck at work till nightfall," she says as we sit at the smoothie shop next to the boxing gym, waiting for our orders. "This is why I need unemployed friends."

"So glad I can be of service."

With Tiwanda's increasingly long work hours, it's harder to meet up during the week. We haven't even attempted to have another after-work happy hour with all four of us. I've enjoyed hanging out with

Elise, though. The class was much more intense than the DVDs and online videos I've been following. Mainly because with those, I have zero accountability and end up taking a break whenever my body feels inconvenienced by breathing under such duress. I haven't completed a Tae Bo set since the day Cory held my hips in place.

"Have you decided what you're going to do next?" I ask.

"Still trying to find clients in need of a web designer. But"—she drums on the tabletop with a huge smile—"I auditioned for a regional theater musical earlier this week, and it went well! That's my focus—getting out there and auditioning as much as possible."

"Maybe you should go on my date tonight. Y'all have more in common."

Elise wrinkles her nose. "No thanks. I try not to date actors if I can help it. They tend to be too dramatic. Also, I don't date men. See aforementioned reason."

"Valid."

The person who makes our smoothies is nice enough to bring them to us since we're the only ones here. Mine is green as a result of my mostly fruit blend and a sprinkle of kale. Elise's is a murky tan color from the banana, almond milk, and vanilla protein powder.

"If he's a bust, call us. I'm hanging out at Tee's tonight. You can come by, and we can start planning your room. First dates are like bad movies—no reason to stick around if you know the ending will suck."

"It's not technically a first date," I point out.

"True. But you should probably still act like it is."

With this sound advice, I go back to my apartment and prepare to meet Anthony. I'm accompanying him to an improv show that a few of his friends are in. Then we're going out to a low-key dinner afterward. I shave, something I didn't regularly do during winter. Now that we're well into spring, it's a good time to spruce up. It's not necessary with the dress and tights I'm wearing, but it makes me feel like I'm putting some effort into taking this seriously, which Tiwanda beseeched of me when she called after work. To my dismay, Met has acquired a new believer.

Anthony's friends gave him tickets for the table up front, which we share with two other people who are also friends of the troupe. The improv show features a diverse cast and encourages audience involvement. It's not an activity I take part in frequently, but it's highly entertaining. Anthony's boisterous roars elicit laughter to jokes I would have otherwise not reacted to. He's the ideal audience member.

It's not awkward being with Anthony, but it's not exactly comfortable either. I thought it might be more of the latter, but having preconceived notions of someone makes them more foreign when you learn who they really are. Even when those notions are based on a previous version of them.

After the show wraps, we wait around for Anthony's friends to come out. I stand by as Anthony strikes up a conversation with anyone in our vicinity. He's charming, and with his face, people are more than happy to chat with him.

The troupe comes out from backstage, some in changed outfits but most with only an added jacket. Anthony introduces me. I tell them I enjoyed their show, providing specific bits I liked. That starts them up, laughing at how hard it was to keep a straight face during the scenes. Anthony loops an arm around my waist and smiles down at me. Being on the receiving end of his admiration is a surprisingly familiar buzz.

"You all coming out with us?" one of his friends asks us and the other pair from our table.

"For sure," Anthony says, then looks at me for my approval. I was anticipating our alone time to get acquainted with *It's Anthony Now*, but he's already agreed to go. If I say no, I'll be a downer. In fact, they'd probably say, "All right, deuces," and I'd be standing here looking goofy while Anthony leaves with them. I nod and it's settled.

The restaurant bar is a few blocks down the way, so our group of eight walks the short distance. Anthony and I start off beside each other, but conversations cause us to reconfigure. While Anthony walks near the front of the group, joking around, I am near the back, chatting with my favorite of the troupe, Linda. I admit I laughed almost exclusively when she was onstage. She's Latina, uses a wheelchair, and has the best deadpan I've ever seen.

"Hey, I heard that!" a male troupe member says of my admission.

"You were supposed to!" Linda yells back. To me, she adds, at a volume loud enough to be overheard again, "Everyone declares me their favorite. He gets a bit touchy."

The restaurant is bustling, but they have us seated as soon as we arrive. According to Linda, the troupe comes here after every show, so they hold a spot for them. We do a little shuffle to get settled around the table. I make sure I'm seated near Linda. Seemingly as an afterthought, Anthony moves to the chair beside me. It's centered enough for him since I'm at the end. He sits and reaches under the table to squeeze my thigh as he speaks to the person on his other side. The man is juggling a lot of people.

Not for the first time, I wonder if he feels pressure to do this. Does he have a need to be something for everyone, or does it come naturally? I'm borderline exhausted observing him in his element. But when he turns and leans in close to tell me something, I understand why I'd want a person like Anthony around, why I cherished having him around in high school. His attention is captivating, whether it's flirtatious or not.

We order a ton of sharable food—platters of wings and potato skins, mini burgers, and spinach-artichoke dip. We drink beers and laugh at each other's bad jokes. Everyone but me is an actor here, but they're not all performative off the stage. I find myself mentally dividing the group into two. Anthony is part of the performative group. Linda is chill. Her humor is a blink-and-you'll-miss-it type. The one couple of the troupe—a White guy and an Asian guy whose names I didn't catch—sits directly across from me and Anthony. They're a split. The Asian man I sort in the performative group. He's animated, funny, and perhaps the only one at the table who can give Anthony a run for his money. His boyfriend quietly laughs along and seamlessly fills in details of their story when prompted. Maybe having one of each type in a relationship is the way to go. It's working for them all right.

Two rounds of beer in, we start singing along to the music playing over the speakers. Even though I've been avoiding my mom, I still send her a risqué selfie of me and Anthony. During the third round that half of us opt out of, Anthony's arm is around me as he tells everyone at our table how we met. It's not what I remember at all, but I don't have any other recollection to challenge him with.

According to Anthony, it happened when we were assigned as partners for a group project in theater design class. I remember taking that class to fulfill the drama requirement, but I'd known Anthony existed for the entirety of my high school career. That class is when *he* had the privilege of meeting *me*.

Regardless, his retelling is very cute. When he's finished and everyone is basking in the light of teenage romance—and as Linda is rolling her eyes—he leans over and places a lingering kiss on my cheek.

A few people in the troupe leave, and the rest of us start voicing our intentions to head out soon too. I've already decided against driving home right away and wait as the last drinks are downed. I open my phone to the group text with Tiwanda and Elise to ask what they're doing. It's not too late, and I'm closer to Tiwanda's condo than my own place. Anthony leans over, blatantly checking out my phone. I black out the screen as I return his attention.

"You ready to go home?" His eyes alternate between my eyes and my lips, as if he wants to claim my mouth right this instant. I swallow as my throat becomes dry.

"Is there anything else going on?"

He grins seductively, reaching out to ghost his fingers across my resting hand. "It can be. My place is only three train stops away, unless you're good to drive."

The simple act of Anthony touching my hand and giving me his undivided attention for more than ten seconds makes my chest stir. I open my mouth before I've decided how to respond. It hangs there for a moment until I settle on an escape route. "I have to use the bathroom."

~

The phone rings in my ear.

"Pick up, pick up, pick up," I mutter.

The three-stall restroom smells slightly of bleach under the potent tropical scent puffing out of the wall-mounted air freshener. I stand in front of the double sink, checking out the basket of toiletries. One of the stalls is occupied, but I can't worry about being overheard right now. In the past, I was able to use sign language to communicate covertly with Joelle. I could still video call Lito, but I don't think he would be helpful for this type of advice.

Tiwanda picks up on the third ring.

"How was it?" she asks right off the bat. The audio quality is like listening to someone talk on an airplane. I put the volume up as high as possible.

"It's still going. Maybe. Quick question: Should I sleep with him?"

"Yes!" says an emphatic voice that's not Tiwanda and very much Elise. I chose to call Tiwanda because out of the two of them, she would give the soundest advice. Now I have a demon on one shoulder and an angel on the other. Jury is out on who gets which role.

"You're on speaker in my car," Tiwanda belatedly explains. "Is he nice?"

"He's nice to everyone."

"That's not a bad thing," Elise says.

"You think he's the one Met sent for you? Your *soul mate*?" Tiwanda asks. I don't have the time or wherewithal to argue the legitimacy of Met right now. It's beginning to feel futile to resist.

"I dunno. But a test drive could help. Ew, sorry. I take that back."

Tiwanda and Elise cackle. To my right, a toilet flushes, and the stall door jostles open. The woman shoots me a conspiratorial look as she gets a pump of hand sanitizer in lieu of washing her hands. I'd normally judge, but I'm happy to continue my call in private.

"As long as you think it'll be fun, go for it," Elise says. "I'll show you his portfolio when we get to Tee's. High school ex is hot. Might be your type, Cory."

I start to point out Anthony being a strong match is the reason for this conversation when a curt, baritone voice speaks from what must be the back seat of Tiwanda's car.

"Doubt it," Cory says, emotionless.

I freeze. My brain is too foggy to rapidly process why learning that Cory is listening to this conversation has me flustered. For some reason, I don't think it's shyness about my sex life.

"I gotta go," I say.

"Wait!" Elise shouts. "What are you going to do?"

I groan as I occupy my hands, taking an oil-blot paper from the basket and pressing it along my T-zone. "I don't know. I guess I'll figure it out once I get there."

"Let's have a vote. Who thinks Cori the Second should get laid tonight?" Elise asks.

"I don't approve of this name." I shake my head at my reflection in the mirror.

Elise ignores me and continues. "I'll start. A definitive yes. Cory the First?"

I swear I can hear his sigh through the car's Bluetooth. "If she's considering a vote, she shouldn't be with him anyway."

"All you had to say was no," Elise says. I can imagine her turning around to shoot him a playful glare. "All right, Tee. You're the tiebreaker."

"I agree with Cory. Ultimately it's your decision—you know that. But for what it's worth, I vote yes."

Elise whoops and I hear nothing more from Cory. I say bye to them, slip my phone in my bra, and push soap out of the dispenser. By the time I finish washing my hands, I will decide if I want to go home with Anthony. It would be fun to revisit this. Our sexual relationship only went so far back in high school. There's no compelling reason to bail. I scrub until the foam starts to disappear, then rinse. Focusing on this task brings clarity around the remaining beer haze. If I focus on the facts, it's an easy decision.

One, I'm crushing on Cory. But this is my specialty: guys who are not for me. It's annoying, especially with Met cosigning it this time. However, it's a feeling I have. There. I've acknowledged it. Second, I'm attracted to Anthony and more than a little curious. It's mutual.

Those are the relevant facts. And suddenly, what I need to do is crystal clear.

CHAPTER SEVENTEEN

Anthony's apartment is farther into the city than mine, and he pays for it in size. It's a studio, but not like the ones I see on Instagram with cute space maximizers. No, this is the normal rent-prices-are-ridiculous kind.

His large television is mounted to the wall. The soft, worn gray leather couch looks comfy enough. Furniture is kept to a minimum. See: not much space to spare. The curtain separating his bedroom area is currently open, revealing his neatly dressed bed.

Anthony returns from the bathroom as I catalog his habitat. He bites the corner of his bottom lip a bit, as if the sight of me in his space makes him bashful. Maybe it's sincere. Does it matter if it isn't?

He must interpret my thinking face as a beckon, because he launches into action, leaning down to press his lips against mine. He's swift. I don't have time to take a breath before he cuts off half of my air-supply routes. I sputter into his mouth, and he pulls back.

"Sorry, wasn't ready for that," I say.

"You wanna sit down?"

"Yeah. Let's start there."

He ushers for me to go ahead of him, thus choosing if we sit on the couch or his bed. I choose the couch, strategically sitting in the middle. I'm here for a reason, after all—to have sex with the hot guy from my past, not a conversation across opposite ends of the couch. Although that might be nice too. Despite being with him for the past four hours and hearing him talk all night, I'm clueless about his life.

"I still don't know how you ended up in Chicago."

He rubs the back of his neck, obviously not following the thoughts that led to the question. But he catches up and smiles as he recalls a fond memory.

"After undergrad I moved to LA with my roommate and two other actor friends. I auditioned a lot. Booked some roles, usually a one-and-done. Then I got a recurring job for a show filmed here. Liked it so much, I moved. There's opportunity here. I had a couple of auditions this week alone. If they're casting elsewhere, I send in recordings."

He points to a space near his bed that I overlooked. A camera is set up on a tripod in front of solid-blue fabric tacked to the wall. An impromptu recording studio.

"Why did you move here?" he asks.

I try to recall my conversation with Ms. Leyda and the clear explanation she helped me verbalize. But Anthony doesn't know Joelle or anything about my life since he graduated high school. I shrug. "Wanted a change."

Then I lean in, lift my hand to his face, and try to remember a time when I held it and naively called him my first love. Our lips meet, tentative at first. Soon, it becomes eager because improvements have been made.

"I never thought we'd be together like this again," Anthony says.

"Did you . . . want us to be?"

"No. I mean, it wasn't something I thought about."

"Oh. Me neither." I kiss him again because it's something to do that feels good. He pulls away after a minute with something else to share.

"Do you remember back in high school, when we'd go off campus for lunch?"

"Um, yes." I use my fingertips to smooth my hair from my temple up to the band holding it all in a curly puff. Heat spreads to my face at the memory. We'd ride off in the car his uncle passed down to him and park in an empty lot, oftentimes at the local church that didn't have anything going on around noon on a weekday. We didn't go there to pray.

"Remember I was the first person to . . ." He drops his hand to my lap and squeezes my inner thigh.

Is this his dirty talk? I'd rather focus on the things he could do now instead of the awkwardness of a decade ago. Also, he's incorrect.

"Technically, you weren't the *first* person."

His head jerks back a bit. "Who was?"

I poke out my chin, raise my eyebrows, and wiggle my fingers like jazz hands.

"Oh." He scoffs. "That doesn't count."

Yes, it does. I was the only one of us capable of doing anything worthwhile at that age. I don't say this aloud, though, because I'm not sure how fragile he might be about his skills of yesteryear. Instead, I say, "You want to remind me how it went?"

His tongue slips out the corner of his mouth as he gives me a wicked grin. He slides from the couch and onto his knees in front of me, positioning his hands on either side of my waist. "I'll do you one better."

~

The bathroom in Anthony's apartment is plain and functional, the bulbs over the mirror spotlighting my missteps only moments later. I groan as the water-soaked paper towel seems to make the spot on the front of my dress worse. I should just give up, go home, and throw this dress away. Even if a cycle in the washing machine can clean it thoroughly, it still wouldn't erase the memory of this mess of a night. What was the point of coming here if in the end I had to *literally* take matters into my own hands?

With a brief tap on the partially open door, Anthony joins me. He stands in front of the toilet and drops his pants. The bathroom is so compact I take a sidestep over to make sure I'm not in a splash zone. I don't need any more of his bodily fluids on me. Maybe he's open to feedback—he is an actor, after all. Aren't they all for improving their craft? My first and foremost comment: absolutely no spitting. Don't spit when you're on your knees. Just ask before trying, please. Don't spit on me *down there*; don't spit on me anywhere. A catchy mnemonic tool at his disposal.

"Who's Cory?" he asks. I bristle. His pee landing in the toilet bowl as surround sound provides an excellent backdrop to my instant panic. His eyes are trained on the porcelain target, his profile calm as he awaits my response.

"What do you mean?"

"That's the name you said as you came." His voice is casual. I can't tell if it's because he's truly indifferent or trying to mask hurt. He's a talented performer; it's impossible to know. It's his fault my brain resorted to supplying images of Cory to block out my reality. How naive of me to think revisiting this would *lessen* my draw to Cory.

I laugh, higher pitched than normal. "Oh, that's me. Remember, my family calls me Cori."

"You said your own name?"

"Yeah." I scrub at the spot on my dress harder than necessary. "You know, because I was doing such a good job. 'Yay, Cori! Go, go!'"

Anthony chuckles, shakes, flushes. "You were all right."

The smile I put on for my faux self-encouragement cheer drains from my face. I know he's probably kidding, but it still annoys me. I made lemonade out of the lemon seeds he gave me! The seeds currently all over my dress!

"We can go again if you want. Give me a minute," he says before he slaps my behind, then walks out of the bathroom.

A minute, my ass. I give up on my dress and get the hell out of there in case he has more stamina than I'm giving him credit for. I don't want to stick around and find out.

CHAPTER EIGHTEEN

What kind of grown woman drunk texts her mom? Or, more accurately, sends her mom a picture in which she's pretending to lick her ex–high school boyfriend's face? Apparently me. I'm that kind of woman.

Thanks to Mom's busy retiree lifestyle, I'm able to put off speaking with her until the following Thursday. She calls me while en route to her dentist appointment. Her mom intuition must be strong, because I'm in the middle of checking the substitute teacher availability board for next week. My three-week gig at Jones & Jackson ends tomorrow, and no new offers have come from the temp agency. Mom must have felt my desperation.

"Sweetheart, you're capable of using your turn signal. Your momma raised you better than that." Every few minutes she breaks out of the conversation to reprimand a driver in her signature disappointed motherly tone. It's worse than cussing them out, honestly. Her tenor changes when she asks, "You're not going there again, are you?"

Instantly, I'm aware she's directing the last comment toward me regarding the picture with Anthony. She didn't dislike him back in high school, so her attitude is inexplicable. Though our date didn't inspire me to rekindle things with Anthony, my defensiveness grows. In the days since, I've had time to reflect on the ways I instigated the lackluster ending. I also may have received a scathing notification from Met:

Fee fi fo fum, I'm sending quality matches, don't be dumb. Perhaps I didn't give Anthony a fair chance, because it sure as hell couldn't be referring to Justin.

"Why shouldn't I? Didn't you see the picture?"

"A pretty face might be . . . *lickable*. But Anthony would be a step backwards for you, Cori. And after stepping back with your career, maybe you should focus on getting that moving in the right direction first."

"Quitting a job that wasn't serving me isn't moving backwards."

"It *was* serving you timely paychecks."

I clamp down on my tongue to prevent saying something smart. My mom supported my move to Chicago when she thought it would come with prompt job placement. Now, I'm going on four months without applying for a single permanent position. I wish she understood that I'm stressed enough without her added frustration.

She sighs heavily enough for me to hear over the background noise. "If you need help for May, I can do half your rent. Not all. I have Barcelona to save for."

"No, Momma. That's what my savings are for."

"Savings are for buying a house or a new car to replace your hunk of junk."

"Bessie doesn't deserve this disrespect." Mom laughs as she always does when I refer to my car by name. It brings a smile to my face—the first she's caused in weeks. "Seriously, don't worry about me. I'll figure it out."

To prove this to myself, I click open a listed substitute job for next week at random. It's a two-week replacement for a second-grade teacher. The regular teacher's maternity leave started earlier than expected, and they're looking for someone to fill in until the prearranged sub is available. I wanted to stick to older grades for subbing, where the responsibility burden isn't as heavy. But I said I would figure it out. Once I start calculating how much I'll earn for the two weeks and what expenses I could cover with it, the decision is made.

Mom hangs up with me as she arrives at the dental practice, and I relocate from the living room to my bedroom. It's becoming my favorite spot in my apartment. Before, I used to spend most of my time out in the living room for its coziness and the television. But since my weekend bargain decorating quest with Tiwanda and Elise, I've been in love with the ambiance of my bedroom. Now I have a beautiful wooden vanity dresser with a mirror and a chair—a great place to do my hair and makeup. I also got an area rug in coral blue, a funky antique lamp, and a body pillow. Tee and Elise insisted on this purchase after I detailed my night with Anthony. They've dubbed it #SpitGate.

We asked Cory for help transporting the dresser, but he was hanging out with his guy friends. He was also notably absent two days ago, which was a Tuesday. I texted to check on him that night, asking if his usual South Side appointment was canceled. He responded, No, it wasn't. I didn't press for further explanation. He's not required to come by, take up my couch space, and eat up my fruit snacks. Though I did replenish my stock with sharing in mind.

I get comfortable on my bed with my laptop and Joelle's envelope. Every few days, I tend to explore the contents. The last trail I followed led to calling Ms. Leyda for information about their final trip as a family—a whimsical weekend in New York City. In a rare moment of Joelle feeling strong, they purchased tickets from accumulated points and charged the rest to credit cards. I saw a few pictures during that trip but none I still have. After we hung up, Ms. Leyda sent me photos. They were smiling and being silly, enjoying the miracle of life in the face of one ending. This trip led to the Met Museum button.

This afternoon, I plan to do more research. If I got that much comfort from a button, I can imagine how much I'll get from investigating each one of these items. Cory was right; it is a gift. But it's not a collection baring the same message. Each thing is tied to a separate story or idea. I might not figure out each one right away, but I'm becoming confident that, in time, I will.

Instead of dumping everything out, I reach into the envelope and select something at random. I groan. It's a four-by-six cardstock advertisement for an event. I consider redrawing, but Joelle would know I cheated. I read the flyer in its entirety. Before, I'd scanned the title of the event, the date, and the enlarged "FREE!!!" Once I saw it had passed, I moved on to the next item. But now I'm wondering . . .

I snap a picture and send it to Ms. Leyda. **Did Joelle attend this? I** ask. She responds quickly. **If she did, it wasn't with me.**

Maybe something she wanted to join but couldn't. The event is a workshop spanning five hours. It would have taken a lot out of Jo to go. I flip over the card. The back details four parts of the workshop.

Part one is a brief history lesson on the economic journey of Black and Brown people. That's followed by a workshop focused on personal finance and planning for families. The third part is a breakaway session for group activities. Finally, there's a small business–pitch showcase while the youth participate in an investment game. I nod my head in appreciation of a well-rounded event. It reminds me of a class I took in college, the Economics of Maintaining a Poor Class. Joelle took the course with me, though she'd already satisfied her requirement with microeconomics. Our majors didn't have much opportunity for overlap, so she took this with me as an elective.

I left every class period angry. Growing up, I was unaware of my mom's struggles in providing for us. Once my parents separated, Mom funneled the money Dad sent into college savings accounts for me and Lito, stretching her teacher's salary for our everyday necessities. It helped matters that we'd recently moved to more-affordable Texas. When I became an adult and had to worry about money, she was candid about her experiences in her early years. That's the reason she's willing to help me, even if it comes with an expiration date. Later in her career, she climbed the ranks and became principal. We moved into a house that was ours. I remember seeing my room for the first time and calling Joelle. "I'm the most powerful princess here," I told her.

And when Jo, sick of my ranting after every class and with every essay assignment I had to research, said, "Do something about it, then," I rolled up my sleeves and made a plan. First, I would finish the assignment. Then, ace the class. Longer run? Graduate and secure a good-paying entry-level corporate job. This, I thought at the time, would build upon all my mom sacrificed for me. We'd gone from lower-middle class to more solidly middle class, and I wouldn't allow my line of the family to slip back.

Only recently did I realize that was never a good solution. And I doubt it's what Joelle meant. Despite my mom's hard work for our household, we have plenty of family still struggling. A single success story doesn't help an entire family, let alone a community.

This free workshop, however, is the type of resource that can generate real change. I wonder where they get their funding from and how much expense went into putting this on. Was there a limit on how many families could enroll? I look for the name of the organization. Their website is squeezed down at the bottom—FinancefortheFam.com. I try to pull up the website.

"Site under construction."

I check the address, and after typing it in anew and getting the same screen, I accept defeat and get in the shower. It's not yet five o'clock, but I have to wash my hair, which adds hours to my getting-ready-for-bed process. I procrastinated up until this point but can't put it off any longer. Vicki and a few people from the office are taking me out for a late lunch in the last hour of my shift tomorrow. I want their final impression of me to be dependable, hardworking, and all with great hair.

I play music and hydrate to prepare myself for a shower double the usual length. Then I go at it. After doing my own hair for months, it's muscle memory at this point. I go through each section of my hair, untwist, focus on cleansing the scalp, retwist, then move to the next. When my arms tire, I switch to a section that allows rest. Back when I had my fancy postgrad job, I'd go to the salon every three weeks to get my hair done. It was my "I made it" moment. I guess I could call this new routine my "Bitch, you thought" moment.

I finish as my fingers start to prune and dry off as best as I can with my hair dripping down and undoing my progress. The music is blaring now that the noise of the shower is gone. I turn it off and immediately hear the heavy knocking it masked.

I wrap my towel around me and hurry to the front door. It's not too late for noise, but maybe one of my neighbors is in a bad mood. Through the peephole, I see Cory, his head bent as he waits for me to answer. *Are you kidding me?*

I thought him showing up in the middle of my workout was embarrassing, but my hair is in six soaking twists, currently sprinkling the floor with water.

"Hello?" Cory says. My hasty approach must have tipped him off. I open the door.

"What did I give you a key for?" I ask as he stands there, gaping at me. After performing a quick scan from my Susie Carmichael hair to my bare feet, he composes himself and focuses on my face.

"To use when you're not here. And"—he flourishes a hand at my toweled form—"you're obviously here."

I roll my eyes and back away. He lets himself in and shuts the door behind him.

"And you're here . . . on a Thursday?"

Half his mouth quirks up. "You know my schedule?"

"I thought I did."

"Sorry. I texted you, figured you'd respond by the time I got here. Then I saw your car out front and tried calling."

"Shower," I say. He nods. Then a silence descends around us that I've never experienced with him. For most of his visits here, we've done minimal talking, and it was always a comfortable silence. The type that made me not mind him coming over to use my apartment. His presence wasn't quiet, though. It was reassuring.

This thing happening between us now is unsettling. It makes me not want him here, making me uncomfortable in my own space. But judging by his demeanor, I know this isn't his intent. He seems to barely want to be here.

"I'm going to go finish," I say with a gesture to my head. "You can work or whatever."

I go back to my room without waiting for a response. Once I'm there, I decide I'll stay. It's nice back here in my cute new room, and it'll take me two hours—at least—to get my hair twisted. Cory and the weird energy he showed up with should be gone by then. I moisturize my skin, throw on some loungewear, and get to work.

An hour and a half in, and I'm on a roll. I'm moving slower than planned, but my laptop is open on my dresser, streaming a comedy show I haven't had time to catch up on. I'm twisting and laughing and tuning out all the things that consumed my mind before. Like the dead end from the flyer, my impending elementary-sub gig, and ignoring Cory in my front room.

I'm doing a great job of pushing all those thoughts to the edge of my consciousness until there's a gentle tap on my bedroom door. It's light enough for me to pretend I can't hear it over the sound from my laptop. But when in the months I've known Cory have I ever been able to truly ignore him?

CHAPTER NINETEEN

"Yeah," I answer, leaving it open to his interpretation if that means he can come in or not. I have both hands employed, unwilling to let go of the two halves of the nearly complete twist. I lean over to pause the show with my elbow.

Cory opens the door a crack. "Okay to see you?"

What an odd way of asking if I'm dressed. It makes my chest seize as if he'll see me naked, though I'm wearing a raggedy T-shirt and cotton shorts. "Yeah," I repeat.

I glance at him standing in the open door before refocusing on my hair in the mirror.

"Wow. Your room looks great now," he says.

"You've been in here?"

"Remember the time I forgot my phone charger? You told me I could get the one out of your room?"

"Oh. Right."

Since the first slipup, he's shown a carefulness to respect my space, to the point of not stepping more than a toe in now. It's awkward, but this conversation is more manageable not facing him. I separate another small section of hair to work with.

"I'm heading out," he says.

"Got a client?" I ask to fill the dead air between us. I'm trying to behave normally and failing, because why pose a question when the answer is known?

He surprises me and says, "No. I'm going home." There's some hesitation in his voice. If he's done for the day, then why did he come over? The logical part of my brain reasons *traffic*. Maybe he sat here a bit to avoid it. That makes sense.

"You twisting all your hair?" he asks.

I hum affirmatively. I still have a good third left, with three clips in my hair to keep it out of the way until I'm ready to twist it. When I finish, I'll have to sit under the dryer a bit. My wake-up time tomorrow will be earlier to separate them and make sure it looks all right. Nothing worse than spending hours on your hair just to have to pull it up into a hair band. Thinking of next steps is an exhausting exercise in itself.

"How long is it going to take you?"

"Another hour. Maybe more if you keep distracting me. Help or get out." I'm teasing. Or at least I try to affect that tone, but it's in keeping with trying too hard to be normal. It sounds serious to my own ears. Cory drops his bag inside the door and strolls into my room, his usual sureness in each step.

"What are you doing?" I look up at his reflection as he stands behind me.

"Helping. It's two strands, right? Nothing fancy?"

"Yes . . ."

"Okay," he says as if it's totally in his wheelhouse. With this much confidence, would I be able to tell if he was bullshitting me? "But separate it for me. I don't know what size you want them."

All right, not a secret professional hair stylist, because he would have been able to figure out sizing by the completed twists if he were. I grin and hand over the section I parted for myself.

"You have to put the twisting cream on it," I tell him, pointing to the open jar on the dresser.

He scoops up a dollop with his free hand. "Is this enough?"

"Too much." I swipe a finger across his and take half away. "I'll show you."

I take my hair back, brushing against his hand in the process. In an attempt to conceal how the contact makes my back snap straight, I give verbal instruction. "I try to twist it around my finger as I twist the two strands, but it's not necessary."

"I can handle that, Cor." I glance to his eyes in the mirror, expecting to catch him rolling them from the tone of his voice. But he's attentively watching my hands work. I don't know that he's ever shortened my name before. I wonder if it was premeditated, a reclamation of his name.

I finish with a final twist to the end of the strand. "Voilà! It doesn't have to be perfect. I'm taking them out tomorrow anyway."

I take out one of the clips, struggling to remember which one I'm currently working on. It's a small piece left of this section. I break it into two and hand Cory the one at the better angle for him.

He gets to work right away, already having the twisting cream ready. I'm momentarily distracted by how good the little pull of hair feels when it isn't my own doing. Also, I'm checking him out to make sure he's doing it right.

He is. I'm impressed. Then I'm annoyed at myself for being moved by something so simple. I focus on my own twist instead.

"How do you know how to do this?" I ask.

"My sister, Euniqua, is two years older. We used to play together."

"What'd you play?"

"Everything. If it was my choice, it'd often be the two of us at a four-person board game, taking two parts each. After her video game obsession, she went through a hair and makeup phase. She had five of those creepy head things with the hair. They were our clients. She was always the owner of the salon, yelling that we had to hurry, and our customers were upset because I couldn't braid. I learned how, of course."

"I expect nothing less of you."

Cory isn't the type to accept incompetence lying down. The pull from him stops, and I think it's because of my comment, but no, he's done.

"Can I start another?" he asks.

"Yeah, I have to mist the next section, though. One sec." I twist faster.

"I got this." He unclips the next section and holds it with one hand as he grabs the spray bottle with his other.

"One spray. I only need it damp." He gives a precise single spray in one spot. "Good, but you need to rub it into the bottom strands as well."

He uses his fingers to spread the water around. I'm starting to tell him it's sufficient when he sinks lower to my scalp. He proceeds to massage in a circular motion. His fingers are gentle and cool against me, sending tingles down my spine and a warmth up my neck. My head dips backward as I let out a quiet moan.

Cory's fingers still. Not quiet enough, then. I straighten, clearing my throat.

"You don't have to do that." My voice is scratchy.

"Hmm." I assume that's his acknowledgment. He breaks off a piece, gets my approval on its size, and clips the rest of the hair away.

"I never liked getting my hair done when I was little," I tell him. "Thought it was the biggest waste of time. Especially when my brother came, crawling around and being happy without the fuss."

"Same. I tried growing my hair out many times, only to give up a month in when my mom got on me about having to pick my hair out."

"How long have you been growing your locs?"

"Four years. Almost quit this too. But I had a friend who went to cosmetology school and later focused on natural hairstyles. She made sure I got the proper maintenance. Wouldn't have had the patience to do it myself."

"It looks good." Quite the downplay of what I really think. That I'd like to take a handful of his hair and use it as a rein to guide his mouth all over my body.

"Thanks," he says after a beat, as if he can read my thoughts. I'll have to keep those quiet, just in case.

"Maybe your sister overworked you."

"Huh?" He understandably does not follow my conversation jump. The more we talk, the less I'm fixated on how good he is with his hands. I'm jumping on any continuation I can find at this point. It's either this or kick him out. But he's already on to another twist, and at this pace, we'll be done in less than thirty minutes.

"The reason you lost patience with doing your own hair."

He grunts, widening his stance a bit.

"After rushing to finish all your plastic clients' hair, you were burnt out at the ripe young age of . . ."

He looks up and to the right, recalling the needed info. "Nine. I stopped doing hair with Niqua then, but I wasn't burnt out quite yet."

"Why, then?"

"I hit the unwritten age when it becomes unacceptable for a boy to play with dolls."

I stiffen as I tamp down my anger. "Who told you that?"

"My uncle. It wasn't directed to me, though. My sister had dragged me off to her room, but I forgot something in the kitchen and went back for it. That's when I heard him. He asked my dad, 'Isn't he too old to be playing with dolls?' Real offhand, kind of joking. But I was a sensitive kid."

"How did your dad respond?" I cut past the fluff of that answer to get to the tipping point.

"I can't remember verbatim. He laughed first and said something like, 'I know. Can't tell Lorraine that.' My mom."

"He didn't stand up for you."

Cory looks up and away from the task of my hair for once, locking his gaze with mine through the mirror. Though he's looking at me, his thoughts seem far away. His lips pull up into a smile, genuine but sad.

"No, he didn't. I never played salon again. I pretended I wasn't in the mood at first. Then one time I yelled at Niqua, said she was annoying. She never asked me after that, and eventually she stopped playing too. I think half the fun for her was bossing me around. A few years ago, before my dad died, I brought it up with him. He'd known I was bi for years and loved and accepted me fully."

"How'd it go?"

He's quiet for a moment, but I'm more than willing to wait. He splits off a new section of hair to twist, which I promptly steal away from him. He tuts at me but gets another piece for himself. Then he continues.

"I learned how to learn from my dad. My mom, she's been amazing for as long as I can remember. She lives her life with the purpose of loving and listening to others. According to her, I'm bullheaded like Dad."

My face scrunches because I haven't seen much of this characteristic. It makes me realize how little I know about him. There's a slow-churning excitement in my gut at the prospect of how much more I might learn, if I'm lucky.

"My dad grew a lot as he raised me and my sister. He went back to school and got his bachelor's, then his master's in social work. He fought against his nature to stay open minded. That didn't come easy for him. And when I brought up the hair thing . . . he didn't remember it."

I gasp. "No."

"Of course not, right?" There's a laugh in Cory's voice, and I realize I could happily listen to him tell stories about his life forever. Maybe we are destined to be lifelong friends. "He did say it was an exchange he could imagine him and my uncle having. He apologized, and we had a good talk about masculinity."

"That's . . . a lot."

"Mhmm."

"Did your mom know about any of that?"

"No. She likes to think she shielded us from our family. Niqua is pan, but my mom didn't pick up on that one as easily as she did me. She says she knew early for me, much sooner than it took to figure out for myself."

The endearment in his voice has me regretting not going up to meet his mom the night we ran into her and her mystery man. "Is she right?"

He nods. "See, I didn't only have crushes on girls. But when I did? I hyperfocused on them to block out the fact that I couldn't stop daydreaming about my best guy friend. In college I did the opposite. Trying to make up for lost time, I guess. It still feels recent that I allowed myself to just . . . be."

Cory's soft exhale mingles with the gentle slip of our hands against slick strands of my hair for a potent moment until he continues, "For the most part, my mom succeeded. She never allowed the loudly homophobic around us. Biases, though . . . they can be quiet. Sometimes your consciousness misses it."

"But the subconscious picks it up."

"Fucking always."

We work quietly for a few minutes. It's too warm a silence to press play on my show once it starts the countdown to timing out. Maybe the energy I thought Cory arrived with was my doing. It would be irrational to have a guilty conscience for my Friday night with Anthony when I'm very single, but stranger emotional responses have occurred.

I start to unclip the final section of hair. We'll only need to make five or six twists out of it, and then we're done. Cory rests his hand on mine, stilling me.

"I'll take care of it," he says.

I let my hands fall into my lap. "Such excellent service at this salon."

"Yeah, yeah." He spritzes the section with water, this time doing better to not aim it at one spot. I'm watching his improved technique closely in our reflected images. When he catches me, I don't shy away. I expect him to refocus on my hair, but he doesn't. His eyes stay locked on mine as, again, he slips his fingers onto my scalp. He pauses for a second. I may be imagining it, but I swear I see a challenge hiding in the slight rise of his eyebrows.

I open my mouth to say, *I told you, you don't have to do that,* but just as I force out a pathetically weak sounding "I," he does *that.* His fingers press firmly into my scalp, moving in slow swoops. I clamp my mouth shut for two reasons. One, if I continue speaking, I'm not confident I'll be able to get out any comprehensible sounds. Two, I'm not willing to give in easily to a contest.

I stare back at him, hoping he doesn't notice how shallow my breathing has become. When my jaw goes slack, I press my lips together to resist the urge to make it known how good he's making me feel, how hard it is for me not to squirm in my chair. But he obviously wants a reaction, so I refrain.

The muscles in my neck loosen, and my head sways in concert with his movements. I feel warm and electric all over. It's too much energy without enough output. My breaths are shaky with restraint. Cory's eyes flick to my tensed lips, the rise and fall of my chest, the pressing together of my legs that I thought was subtle enough not to be noticed.

Forget it.

I let out a relieved sigh, a tempered response. When he looks into my reflected eyes and there's not triumph there but lust, I lose it.

"Are you kidding me?" I groan. I never realized a scalp massage could be such a turn-on. The guys I've previously dated were barely allowed to touch my hair.

I reach up to rest my hand on his. His movement stops immediately. I turn in my chair to look up at him without the aid of the mirror we've been communicating through the past twenty minutes. He's less certain here, looking around before finally meeting my eyes. His hand twitches in my hair.

There are a dozen questions vying for the top position, but none seem likely to provide the answer I want right now. Instead of speaking, I reach up and clasp his shirt. It's only now I notice he's not wearing his usual scrubs. He's dressed casually in sweatpants and a T-shirt. How long has he been done with work today? It's a brain exercise to consider this, but maybe he didn't come over here to wait for traffic to clear.

I don't know if I pull him to me or if he moves of his own accord. Perhaps it's a joint effort, because his mouth is on mine in record speed.

It's quite possibly the messiest first kiss I've had with someone. Cory tilts my head back with the hold he still has on my last untwisted section of hair. Everything about his positioning is dominant, and he takes advantage of it as he devours my mouth. I try to match him, try to press back into him harder, slip my tongue into his mouth, but at this angle I feel like I'm a baby bird at feeding time. When my chair starts to tilt back, I pull away with a startled "Whoa."

Cory makes sure all chair legs are firmly on the ground and steps back. He's blinking like he's trying to reorient himself to reality. But I don't want that yet. I haven't indulged myself. And since I'm unsure I'll ever get the chance again, I must act.

I stand and push Cory until the backs of his legs are against the side of my bed.

"Sit, please," I say.

He does, eyeing me warily. Unsure if he should get excited or leave while we both have a sliver of deniability, probably. I step closer to him. We're about equal height now since my bed sits high. His locs are up in a hurried bun. I locate the hair band and free them, tucking a few behind his ear, letting that hand settle on his neck.

Then I press my knee into the mattress beside his thigh and climb onto his lap. He's not sitting far into my bed, and for a moment, I worry I'm going to slip off. But he hooks his arms around me, securing me.

I brush my nose against his. "Thank you," I say. And then I kiss him properly.

His lips are more effective than his fingers in my scalp. Maybe. I'm not sure. I'm not sure of much right now, but I think if he combined the two actions, I might short-circuit. As it is, his hands are currently occupied. One arm is still hooked around my back, his hand splayed on my side. The other is feeling on the upper part of my ass. I might not have done all the power squats in my exercise videos this week, but he's still into it.

I grind against him, hoping to release some of the built-up tension I've carried since the first scalp massage. It seems to work, so I do it again. All the while, I'm changing the pace of our kiss. We don't have to be frantic anymore, as neither of us seems to be a flight risk at this point. I kiss him slowly, deeply, our tongues teasing each other.

"Should we . . ." I skim my teeth across his lip.

He growls and, for some surely devil-influenced reason, stops. Maybe he misinterpreted. I meant should we take our clothes off, not should we stop. His roaming hands still, and his lips leave mine. Other than that, there's not much change in his positioning, but the vast separation is clear. His arm falls aside as I stumble off his lap.

"I need to get home." He scratches the side of his nose.

"Yeah, okay." I don't ask what caused his sudden change in demeanor because the thing is, we both know it shouldn't have started in the first place. "Lock the door?"

"Of course."

He almost leaves his shoulder bag on the way out but stutter-steps as he remembers it. I stay put until I hear the turn of the lock sliding into place. Astonished, I drag my feet back over to my chair and shake my head at my reflection.

Great going, I admonish myself. Now I have pent-up energy, a section of hair I need to finish twisting myself, and complication of what was the easiest burgeoning friendship of my adult life.

CHAPTER TWENTY

"Don't let them think they can get over on you. If they perceive you as weak, we're done for."

I nod at the teacher's aide, Ms. Powers. She's a bit on edge after I confessed my lack of previous subbing experience. I reported to school an hour early to meet with her and discuss the lesson plans she emailed over the weekend. The good news is, I still understand second-grade academics. For many subjects, they're building on foundational concepts they've been working with all year. Bad news: these kids need to stay occupied at all times. Otherwise, we lose control of the classroom. Ms. Powers already accepted an offer to return next year as a fourth-grade teacher, having recently passed her certification test. This, too, qualifies as good news because she is more than willing to take the lead with class.

By the time we finish updating the responsibility chart and setting up for our first activity, it's time to gather our lot from the cafeteria. Usually, Ms. Powers explains to me, only one of us will go and pick them up. The other stays behind to finish prepping the room. Today she'll show me the best route to go, and tomorrow I'll do it on my own. She leads me through the halls of the old school building, toward my doom. The kids keep the excitement of seeing a new face at bay on the walk back to the classroom and even through the first activity. But if I used a line graph to plot the relationship between time and the number of random questions directed my way, it would show an exponential increase.

"Ms. Evans, do you have a dog?"

"Ms. Evans, are you married? My dad is getting married, but my mom says I don't have to go if I don't want to. But I'm going because my dad will be happy, and I get to bring the ring to him."

"No dogs," I direct to the girl with beaded braids. "Weddings are fun sometimes," I tell the future ring bearer. "I'm not married."

The latter child, whose name definitely starts with an *R*, goes back to hiding behind his book. He tends to speak in spurts. We're doing station work, and I'm checking on the two children in the story-time area. They flip through books and interrogate me.

"Do you have a bae?" the girl asks.

"'Bae'?" I try not to laugh.

"Yeah, like a boyfriend. Or a girlfriend. My sister's bae is a girl."

"I don't have a bae," I say. "What's the book you have about?"

"Trucks. Do you like anyone?"

Failed attempt at refocusing. Corinne zero, child one. I mean to tell her no and try again to discuss the book, but I look into her little squishy face, and I cannot lie to this child. "Yes," I admit. "I like a guy."

"Did you tell him?"

"In so many words, yes."

She puckers her lips. "Did he say he likes you back?"

"No."

"Were you sad?"

I hesitate. Was I? At the time, I was more confused than anything. I finished up my hair, got something to eat, and then went to sleep early. The following day, lunch with my J & J coworkers was great and boozy for those of us not returning to the office. I stayed in my apartment most of the weekend. Elise went to San Francisco to celebrate Cambodian New Year with her sister. Tiwanda was busy with a work project she had to use her weekend to finish. Cory never contacted me and vice versa. As far as I'm concerned, he should be the one to reach out and explain his abrupt exit. But with this noncommunication, I suppose we're both deciding to pretend it never happened. Which is probably for the best.

"Yes," I tell her. "I'm a little sad."

Cory, as great as he is, is a romantic waste of time. He's AM—After Met. He's also the top reason I'm holding on to denial of the app when it would be much easier if I believed as resolutely as Elise. My mom once told me I was attracted to people not because of what they have but rather what I lack. If that's true, then Cory must have some damn sense because I can't seem to find mine. My thoughts keep wandering to what could have transpired if he didn't have the clarity of mind to stop our kiss.

I had these pesky musings all throughout the weekend. Again, the cycle leads to anger that the Met app exists, taking up an unknown amount of storage on my phone. I try to delete it again during my lunch break, but it won't be shaken. The attempt is immediately followed by a shady Met Tip: Deleting me won't delete your problems. Let Met help.

What would I have done without Met's *help* telling me Cory is ineligible? Without this crap app, would I have made a move? Ask Cory out instead of waiting for another person from my past to materialize? Improbable, but it sucks not having that option because there's a seed of doubt that it would be doomed to fail. Even if Met is bullshit, enough coincidences have happened that seemingly legitimize it, and I'm now behaving accordingly. Self-fulfilling prophecy and all that.

Our class elective for the week is art. My line leader, Chloe, and I are tasked with leading the class to Mx. Martin's art classroom on the first floor.

"It's Mx. because they're not a boy or girl," talkative little Brandon explains to me as I'm trying to get them quiet and lined up.

"Brandon, is now the time for talking?" Ms. Powers asks. She desperately needs this thirty-minute break from the kids. With a new teacher in class, the children are understandably struggling. Some are simply more talkative than usual, others are showing their ass. We had two separate outbursts today.

We wind through the hallways, the children trading shushes with each other the entire journey. The art-room door at the end of the hall is open, welcoming us like a beacon. Although I want nothing more than to allow the children to run inside while I speed walk in the opposite direction, my mom wouldn't let me live it down if I got dismissed from a substitute-teaching job.

I professionally stick my head in the room and ask, "You ready for them?"

Mx. Martin lifts their gaze from the papers on the desk and I freeze. I can't place them right away, but there's a ping of recognition I've come to fear. False alarms set me on edge. Once, while out grocery shopping, I saw a guy who resembled a celebrity and almost rammed into an innocent bystander with my cart. Another time, I thought I saw my former middle school teacher. That would have been awkward. I expect logic to catch up and assure me I don't know this person. Before that happens, Mx. Martin tilts their head to the side as if going through the same inner questioning.

"Yeah, bring them on in," Mx. Martin says. I wave the kids inside, and they scurry to their assigned tables. Some high-five Mx. Martin in passing.

Mx. Martin has light-brown skin and short curly hair, and the way they dress makes it clear painting isn't their only artistic outlet. They're wearing burgundy ankle pants with sleek brown loafers and a loose-fitting mustard-yellow shirt. The wide collar makes it hang off one shoulder a bit, exposing a tattoo that runs in a tidy line from the base of their neck to the curve of their shoulder.

"I think I know you from somewhere," they say between announcing directions to the students. "Can't figure it out, but I will. See you at one forty-five?"

"Right, I'll be back for them," I drone.

"Don't sound so enthusiastic." They smile and walk backward toward the center of the room. I leave the classroom, wrestling with myself not to acknowledge how cute they are.

When I return for the kids, they are in the midst of cleanup. A child from each table goes to dump the paintbrushes and water cups in the sink. Table by table, they bring their watercolor paintings to the rack to dry. There's a lot of activity, but it's organized. Mx. Martin is a superhero.

"I got it," they say.

"Good, because I got nothing." I spent the past thirty minutes running through possible options, all the while feeling guilty because . . . Cory. If I met Mx. Martin before Met app, then automatically they are more likely to be my soul mate than Cory. Despite knowing how he can get my heart pounding after a few touches, Cory has zero chance. I texted Tiwanda and Elise, giving them a heads-up on my potential third match, purposely choosing the group chat that didn't include Cory.

"Do you live in Hyde Park?" Mx. Martin asks.

"Near it."

"Well, on weekends, I sometimes teach a tipsy painting class there."

My mouth drops into an O as I recall the two paintings hanging in my hallway right now, a result of the outing with my mom when I first moved. But I'm sure Mx. Martin was not our instructor. We were led by a woman with fuchsia hair who got annoyed when we insisted on changing all the colors for the predetermined picture.

"What painting did you do?" they ask knowingly. "Table three, you can wash your hands."

"The sunset sky one."

"I don't teach that, but I was probably around helping. I usually check people in, help replenish paint or wine."

"Oh yeah," I say, finally able to place them. Pre-Met then, and therefore my third potential soul mate. And as intriguing as this artist is, I really am too tired for this. I gather my children and say goodbye, not making any attempt to schedule a date.

The second day of subbing I see Mx. Martin during my morning cafeteria duty and learn their first name is Devin. They circle the cafeteria, not getting more than a few steps before someone stops to talk to them. Sometimes it's fellow teacher-monitors but most often it's children from all grades. Each time, Devin is engaged, genuinely interested in what the children have to say. I know teaching isn't for me simply because I could never match that level of caring.

The third day, it's my turn to take the children to art class again. When I come around to walk the group back to the classroom, Mx. Martin says, "Who wants Ms. Evans to come check out their paintings?" Nearly all hands go up, and Devin leads me around the room, pointing out what each child did well in their painting. "See how measured Bianca's brushstrokes are?" "Ezekial has worked really hard on his cloudy effect." A unique comment for every single child. And since they are multitasking goals, it doesn't surprise me that Devin is able to direct cleanup as we make our rounds.

I don't see Devin again until the end of the fourth day. Ms. Powers had to take off as soon as the school day ended to pick up her niece from another school, leaving me alone to straighten up the classroom and get ready for Friday Fun Day, a school-wide day of play.

I'm sitting at one of the clusters of children's desks because the two adult-size desks—which Ms. Powers and I use interchangeably—have too much going on. But since we've taught the children to clean up after themselves, their desks are perfect for the task at hand. I have sheets of laminated fake money I'm cutting out for one of the games tomorrow.

The classroom door is partially open, as other teachers are also prepping for Friday Fun Day, and occasionally one of the teachers from a neighboring classroom will come by, looking for a specific material. There's a tap on the door now as Devin enters.

"You came here at a great time," they say.

"Is it?" I grin. "Sounds like a day of chaos to me."

"Yeah, but it's organized chaos. Can I help?"

"Please! There should be another pair of scissors on the desk in the corner there."

Devin locates the scissors and gets settled in the seat diagonal from me. I hand over a stack of money. They hold the top paper up, turning it this way and that. "Who arranged the money on here like this?"

I laugh because I spent the first ten minutes of cutting with that very same grievance coursing through my veins. Whoever did this tried to squeeze as many dollars and coins as possible on the paper. Some bills are horizontal, while others are vertical. Mock quarters are squeezed in wherever there is space. It's economical but makes it impossible to use the paper cutter. Hence the manual cutting.

"Seriously, we need to go get whoever is responsible for this right now. They should be helping us." Devin starts working, though, trying to figure out the best way to go about this.

"You don't have anything to set up for tomorrow?" I ask.

"I'm finished. We're doing balloon painting with darts. I've had the canvases ready for about a week now."

"Overachiever," I mumble.

"Planner. I had my fifth-grade art class help me with filling the balloons and attaching them to the canvas. Work smarter, not harder."

"Seems like you have to do both around here."

Devin makes a sound I interpret as *No shit*. I sneak looks at them as I clip the money. Today they have on tiny gold hoops, two on each earlobe. They're wearing a cream sweater, which seems risky with their line of work. Maybe they took it off during classes, because a denim collar overlays the neck of the sweater, exposing the button-up underneath.

"What made you get into subbing?" Devin jolts me from my not-so-subtle observation.

"My mom is a retired teacher, and she basically strong-armed me."

"This a side gig?"

"One of many. Still figuring out what I want to do full-time. I moved here from Houston at the end of January."

"From Texas to Chicago winter? Why?" They shake their head. "I moved from California over a decade ago, and I still regret it sometimes. When it gets really cold, I regret my mom moving us from Panama when I was a baby."

"Uh. Well."

Devin looks up from the laminated paper money. In this moment, I know with certainty they wouldn't trivialize the journey that led me here. And though I've barely conversed with them, they're one of the rare people I've met who I'm comfortable enough to trust quickly, not waiting whatever arbitrary time period for them to earn it. Not even Cory received such immediate trust. I shake the thought of him from my head.

"I can't guarantee it'll make sense when I try to explain it."

"Give it a go," Devin says, resuming cutting.

"I lived here for eight years when I was a kid. It's where I had my first real best friend. And then my parents split, and we moved to Houston. So that's home. One of them, I guess."

"You can have as many as you want."

"Well, that best friend died last year. We kept in touch all those years, went to college together, graduated, then right as we were starting our adult lives, she got sick. Came back home here to . . ."

Devin hums their understanding.

"And so I decided to move here."

"I can see how that could bring some healing."

"That's what I'm hoping for, anyway."

We continue trimming the stack of fake money, with Devin telling me why they enjoy working for this school and all the side jobs they do to feed their passion. I trade stories of my temp jobs.

With Devin, it's like I've come to this job with a friend in waiting. My dialogue with Ms. Powers is limited to classroom topics. I don't know much about her outside life unless it coincides with what's going on inside. During lunch, I sit near the other teachers but try to zone out and get some alone time in my brain, if not in the physical environment. This conversation with Devin is providing me a social aspect I haven't known I needed.

"What kind of work did you do before?"

I prefer this question to its commonly asked inverse: What do you want to do now? Devin seems to understand that would be a frivolous question to ask.

"I was a financial analyst. Majored in economics and ended up at this huge company. It was fun for a while. Steady paychecks with more than I knew what to do with. Company happy hours every other week. Company lunch every Friday."

"I'm sensing a trend here," Devin says. They're still focusing on the page in front of them but wear a slight smile.

I sigh. "Did you always know you were about this life?"

"You mean the broke life?" They guffaw. "I was about the 'do whatever it takes' life. I always had the conviction it would be worth it. My mom was an artist, though she never sold her work. My dad tried to be a musician before he got a steady job in manufacturing. They're my biggest supporters."

"My mom is straddling the line of supporting me getting my shit together and pressuring me *to* get my shit together pretty well."

I dump my scraps into the recycle bin as Devin cuts out the last fake coins. Ms. Powers left behind plastic bags to separate each denomination into, and then I am free to go. Devin scrolls on their phone as I put the last of the supplies away.

"Thanks again for the help," I say. "See you tomorrow for Friday Fun Day?"

"Yeah . . . unless you want to come to Teacher's Happy Hour."

"There's a teacher's happy hour?"

Devin nods slowly. "I think you need it. Come on."

CHAPTER
TWENTY-ONE

Teacher's Happy Hour is with 100 percent less alcohol than I expect and 200 percent more sweets.

After leaving school grounds, Devin leads me on foot several blocks away to Baker's Dozen, a bakery opened a year ago by a local Black family. Apparently, in the closing hours of every weekday, they sell perishables 25 percent off and 50 percent off if you're a Chicago Public Schools worker. When I ask if being a substitute teacher counts, the owner says, "Of course!" and throws in a free cookie.

Devin waves at a few other people but chooses a separate table as we wait for our ordered lattes.

"Are they teachers too?" I ask.

"Yeah. But every time I sit with them, they like to tell me how easy my job is in comparison to theirs."

"Great seat choice, then."

I bought a bunch of doughnuts and muffins to last me the next few mornings. For now, I pick one to nibble on as I chat with Devin. It feels like a moment I've experienced only once in my life. Back in college, I'd been set on cramming for a test but ended up chatting with a guy trying to do the same in our residence hall common room. We had a whirlwind collegiate romance for three months afterward. For a moment, we both imagined we were experiencing what it was like to find the one in college. And then, he turned out to be someone who constantly downplayed my feelings—all of them.

If I was excited, it "wasn't a big deal." If I was upset, I needed to "calm down." If I was obsessed with something, it "wasn't all that." Finally, Joelle told me to cut him loose. And after he said Joelle's opinion of him was "not that important," I took her advice.

Joelle and I depended on each other heavily for love-life shenanigans. Neither of us fared well. Maybe this explains why I struggle with Met app–related matters. Joelle would have supported this app with as much conviction as Elise. She always said it costs nothing to believe. In fact, she'd probably have a favorite picked out pending the fourth match. And she surely wouldn't support me getting distracted by Cory when there are such high stakes.

Devin and I leave the café and walk back to the school. My hands are full with a box of baked goods cradled in one arm and the remainder of my chai latte in the other.

"This area is cool," I say, more observant of the storefronts than before.

"I moved from Hyde Park over here to be closer to the school."

"Good change?"

"I'm getting used to it. When I first moved, I distributed my business cards to a lot of the places around here. My niche is teaching art, but I do some graphic design, too, and sell some pieces. I've already done some work with a few." Devin points to a small storefront we're approaching. The glass is decorated with a painted picture of a park. It shows green hills, families hanging out, and dogs on leashes. We come to a stop as I examine it further.

"You did that?"

"No, but it's what first drew me inside. Turns out it's a nonprofit. I do some pro bono classes with them once a month, usually. We're on a break now, though."

We start walking again. "It's a nonprofit focusing on the arts, then?"

"Actually, no. It focuses on double generational financial wellness. I do a workshop on how you can turn your art into a living for middle and high school students."

I come to a stop quickly, my box of baked goods almost flying out of my hand. "What is it called?" I ask as I backstep to locate the sign. There isn't one.

"Oh, they're rebranding. There hasn't been a new sign for a few months now, or a website. Wanna go in?"

I nod, unable to speak over the shifting gears inside me that sound suspiciously like everything sliding into place. Devin presses the doorbell. It takes a minute for the door to open. A guy welcomes us inside and greets Devin warmly with one of those handshake-turned-into-half-hug maneuvers. He introduces himself as Pedro.

The reception area inside is as artistic and hip as the mural on the outside. There are colorful paintings of children in various shades of brown arranged in a straight line that continues across all four walls. This place has good energy.

"I know, I know. But we'll be back soon, stronger than ever," Pedro says before Devin has said anything.

"I didn't come here to get on you. I know you all are working."

"It's down to three of us now. We recently won a grant. It's a little less than the funding we hoped for, but we can make do. Aisha wants to apply for a few more, but Heidi left and we're working double time to all cover her job. We might have to push the June relaunch back."

I'm following their conversation as best as I can, and from the bits I get along with gaps I try to fill myself, I'm jittery with excitement. Or maybe that's the sugar from our bakery run.

"What did Heidi do, exactly?" I cut in.

"A fucking lot," Pedro says. "She applied for the grants, handled our budget, a good chunk of the marketing. The list goes on."

"So . . . like a financial person?"

"Yeah."

"I'm a financial person," I announce somewhat proudly. Pedro doesn't react as enthusiastically, not understanding the relevance. "Is this Finance for the Fam?" He nods. *I knew it!* "My best friend left me a flyer of the workshop y'all had last year. It was an all-day thing."

"That was our top event."

"I tried to pull up your website from the flyer, but it wasn't found."

"We're in the process of finding a web designer."

"Right, Devin told me. My point is, this is where she was trying to lead me. I have a finance and economics background, and I think the work you're doing is super important. You lost Heidi. Can I apply for the job?"

Pedro regards me skeptically as a slow smile grows on Devin's face. We both face Pedro, awaiting his response.

Pedro laughs, a little stunned. "Are you sure? Heidi's job has taken all three of us to do it, and we're still coming up short."

"I'm not implying it would be easy, but . . ." I huff out a gust of air, frazzled that I have to convince this guy when the realization hit me like a freight train. "It sounds like you all are trying to do your own jobs, plus a third of Heidi's. Of course it's difficult. If I could help, it could give you time to focus on other things."

It's dead quiet as Pedro visibly doubts this.

"We were planning on filling the position before fall," he says. "But I have to check with the other members of the board. We started this together, and we're protective of who we let in."

"Certainly, that's understandable." Now that I have my foot in the door, I change my tone to business professional and not *please hire me I'm desperate.*

"You would have to apply and interview with all three of us since it's a salaried position. Full transparency: it's not much, but it's impactful work."

"You don't have to convince me," I assure him.

"Just warning you, it won't be like the finance dollars you were making."

"Oh." I titter. "I let that go a long time ago."

CHAPTER
TWENTY-TWO

As soon as I step in my apartment, I pull out my phone to share my good news—only deciding who to tell is more of an issue than I initially expected. I first thought to tell my mom, but I don't want to get her hopes up. Her expectations and interview tips translate to increased stress levels.

Lito is the only other familial option, but since he's been ribbing me on my employment status these past months and recently told me he was offered the internship here but doesn't plan on accepting, he doesn't get to know anything until it's concrete. Also, he's known to have some reservations about working for nonprofits, and I don't need that negativity right now. Not when I'm in my rose colored–lens phase. Everything is magical and falling into place when all I've done to make it happen is exist. That was enough.

I decide—as I throw off my jacket, free myself of pants, and fling my bra across the room—that this is what friends are for. Specifically, local friends. My finger hovers above my recent texts as I try to decide whether to send it to the group chat with only me, Tiwanda, and Elise or the one that includes Cory. I imagine they have one that doesn't include me. I shall persist and show them how amazing I am until that chat is obsolete.

If I'm being honest with myself and put my petty feelings aside, there really is no debate on which is the appropriate chat to use. Cory and I haven't communicated in a week, but I want him to be in the loop on this.

I found a job to apply for!

Elise's response comes first, a string of emojis and a dancing GIF. It's followed by a regretful, Nooo does this end our random midday hangs??

Tiwanda is not long after, which I hope is an indicator of a more manageable workload. She wants more specifics. What's the company, job position, salary? Can they hire me too?

I text back that it's a nonprofit, salary can be inferred from the aforementioned, and that I still have to convince them to hire me first. She replies with a GIF of a woman banging her head on a desk repeatedly. Maybe her workload hasn't improved, then.

I await Cory's response. Well, I stay on my phone and swipe through my other most used apps as I try to convince myself that's not what I'm doing. After five minutes, I get up and go check my fridge, though I'm well versed on its contents. In my excitement about the possible job, I'd forgotten to stop at the grocery store. I eye the box of doughnuts and muffins on the counter, considering them as a hassle-free dinner.

My phone buzzes. Not the short message one but the long, insistent one reserved for phone calls. I go check if it's a scam call, but it's Cory. Calling me for the first time since he'd asked for permission to enter my apartment.

"Hello?" I try my best not to sound on edge, but I only had seconds to pull myself together before I would miss the damn call.

"Hey." Wow, he has this nonchalant thing down. "First, congratulations."

"I haven't gotten a job yet."

"I know. Congratulations." He emphasizes it this time but provides no further explanation because really, it isn't necessary.

"Thanks," I say, and mean it.

"Second, have you figured out dinner tonight?"

"No . . ."

"Good. I'm in the area, and I'm bringing food. If that's okay?"

I can't agree fast enough. We hang up and I tell myself not to freak out while running to put on a good, comfortable after-work outfit that's cute but not too cute. It obviously doesn't matter—we were literally all over each other when I was in an old T-shirt. Still, it's more a preparation for myself than Cory's benefit. I can't very well greet him in my underwear, now can I? Or . . . could I?

By the time Cory arrives, I have decided no, I cannot wear underwear to dinner. I put on yoga capris and sat my ass on the couch to watch television instead of pacing and overanalyzing this visit. But then I ended up getting on my laptop and researching organizations both in Illinois and elsewhere that focus on financial literacy. I fell into a rabbit hole that included putting library books related to running nonprofits and grant writing on hold.

Cory comes in with one large paper tote bag of food that smells mouthwatering. The only hint I got was a text asking if I liked seafood. I eagerly help unpack the food and lay it all out on the counter as he uses the washroom.

There's a seafood pasta, bread rolls, salad, and a surprise second entree—some type of ravioli.

"Which one is mine?" I ask Cory as he rejoins me in the kitchen.

"Possessive much? We're halving."

"I was planning on getting some of yours anyway. Guess I can share mine too."

He shakes his head at the counter, but his eyes flick up and meet mine. It inspires a jolt in my chest that reminds me nothing about this is a normal friend visit. But I can see how hard Cory is trying to make it so.

We pile pasta on plates and salad into bowls and throw down. After expecting to have a dinner consisting of half-price pastries, this is an immeasurable improvement. He not only humors me but is whole-heartedly interested as I recap everything leading up to this possible job. Starting with the flyer in Joelle's package and ending with another teacher showing me a place they volunteer art services. I skirt around the detail that said teacher is a potential soul mate. After reliving everything with Cory, I'm somehow more enthusiastic about the position.

"Thank you for this," I say as I fork a second helping of pasta onto my plate.

"You deserve it."

"After I get the job, I definitely will."

"It's not illegal to celebrate twice."

"Sure, as long as it involves you bringing food."

"Anytime."

I glance at him, but he's focused on his plate. He said that last part breezily, but might it hold weight? How, when he spent the last week barely responding to my comments in the group chat? I must broach this conversation because I can't guess what he's thinking. If I did, I'd say he didn't spare a thought over what happened the last time we were together.

"So," I begin as he sets his fork down.

"You really believe in that?" he asks.

My expression goes slack. I try to rewind the conversation a bit in my head and replay what I must have missed. Nope, nothing there. "Believe . . . what?"

"In your soul mate app."

My head rocks back like a reflex. "Um. No? I don't. Not really."

He eyes me suspiciously.

"Well, it is strange. It has kind of proven itself."

"You've had three coincidences. That doesn't mean this app is real."

I groan inwardly. Tiwanda or Elise told him about Devin. No wonder this topic is on his mind, given it's the first time I've seen him since we kissed. I haven't confessed to Tiwanda or Elise why I started to believe in Met. If I told either of them having this app pestering me helps fill the void of my dead best friend, they would think I'm off my rocker. It's better to appeal to Cory with logic.

"Before the app, how many people did I run into who I knew already? Hell, when I lived in Houston, the city I grew up in for over a decade, I ran into one person from high school in four years. One!" I hold up an index finger to stress this point.

Cory shakes his head with a half-formed eye roll. "This speculative app tells you it's sending your soul mate, and because of that, you sleep with whoever comes along?"

I think I actually freeze. For a moment, all the organs in my body stop functioning. But then my brain snaps back to alert and reminds my heart, my lungs, and my nerve endings, *We have to keep going so she can curse him out!*

"I'm sorry," Cory says as I kick back into gear again. My face must have alerted him of the danger but, *oh, hohohoho*, he can't avoid it now.

"Excuse me? Who I sleep with is none of your business." My subconscious decides to chime in that it could've been his business if he hadn't dipped out last week, but I ignore that. From the glint in Cory's eyes, I think he's had the same thought, but he's smart enough not to voice it. "This could have waited until after I finished eating. Or, you know, maybe never." I angrily stab at my plate.

When my food falls off my fork halfway to my mouth and I continue the motion hoping Cory doesn't notice the flub, the asshole laughs. He tries to cover it up with a fake cough, but he's not very good at it. Anger flares in me anew.

"Why do you care? About the app, about my sex life?"

"Are you kidding? We . . ." His mouth stays open for a few seconds as words refuse to come out. He closes his mouth, resets, tries again. "Why did you kiss me if all you care about are the people the app sent you?"

"Maybe I'm not focused on the app, as you seem to believe."

That skeptical look of his again. It shouldn't work to get me to reveal more twice, but . . .

"I kissed you because I wanted to. Same as with everyone, app related or not," I say.

"Right." Cory stands. "That makes sense."

"You're leaving?" I ask.

"I think I should, yeah."

"Fine, but leave the leftovers. I'll accept this as repayment for you ruining my supposed celebration."

This causes him to pause. He turns to me, lips tensed, eyes squinting as if he's trying to read the small printed manual on how to approach this error.

"This wasn't the right time to talk about this."

"Ya think?"

"I really am sorry. I didn't plan it going like this. I mean, it's my fault but . . . yeah. Maybe I should stick to writing my ideas down."

His apology is sincere, if confusing. I'm still scratching my head as he rinses the dishes he used, places them in the dishwasher, and goes to put his shoes back on.

"I'll see you tomorrow at sober game night?"

"Sure," I say, now wary of the get-together Tiwanda planned. It's the first time we'll all be together since Elise's liberation celebration.

Cory lets himself out. It's only after he's gone and I'm showered, getting ready for bed, that I realize he never told me how he imagined the conversation going in the first place.

~

Friday Fun Day is a huge success. The children enjoy themselves, there are no serious injuries—which I hear is a first in its eight-year history—and I manage to have fun. For most of the day, I'm inside the gym with the inflatables. There's an obstacle course, a slide, and a jousting pen. I personally thought the jousting pen was a strange risk for a school with injury reports the past seven Friday Fun Days. But, as the kids say, no one died.

I'm feeling so charged after a day of meeting and genuinely connecting with the other teachers that when Devin asks if I have plans for tonight, I don't consider lying. In fact, I take it a step further.

"Having a mostly sober game night with my cousin and friends. You want to come?" I ask jokingly, thinking it sounds like something no one would volunteer to be part of with a group of strangers. Elise warned me how competitive this night usually gets. That's the reason it became a mostly sober game night. The last time it was a drunk game night, Cory's ex Brian ended up tripping down the stairs and spraining his ankle.

Devin surprises me and says, "Sure, I'd love to."

We carpool to Elise's far-as-hell apartment on the North Side. Devin controls the music, and we switch between singing along to songs and turning the music low to chat about something random. At one point, we're joking about my driving snafus, which I swear never happen when I'm solo. Then we stop at a grocery store nearby and pick up our share of the required snacks.

As soon as we arrive at Elise's apartment, the carefree feel of the carpool is dead. At least it is for me. Because I'm kind of showing up with a date to a friend hangout that includes Cory? I can't with myself.

Elise, Tiwanda, and Cory are all there when we arrive. I introduce Devin, and they easily make an effort to connect with each person. With Cory, Devin notices he's wearing a Northwestern shirt. They're both alums, Devin for undergrad and Cory for his doctorate program. There was no overlap, but still. Devin makes their connection with

Tiwanda, something about the boutique jewelry they both have on. From a picture hanging on the wall, Devin figures out Elise is also from the West Coast, so they converse a bit about that. *Seriously, how do they find ways to relate so smoothly?* I make eye contact with Cory. His face mirrors my thoughts. I suppress a laugh, and he returns my smile, shaking his head ruefully.

"What are we playing first?" I ask as I check out the spread of chocolate truffles on the kitchen counter. Tiwanda made each of the four types herself. I choose the raspberry-infused one first, then hungrily reach for the others.

"We're waiting for one more," Elise says.

I scrunch up my face because I was the only one in the group chat who said anything about bringing someone. It's not against any rules, but it's odd it didn't come up when Tiwanda assigned snacks for each of us to bring. Neither Tiwanda nor Cory seems surprised by the additional player. Tiwanda sighs, and Cory is blankly staring at something on his phone. Did they discuss this in the group chat that doesn't include me?

The doorbell rings, and Elise goes to the door. I don't bother to hide my curiosity. I think I recognize her friend, but I'm having trouble placing him until she says, "Bebe Bri!"

As in Brian. As in Cory's ex. My jaw drops. Cory's doesn't. He stands and goes to greet Brian too. It's a brief side hug but . . . what is going on?

"They're trying to be friendly again," Tiwanda says in my ear. I turn to her, aghast. She simply crosses her eyes and grabs a deck of cards. "All right, grab food if you want it. I'm ready to play."

We start with a partner game that requires a secret signal between you and your partner. You then try to use it discreetly throughout the game without the other teams picking up on it. We draw for teams to make it random. I'm with Brian, Elise is with Devin, and Tiwanda and Cory are partnered. Each team gets a minute in Elise's office to come up with their signal, and as our time runs out, I hastily agree with Brian's dumb idea to touch our hair. I expect Tiwanda and Cory to win, from simply knowing each other the best out of all the pairs, but Devin and Elise shock us all by winning. After the game is over, they refuse to share their signal. As they celebrate their victory, I try not to look toward Cory but fail. I can't help but smirk at how scornfully he's watching them. We obviously both agree Devin is ridiculously perfect. This night isn't as awkward as I expected it to be, and I owe that completely to Devin.

"Your friends are great," Devin tells me when we're in the kitchen alone, getting more snacks and beverages. The kitchen isn't completely connected to the living room, providing a bit of privacy. If I stand in the opening, I can peep a sliver of the couch where Brian is taking a seat beside Cory. I bristle, like a porcupine ready to ward off someone for coming too close. When Cory's eyes flick to the kitchen entrance, I take a clumsy step away.

"They're all right," I grumble. Devin takes this as a joke.

Back in the living room, Elise is setting up the next game. It's Taboo, the game in which you describe words without using the ones listed on the cards. We split up into teams, me with Brian and Cory. *Awesome.* The threesome no one asked for. We decide on a short game to fifty points. Toward the end, it's neck and neck, though our team strategies are wildly different.

Tiwanda, Elise, and Devin give neutral clues anyone could answer. Our team relies heavily on personal connections. Which means when Brian is up, I'm almost silent. When Cory is up, however, it's a battle of who can answer the fastest.

For the last one, we need six points to win. It's a stretch since our best round was five points. Cory is up giving clues; Tiwanda is breathing down his neck, making sure he doesn't say any of the forbidden words. Devin is watching the tiny hourglass like a hawk, crouching to get eye level with it. Elise is chilling, eating cheddar popcorn and enjoying the show.

Cory stretches his arms and rolls his neck before okaying Devin to start the time.

The first clue is directed toward Brian. "What your sister does," he says.

"Accountant!" Brian yells like it was a particular feat figuring that one out.

The second clue is meant for him too. "Something you hate doing," Cory says, pointing at Brian. I'm sitting here useless in my ready position, forearms resting on my legs.

"Cleaning!" Brian yells. Cory shakes his head. "Driving! Working."

"It happens . . . after the sun goes down."

I raise an eyebrow, precisely when Cory looks at me for the first time this turn. He shakes his head, a minute movement meant for me, though other eyes are on him.

"Oh, sleeping!" Brian yells.

I choke on air. But I pull it together because the next one goes to me. "Your mom's old position."

"Principal," I say. Correct. The following one is back to Brian. Then me again. But for the final one, the word that, if guessed correctly before the time runs out, will declare us the winners is related to Cory himself. I know a challenge when I see one. Or when it lives in my head, whatever.

"Something you eat after dinner."

"Dessert!" we both yell.

"That, but specific. I love it. My dad would make it."

"Spaghetti!" Brian shouts, loud and wrong. I'm momentarily stunned at his ability to forget the previous clue.

"Strawberry shortcake!" I yell simultaneous with Devin yelling, "Time!"

We then debate for the next ten minutes if I said the answer in time, but I don't care. Because Cory sits next to me on the couch and bumps his fist into mine, and I know I already won.

CHAPTER
TWENTY-THREE

Game night is over, and we're all sitting in the living room, chatting like it's not nearing one in the morning. I'm next to Devin on the shaggy rug, and we're both so worn out from the combination of Friday Fun Day and sober game night that we're leaning on each other for support. Devin is the reason this group is working, hands down.

When Brian made a laughing-but-serious joke about friends choosing sides postbreakup and Tiwanda visibly began gearing up to kick him out of Elise's apartment, Devin jumped in and told a hilarious story about their college friend group. When two in the group broke up, Devin tried to sneakily see each half separately. But they got caught, which led to the couple getting back together in their shared feelings of betrayal. Now they're married.

"Did they thank you at their wedding?" Elise asks.

"Wasn't invited," Devin says.

We all start making declarations to leave soon, except Tiwanda, who's staying the night. I would, too, if I didn't have Devin to drop off. Brian took the train here. I can't stand him, but it's all of us against city transportation. You help when you can.

"I can give you a ride home. You live on the South Side, right?" I stand to go to the bathroom before Devin and I head out.

"It's all right. Cory's got me."

Oh, does he, now? I can't bring myself to look at Cory because I don't know what my face looks like right now. Any response would be the wrong one, so I say, "Okay," in the most neutral voice I can muster and find solace in the walk down the hallway to the bathroom. When I come out minutes later, Cory's a few steps away from the door, posted on the wall.

"Needed to use the restroom," he says.

I exit and extend my arm as if welcoming royalty to the throne. His body doesn't move, but his face transforms into one of concern. His eyebrows furrow as he observes me. In the awkward silence, I drop my arm. Cory reaches out to catch it. "You all right?" he asks. I shake off his touch.

"Fine." I glance down the empty hallway. Our friends' voices from the living room are indecipherable. This is the first time we've been alone all night—might as well air my grievances. "Brian is here."

Cory squints at me. "Yes," he says, as if I'm the dimmest bulb in the lamp.

"That would have been useful information to share."

"I asked Elise if it was okay. Tiwanda knew too."

I raise a hand like I'm a waitress carrying an invisible platter.

"You don't know Brian," he says.

"I know you."

His head flinches back, seemingly realizing his fault. He drops his gaze to the floor, then back up. Any breakthrough I thought occurred moments before is gone once he meets my eyes again.

"Is Devin a friend?"

"What does it matter? I told *all of you* I was bringing them. Devin's been great. Brian was the one being weird all night."

"You don't know his normal, so your judgment is negligible. What's weird is knowing exactly what to say at all times. I'm talking about Devin."

I scowl, more because he felt the need to specify than the statement itself. "Don't be a hater."

"You were thinking the same thing; I saw you."

"Seeing me equates to reading my mind?"

"Most of the time, yeah."

I resist the urge to smile but ultimately am unsuccessful. I'm annoyed with him, yes. But he has a point. The times we locked eyes tonight, I felt he understood me without verbalizing and vice versa. Still, Brian? Also, I'm a tad peeved about the last time I saw him, when he insinuated that I was indiscriminate in my sexual relations. His apology might have turned down the flame, but I'm still simmering.

"Where did you find Devin? How can one person get along with everyone?" Cory says. He's animated, moving his arms as he speaks. I break and laugh. His joking, incredulous voice is contagious.

"We met at the school I'm subbing at. Well, technically before that—out painting with my mom. I think it's a teaching thing, though." You might not like all the kids, but they shouldn't know that.

The smile washes off Cory's face. "Wait—you've met them *before*, before?"

I nod slowly.

"This was a date?"

"No." I check the hall again. "We're all hanging out."

"A trial run, then. See if your *soul mate* would fit in with your friends."

I cross my arms. It's not an unreasonable idea, though it wasn't a consideration at all. This is the second time he's freaked out about this soul mate idea, and I'm growing tired of it real fast. I haven't figured out if I want to put all my eggs in the Met basket, and getting this shame from Cory isn't helping.

My nonanswer gets under his skin more than any words could. He steps inside the bathroom and shuts the door in the vicinity of my face. I clench my fist to bang on the door, but by all that's holy I pull myself together before giving him the reaction he wants.

It doesn't make sense. I thought Tiwanda or Elise had already told him I'd met my third Met match? Maybe they didn't tell him particulars, including Devin's name and where we met. If Cory was unaware, then I grudgingly understand his perspective but not to this extent. We're friends who have made out, and it's clear he's uncomfortable starting anything with me while I have the Met situation going on. That forfeits his right to behave like this.

I interrupt Devin midconversation to make my escape before Cory is out of the bathroom. Tiwanda eyes me as I hasten Devin along, but Elise assists by walking us to the door.

My thoughts are so consuming that I don't notice there's no music playing in the car for the first five minutes. Devin pulls me out of my Met-app-and-Cory loop as we're sitting at a red traffic light.

"Is it exhaustion or Cory?" they ask me.

I snort. "A lot of both, I think."

"And Cory and Brian are exes. That was weird."

"It was, right?" I glance at them, overexcited someone agrees. "'No thanks, I don't need a ride,'" I say, mocking Brian. "'I'll make Cory drive thirty minutes out of the way and then turn around to—'" I stop abruptly as my brain populates the solution. Cory's going to stay at Brian's apartment overnight. The light turns green, and I hit the gas harder than I mean to. Bessie vrooms as she goes absolutely nowhere.

"Doubt it," Devin says to my unspoken worries.

My shoulders slump and I hand over the cable for Devin to plug in their phone for music. Though the opposite side of the highway is severely backed up, our side only experiences a slight slowdown due to people's nosiness. It's not too horrible a trip from the North Side. When I get home, I find I have enough energy to shower. The warm water invigorates me as I wash off the day. I take my newfound vigor and direct it at cursing Cory in my head as I moisturize and slip on a nightie. He messed up the connection with my most eligible Met match. More upsetting, I allowed it to happen.

I pull on my bonnet, climb into bed, and connect my phone to the charger. I open Met, willing it to send a notification. When I'm awarded with a chime, I nearly fumble my phone. Met Tip: Choose or lose. The first time I'm seeking its support, and it gives me something as useless as this. I set the phone on my nightstand and close my eyes for about two seconds before a call comes through. Tiwanda. Oh crap, I never texted the group I made it home.

"Hey, sorry. I made it."

"I figured, but I saw an alert the highway is closed because an eighteen-wheeler flipped. Some cars involved too. What?" She leans away from the phone on the last word. "Oh. It's heading towards downtown. Okay, now I don't have to call Cory. Speaking of, did you want to talk about—"

"I'd rather be stuck behind the eighteen-wheeler traffic," I say.

Tiwanda laughs. "Great, we agree. Good night."

Before I replace my phone on the nightstand, it begins vibrating again. *Wow*, I think as I glance at the screen. *The devil really has it out for me tonight.*

Cory's voice is hesitant on the other end of the phone line. "Are you at your apartment?"

Where the hell else would I be? "Yes?"

"I-90 is closed."

I look up at my ceiling. "One, I said I'm already home. Two, Tiwanda called about this, but it's not on the side of the highway we were on."

"Yes," Cory says in his forcibly patient voice. "But it is the side I usually take to get home. The GPS estimates forty-five minutes with the extra traffic, going Lake Shore Drive instead."

"What? Where are you?"

"In my car. Outside Brian's."

Oh. I start to make a case for one of the streets that runs all the way through the city, a perk of Chicago's grid system, but realize if I'm barely awake now he probably feels similarly. "Let yourself in." I hang up, then rise to grab my spare comforter and a sheet out of the closet. I sacrifice a pillow from my bed. All of this I pile on the couch. Then I climb into my bed for a second time. I lie there, eyes closed, battling my exhaustion, finally succumbing to the bliss of a dreamless sleep the moment I hear the front door open and close.

CHAPTER TWENTY-FOUR

I normally sleep confined to one side of my queen-size bed. This morning, however, I wake up in the middle, my blanket hanging off the side, tangled in the sheet. Rough night, I guess. I'm so well rested that my body practically sings with relief, though it's only . . . I reach to check my phone. 8:52. Dammit. I couldn't manage to "sleep in" until nine. Meh, it's close enough.

Instead of staying in bed an extra hour, I get up and pad to my bathroom. It's Saturday, but I have tasks to get done. Mainly, fill out the application Pedro emailed me and make a trip to the library for some nonprofit-related books I have on hold. Homework for the substitute teacher on the weekend—how apt.

It's not until I'm standing outside my closed bathroom door that my lackadaisical brain catches up to my functioning body. Amazing how seemingly small details can alert me when something is off. Case in point, when not in use I leave my bathroom door cracked almost always. Never fully closed. Living in a house with a half dozen people and two bathrooms made us come up with an impromptu system I subconsciously brought to my own apartment. Bathroom vacant, door partially open. Bathroom occupied, door closed. Don't knock, don't ask how long they'll be.

So when I'm faced with my closed bathroom door, my first thought is *I have to wait.* This is quickly followed with the counter-thought *I'm the only person who lives here.* But light emanates from underneath the door. Just as I remember I have a guest I don't particularly like right now, the door swings open.

Cory confines all his surprise at me standing here to his face, a slight lift of his chin and jump of his eyebrows. I hurriedly back myself against the wall because there is *a lot* going on here. Potent steam wafts out of the door, bringing with it the fresh scent of my citrus-vanilla body wash. Cory stands in front of me with nothing but a skimpy towel around his waist. I divert my eyes from that sight and focus on his face. His hair is pulled up into a high bun, his beard gleaming with moisture.

"What are you doing?" I ask him.

He partially raises his arm but puts it down before he completes the full gesture, perhaps thinking wiser than to sass me right now.

"I took a shower," he says instead.

"You couldn't have, I don't know, gone home to shower?" I wouldn't normally care if a friend decided to use my shower, but in this moment, I do. "And you have to turn on the vent, or it gets too damp in there." I step forward to reach for the switch on the inside wall. The vent starts with a loud shudder. I retreat as I realize Cory didn't move in response to me like a normal person would, leaving me close enough to feel the heat radiating from his skin.

"I didn't want it to wake you up," he says. I pout at his consideration.

"That's a decorative towel." I allow my eyes to dip in reference for a millisecond.

"It was rolled in a basket."

"I'm aware." My mom convinced me I needed them for my bathroom when she helped decorate. Truthfully, I don't understand its purpose either. "Are you done?"

"Uh. Yeah."

We awkwardly shuffle to trade places and not touch each other. I don't know what I'm afraid will happen if we do. I start to close the door, but Cory's voice halts me.

"You don't, uh, have lotion I can use?"

I sigh. "In my room on the dresser." I reach for my toothbrush and notice a new addition in the holder. "I see you found the toothbrushes I bought for my mom and brother," I call out before shutting the door.

In the bathroom, I brush my teeth, wash my face, and pull my hair up into a loose pineapple puff. The routine calms me and gives me time for self-reflection, regardless of if I want it. I wasn't a good host to Cory, no matter how valid the feelings that spurred my behavior. He was a hapless victim of my morning mood. I want him to feel welcome in my apartment. He has a key, after all. Lately, we've reverted to being snippy with each other. It's not enjoyable. I hate that being irritable was my crutch reaction to him looking delectable standing there in that dumbass decorative towel. I seek reinforcement from my own reflection before leaving the bathroom.

Cory sits on his side of the couch in dark-gray scrubs. The dressings for the couch I'd left for him are now refolded and in the chair.

"You have clients today?" I ask, opening the fridge to take out my water pitcher.

"No, this was the only change of clothes I had in my car."

The snarky thought *I know of a place where you'd have more clothing options* enters my brain, but I suppress it. See? Progress.

Instead, I say, "Do you want something to drink? I'm going to make a breakfast smoothie."

"Actually, the reason I didn't go home is because I was hoping we could go to breakfast." I raise my eyebrows. "I wanted to thank you for letting me stay here."

I shake my head. "You don't have to thank me for using my couch."

"And your shower. And your fancy towel. And your mom's toothbrush."

"And my lotion," I add with a teasing smile.

"I also wanted to apologize."

"Simultaneously?" I bring my glass of water over to the couch and sit with him. He looks over at me for a moment before responding. His locs are down now, just how I like them. I take a sip of water, but it's not quenching all my thirst.

"We've been . . . off lately, right?"

I squint at him, then look away. The idea of being "off" implies there was a time we were "on." What does being on look like for us? Well, there's the communication. Him texting to check if he can come by. When we're together, it's talking about a wide range of things. It's me talking about Joelle and my family, and him and the story of his dad and telling me about the progress of his article for the physical therapy journal. We were really "on" when I was in his lap on my bed. But it's also the peace that came with his presence. Feeling as comfortable with him here as without him. I did everything I do alone, short of walking around nude. What changed since then? Some words Cory obviously regrets, yes. But something else I can't quite pinpoint. Maybe it's the expectation of finding who Met has deemed my romantic soul mate, rendering whatever me and Cory might start useless.

"We've been off," I agree.

"I've talked with my therapist about it and—"

"Wait." I cut him off, sit my glass on the coffee table, and draw a leg under me to face him fully. I beam at him. "You talked about me with your therapist?"

He extends a leg out to bump mine. "Yeah, yeah, but it was really about me."

"Of course."

"I've been acting impulsively lately." My gut swirls with dread as I prepare for him to apologize for kissing me. "We discussed what

171

happened, and I need to make it clear. What I said Thursday night was out of line." I give him a stern nod, and he continues, "I feel this pressure the more I'm around you. We're not dating, I know I have no claim on you but . . . I wish I did."

"Huh?" The easy way he slipped that in makes my heartbeat stampede.

"I know you have the app and the people you're seeing, but do you really trust an app more than your own judgment?"

"You think I'm dating all these people?"

"I was in the car, remember? When you took a vote on if you should sleep with another guy?"

My stomach flies to my throat. I press my lips together to keep from giggling. He looks fed up with my shit, and honestly, I am too. I lift a hand to my face, trying to covertly cover my mouth. Cory narrows his eyes at me, and I lose it. My giggle turns into gasping laughter at the sight of his blank face. He sighs and lets his head fall back on the couch, staring up at the ceiling as I struggle to pull myself together.

"Technically"—I hold up a finger—"it was Elise's idea to vote. I didn't know you were in the car. Plus, the vote is irrelevant. It was ultimately my decision. And since you're so concerned about my dating life, yes, I do trust my judgment. Asshole."

"I'm not"—he lifts his head from the couch and turns his entire body toward me—"'concerned' about your dating life. I want to *be* your dating life."

I realize I never responded to his earlier declaration of wanting to be with me. The first stunned me, but this time makes my heart go soft even while an almost painful, searing flash hits my chest. I have to pause for a moment and allow the unsettling feeling to subside. The way he's being consistently open with me inclines me to reciprocate.

"I don't know about us," I confess.

"Same. But don't you want to find out?"

There are lots of things I'd like to find out. Revolving thoughts of my prospective job with Finance for the Fam, the package Joelle left me, Met, and, yeah, Cory have taken residence in my brain. Am I wasting my time placing even part of my trust with Met when I have Cory in front of me, saying his wants match mine? I shift my positioning so that my knees press into his thigh.

"I've wanted you since voting night. Well, even before, but it was crystal clear that night."

He shakes his head a bit, not understanding.

"I went to Anthony's place, and we were on the couch . . ."

He waves a hand. "I don't need to know."

"Oh, you most definitely do. Especially since you still give me crap about it. But I'll give you the abridged version. It was the most anticlimactic cunnilingus of my life."

He blinks, his gaze shifting with each occurrence, then squints at me. "You didn't come?"

"I did, but by my own doing. And yours. Had to make it worthwhile."

He nods, then stops abruptly when he notices the limited information he has doesn't quite make sense. "Wait, what do you mean *my* doing?"

"Well . . ." I want to adjust the thermostat because it's suddenly too warm in here. "I closed my eyes and pictured you while he was fumbling down there." Cory doesn't react as his gaze bores into my eyes. I have to break away to continue. "When I did get off, I, uh . . . I said your name." I finish in a rush, forcing the words out.

A short burst of air escapes his parted lips. The sound convinces me to face him again. The expression he wears is something like wonderment.

"Not what you had in mind, huh?" I prompt.

"I actively made sure *not* to have anything in mind."

"Now you have an accurate account. Thanks for your assistance. You put in remote work that night." My lips are pursed in a coy grin.

A smile grows on Cory's face as he places his hand right above my knee, near the hem of my nightie. "You're not giving me enough credit."

To say I suspected as much would be an understatement, but I play it cool. "How would it be any different?"

He flashes me a cocky grin. "For one, you wouldn't describe it as a mental exercise afterwards."

"I never said that!" My rising pitch gives my denial away. "Okay, but there was potential there. Maybe with some extra coaching. Teach him how to be a team player." I shake my fists like I'm holding imaginary pom-poms.

Cory's eyes roam over my face before he gently shakes his head with a soft, "No."

"It's unrealistic to expect Anthony to know what I need right out the gate."

"I'd expect him to pay attention to when something isn't working." I bounce my head to the side, conceding his point. He sighs. "Look, I don't care about this dude. Just you."

"I care about you." My response comes forth naturally, yet the reserved hopefulness in his posture hints at his doubt.

"Then what about us? Do you want to find out?"

The hand still resting on my thigh shifts a bit, and the slight movement shoots up my leg, spurring action. I rise to my knees on the couch before settling myself in his lap, straddling him just as I did the first time we kissed.

"Let's find out." I lower my mouth to his and kiss him sweetly, being sure to savor it in a way I didn't last time. After a shared gasp of relief, it spirals deeper, beyond my control. Cory's full lips make an excellent case for us. His hands press firmly into my lower back, creating an impression of safety. I pull back for air.

"Good so far?" he asks.

"Great." I dip my head to kiss more, but after just a brush of our lips, he widens the space between us. I question his daring grin with a sulk. He carefully transitions me from his lap to lying on my back. I hitch myself up on my elbows, already missing how comfortable it was perched atop his thighs.

"It's only fair I get a chance to redeem myself for being associated with your '*most anticlimactic cunnilingus.*' Since you used my image without my consent and all."

In the spirit of fairness, I excitedly agree.

CHAPTER
TWENTY-FIVE

I roll over and collapse onto my back beside Cory, chest shaking with a breathless laugh. After starting on the couch, we quickly realized we needed to move into my room for more space. A small content smile rests on Cory's face as he, too, catches his breath. Regardless of how everything else turns out, I'm positive we both agree this aspect of us works.

"I wish I made those breakfast smoothies before," I say.

"We can still go to breakfast. I promise that's not what I had in mind for nourishment."

I laugh and allow him to pull me toward him. He kisses me with languid exploration. When I told him I wasn't sure about us, I worried Met—if real—meant we were destined to fail. But if I think of the time Cory and I have spent together, including solely as friends, it's obvious any amount of time with him would be worth it. I nestle closer to his side. Just in case our time together is limited, I want to hold on to this improbable man for as long as possible.

Against all odds, Cory and I make it out for sustenance. After sharing a quick shower, in which we manage to stay mostly on task, we get a text from Tiwanda to meet her and Elise for brunch. They choose a restaurant about halfway between my place and Elise's.

I figure I should tell Tiwanda and Elise about me and Cory right away and without fanfare. I text them CORY, followed by a series of emojis: eyes-wide face, eggplant, droplets, tongue, praise hands. A vibration not connected to the phone I'm holding sounds from across the living room, near where Cory is bending to put on his shoes so we can leave.

He pulls out his phone and tilts his head to the side as he reads whatever has come through. One corner of his mouth lifts in a grin. "You texted the wrong chat."

"Did I?" I give him a coquettish flutter of my eyelashes. Cory stares at me impassively until I relent. "Okay, yeah, I did." The back of my neck warms from the blunder.

At brunch, we all largely ignore our coupling in favor of other topics. Elise received a call earlier officially casting her in a play. We pepper her with questions about her role. When Cory casually places his hand over mine on the table, Tiwanda addresses it. "Are you two doing this for real?" She's clearly trying to distinguish if we are hooking up or labeling.

"Yes," Cory says confidently. I concur with a single decisive nod.

Tiwanda smiles in a way that's also on the verge of laughing at us. Elise opens her mouth to protest—I suspect in defense of Met—but Tiwanda deters her. I can't hope they'll let it go this easily forever, but I'm glad not to have the conversation now. The three of us connected over trying to figure the app out together. It's going to be tough for us to put it aside without reaching a conclusion, but it's for the best.

I wish I could talk to Joelle about this. She might understand why I have to give this thing that has been building with Cory over the past few months a try. It's hard not to play into what could have happened if I'd made different choices. Imagine if I had been more open to Joelle's idea of us living in Chicago postgraduation. Mom would have no doubt made sure Tiwanda and I connected, which would have led to me meeting Cory sooner. Joelle would've had the chance to meet him. I could have gotten the approval I feel incomplete without.

Cory goes to his own apartment after brunch, and I go home alone to tackle the short to-do list I abandoned earlier. The application Pedro sent me—created for this occasion, since it's their first time hiring anyone—is unsurprisingly thorough. They don't ask for my entire work history. Instead, they have items like *Part of this position includes knowledge of filling out grant applications. Is this something you've had experience with? If so, please list the corresponding role.*

It's a new type of application, and I take a new approach filling it out. Instead of stretching to apply my experience to match every job requirement, I am honest where I fall short. If it is something I've already started researching, like grant applications, I include that.

I work diligently on the application until it's finished, then I send it off. All the nearby libraries have long since closed for today. But I do have my trusty friend the internet, and I use it to find helpful videos about nonprofits.

I am broken from my productive trance when Lito returns my call from days ago.

"Make sure my room is ready for me," is the first thing he signs.

I put an end to his demands with a repetitive slicing motion near my throat. *"You get the couch."* My mind flashes to how the couch was utilized this morning, and I amend, *"Kidding, I'll take it."*

Lito and my mom are scheduled to arrive a day apart. Lito first, then Mom. Lito expects the grand tour of Chicago he was robbed of when he came for his interview. He has no recollection of living here, since he was just shy of three years old when we moved. The few times we visited as a family, he embraced the city more like a visitor than a former resident.

"I spoke with Dad yesterday. We had a good VRS interpreter, and he video called me from Monique's phone so we could see each other." I

flash him a smile. He prevents me from expressing my delight any further: *"Chill out. We still have to keep working on it, but . . . I'm hopeful. Whatever. That aside, anything I should know before I get there?"* Lito takes care to sign clearer and a notch slower than his usual, hinting he has something in mind.

"What do you mean?"

"Mom's going to be there. You're still jobless. Something else going on?"

"Like . . . ?"

He twiddles his fingers as he thinks, then flippantly signs, *"I don't know, maybe you decided to go back to school or something."*

"Would that be a bad thing?"

"With no direction, yes."

"Thank you, career counselor."

"I charge by the minute."

Lito is obviously taking a study break to call me, because now he dips his head toward the side of the screen, writing in a notebook beside an open textbook. Maybe it's because I'm in a great mood after the start of my day, but I feel an impulse to divulge information. Lito can be a nuisance, and he's guaranteed to use information against me, but it's always in a lighthearted-teasing type of way. Most importantly, he never discloses any dirt he has on me to aid our mom. After devoting an hour and a half into filling out the application, I want to share the news with him even if it's still at the hope stage.

When I have his attention I sign, *"I found a job."*

"Could have led with that." He silently applauds me nonetheless. I hold my hand up.

"I don't have the job yet."

"Okay, I don't think that's what the phrase 'I found a job' means."

"It does in this case. It's for a nonprofit focused on financial literacy."

Lito laughs. *"A nonprofit? In Chicago? You should have stayed in Texas if you were going to earn nonprofit money."*

"Yes, it is a really great cause. Thanks for asking."

He rolls his eyes, the action marking a rare moment that I notice the similarity of our features and mannerisms. We're both a mix of our parents, but people are quick to make a surface-level assessment and say he takes after Mom because they have the same medium-brown skin tone, while my deep-brown complexion mirrors our father's.

"Of course it's a great cause. Mom doesn't know yet?"

"I only sent in the application today. If everything goes well, I'll let her know. If it doesn't, I'll never tell."

"Got it. I'll forget you told me this until you give me more information on how to proceed."

"Appreciated."

"Anything else you're hiding in Chicago? Don't tell Mom I told you, but she suspects you're getting around."

My mouth drops open. "She told you that?"

"Yeah. She was like, 'What's that sign you showed me? With the pinkie? The one that means you sleep with a lot of people?' I told her, 'Mom that's more for people with penises, but I guess that works.'"

I laugh in earnest, envisioning that signed conversation easily because Lito has taught us many ASL phrases and idioms over the years. Mom and I still fumble a bit before using them in the right context.

"Well, she'll be happy to know I also found a boyfriend."

"So this means you don't have said boyfriend yet?"

"Ha ha."

"Wait—you're serious."

I scowl at him, hoping it's impactful through the camera.

"Oh, hohoho." Lito laughs. "This is going to be freaking great."

On Sunday, after talking with Ms. Powers for nearly an hour about the lesson plans for the coming week and prodding my dad for more details about his conversation with Lito, I start my laundry and other housekeeping duties. For my mom's visit, I can't start prepping early enough. She is steps ahead of me despite my readiness. A few days ago, I received an unannounced package containing a blow-up mattress. It's one of the fancy ones that inflate to about two feet off the floor.

Around two in the afternoon, halfway through laundering and almost finishing a Netflix-show binge, there's an insistent knock on my door. I know it's not Cory because he's at his mom's house, about an hour away from the city.

"Open up or I'll use my key!" I hear Tiwanda's muffled voice from the other side of the door as I approach. Then there's a low pounding, like someone using their foot.

"I'm coming!" I yell.

Tiwanda and Elise are standing at my doorway when I swing the door open. They push past me, both their hands full.

"Come on in," I say belatedly.

"We have stuff!" Elise says. I join them at the kitchen counter, where they've started unpacking the bags. There are containers of food in varying sizes in Elise's bags. Tiwanda pulls out gloves, pots, measuring cups, and an array of random items. "My aunt made a food drop-off at my mom's request. She's worried about me now that I'm unemployed but not coming home. As if that job was the only thing keeping me here."

While Elise's older sister lives in San Francisco, her parents and younger sister live in Seattle. The few aunts she has here are in the perfect position to ease her mom's worries of Elise being so far away from her family on the West Coast. I suspect Elise enjoys being on the receiving end of those concerns because she's a middle child. She cites birth order as the reason she joined theater—not getting enough attention between her brilliant older sister and her rule-bending younger sister.

"Also," Tiwanda says, "we're making soap. And body scrubs too." She says the last part in an appeasing way, and by the happy-go-lucky grin on Elise's face, I can assume this was a request of hers.

"Why are we making soap?" I ask.

"Because it's relaxing," Tiwanda says.

"I thought . . ." I trail off and shake my head.

"What?" Tiwanda prompts.

"Nothing. When I saw you two at the door, I thought this was an intervention or something." I laugh. Elise and Tiwanda do not. "Oh no."

"You thought we were going to let you two announce, 'Oh yeah, we're exclusively boning now,' and that be it? No, no, no, no, no."

"Tiwanda and I said it would happen; we just didn't think you were going to be this serious about it," Elise says.

"I don't know. It felt right." More specifically, like it would be pointless to put on the facade of casualness. If Cory was an option, he was my only option. Which should suck. It *should* feel restrictive, but it's the polar opposite. Since Cory initiated this official labeling, I can reasonably assume he feels the same. Plus . . . "Cory gets jealous, so."

Tiwanda and Elise stare at me, amused yet knowing smiles on their faces.

"Why didn't you two ambush Cory?" I ask. "You've known him longer."

"Wrong. I've known you my whole life, cuz," Tiwanda says with a wink. "Also, we did. Yesterday."

"We told him not to warn you," Elise says.

I gawp as if offended by this information, but I'm thinking maybe I found my soul mates after all in having Tiwanda and Elise as friends. That follows none of the rules of Met, but still. Last night, I tried deleting the app again. It's become a weekly routine at this point. For the first time, the app gave me the option to do so. Maybe it somehow knows my relationship status, like the other information it has on me. If I deleted it, would Met still send my final potential match? If I didn't delete it, would Cory think I'm leaving the door open to walk out of our relationship? Though guilt begged me to act wiser, I canceled the request.

"So," Tiwanda says, construing either my thoughts or the preoccupied expression on my face, "we're ignoring Met?"

Gathering my resolve, I nod once. I expected the question to be brought up, but I didn't think it would feel like a trusted friend telling you they expect your relationship to fail. It's also possible I'm projecting.

"I can't trust an app more than myself, right?"

Elise winces. "From my list of exes, I'd trust an app more."

Tiwanda pauses and tilts her head to the side. "The app was meant to guide, not tell you exactly who. I guess Met wants you to trust your own judgment. You've met three; why not wait for the fourth?"

I have no good answer for this. Most of the reasons that pop into my head are selfish. Cory and I never seemed inevitable to me. *Improbable* is more like it. And when the opportunity was mine for the taking, it felt crucial to act decisively. Tiwanda's eyebrows are furrowed, her bottom lip drawn into her mouth.

"I'm not going to hurt him," I say. Cory is her best friend—of course she'd be concerned for him. Especially if she suspects I may leave upon meeting my fourth Met match.

Tiwanda lifts a shoulder, discarding my previous statement. "I'm not only worried about Cory. We want you to protect yourself."

Elise nods in agreement.

Before it gets too mushy, Tiwanda calls us to action. We put the food in the fridge to enjoy after we complete the task at hand. Tiwanda takes the lead, tying her newly done braids back and putting on an apron. She tells us what to do: *Fill this with water. Eight ounces of castor oil. How do you work your stove? Low heat, please, Corinne. Hand me the lye.*

There's not a recipe for me to reference. It's all in her head. I accept being a cog in the engine. On the side, she directs Elise on what to add to make a large batch of body scrub we can divide among us. This process is easier, evident by the fact she lets Elise do all the steps herself.

Finally, Tiwanda allows me and Elise some autonomy regarding soap making. She scoops out some of the mixture into two smaller pots and lets us go at it. I add lavender, vanilla, and mint oil to mine. Elise chooses a citrus blend. Tiwanda makes a mix with scents of rose and decadent chocolate. We pour the mixture into rectangular, oval, and heart-shaped molds. I set them in the corner of my counter—a safe place to solidify unbothered.

We warm the red-curry chicken and rice Elise brought in the microwave and then eagerly take turns spooning helpings from the containers. By some miracle, we quickly agree on a movie to watch while we eat. It's something we can laugh at and talk over, which we do for the most part.

The chosen movie has a character with an aggressive stance of putting positivity out into the universe, going as far as blaming unfortunate incidents on negative energy. When Tiwanda and I turn up our noses at this, Elise forces a law-of-attraction exercise upon us. Our skepticism is another thing we share as cousins. Elise shouldn't blame us. No amount of positive thinking is going to bring Joelle or Tiwanda's parents back.

"You laugh, but which one of us just got her dream theater role and which of us is working at a job she hates?" Elise cuts her eyes to Tiwanda, who sobers immediately. "Or isn't working at all?"

"Hey! I'm applying somewhere. And I thought you liked having a friend not working."

"I do." She makes a kiss face at me. "But you know what I mean."

After being called out, we humor her. It can't hurt. I find a notebook in my room and tear out sheets of papers for each of us since Elise insists we write it out instead of typing it into the notes app on our phones.

She calls the activity Directing Your Own Life, something her spiritual guide assigned her nearly a year ago. Apparently, that's when the process of readying herself to quit her day job and commit to acting began.

On our separate papers, we write down a list of four things, leaving space to fill in details: main character description, setting, time, and at rise. For each, we are to write as if our aspired life is being dramatized on a stage. Character description is straightforward—our appearance and mannerisms, such as if we're standing tall or hunched over. Setting can be as general as the city we want to be in or as specific as our immediate environment. The section for time is where we indicate how far into the future we imagine this to happen. We have pretty much free rein for the last part. Elise tells us to write what is happening onstage as the curtains rise—whatever scene comes to mind that depicts our dream lives.

We spend fifteen minutes with the scratching of our pens against the paper as white noise. I'm on the side of the coffee table directly in front of the couch, so I lean back, pull my knees up, and utilize the hard surface of the nearest book I could grab. Tiwanda is beside me, using the short edge of the table. She shifts and sighs for the first five minutes until finally settling down into a rhythm. Words come slowly to me at the onset, but as the timer runs out, I'm scribbling aspirations I didn't know I had in the at-rise section.

"Time is up!" Elise says, though we can all clearly hear the timer on her cell phone elapse. "There isn't pressure to share but it's encouraged. Putting it on paper is one step, telling trusted people who can hold you accountable is the next."

Tiwanda leans over and tries to peek at my paper, but I hold it to my chest. She does the same on her opposite side. Elise makes no move to shield hers. Tiwanda's mouth drops. She lifts the paper with two fingers, showing a completely full first page and a good chunk of the backside filled. "How often do you do this?"

"About every other month, or whenever I need clarity to make sure I'm turned in the direction of the life I want. You know?"

"No," Tiwanda and I say together.

She brushes off our dissent with a saucy hair toss. "Each time I do, it changes. I'll go first."

Elise describes her future self as having fifteen extra pounds of muscle, a sunshine demeanor, and a new haircut. The setting is a movie set. Time frame is six to nine months from now. At curtain rise, she's interacting with her fellow castmates between takes, one of them remarking on how they can't believe it's her first feature-film role. The cast is then called to their places, and they run an emotional scene for the tenth time, this iteration to the satisfaction of the director. Everyone celebrates the completion of filming. She even wrote a second scene that involves her going out with the cast afterward.

"I love theater, but I want to challenge myself with film," Elise says. "Who wants to share next?"

Tiwanda volunteers. Her future character has colorful hair, braids with a silvery lilac ombré at the ends. It's a style deemed inappropriate in her current workplace. She walks around lightly, like she isn't constantly going over a massive to-do list in her mind. Setting is a storefront in the bustling Hyde Park area. Elise and I are both impressed at the detail she uses to describe the shop's interior: a bright atmosphere with pops of color, homey despite its culinary-kitchen level of cleanliness. She set the time as a tentative six to twelve months forward. At curtain rise, she enters her establishment and cuts on the lights. She plays music as she preps for her afternoon chocolate-making class and private birthday evening event—tipsy soap making.

I never knew she had dreams of turning her hobbies into a business. Now that she's shared them with me, I can easily picture her running a small business, especially with her talent and knack for organization.

Elise and Tiwanda turn to me expectantly. Resigned, I rattle off what I wrote. My character has characteristics I admired in Ms. Leyda—an air of balance and acceptance. I surprised myself by immediately writing Chicago as the setting. At some point, I let go of the suspicion that this would turn out to be a failure of a move, and I would hightail it back to Houston. Time is ten months from now, or more specifically, Joelle's birthday. For the start of my scene, I'm taking out a perfectly-baked-from-scratch batch of brownies from the oven while I chat with Pedro on the phone about an upcoming Finance for the Fam workshop. It's my imagination, so I'm able to cut into the brownies and get a taste of the chocolate swirled with caramel without waiting for them to cool down. The moment is bittersweet, but then there's a knock on my door. I let in Tiwanda, Elise, and Cory, and they fill the space with their collective energy, ushering me into a new scene.

"It's a little basic," I say when I'm met with their silence.

Tiwanda shakes her head.

Elise reaches across the coffee table to squeeze my forearm. "It's perfect." She places her other hand on Tiwanda's shoulder. "Now, let's go out and attract some good shit, ladies."

Afterward, we clean my kitchen, packing away Tiwanda's supplies and Elise's now-empty containers. We're all dragging our feet to get them out the door for different reasons: Tiwanda has another busy week of work ahead of her since she kept her work cell phone off all weekend. Elise says she hates weekdays still because now none of her friends are available to hang out with her. I'm facing my second week with the second graders, but mostly I know as soon as they leave I'll miss having them here.

Not often in my life have I experienced the complete conviction I've done something right. That I've made a decision that put me in the right place, at the right time. People say everything happens for a reason, and maybe that's true. But a lot of events happen daily, most of them with little perceptible consequence. I thought being in Chicago would bring me closer to Joelle, to what I'd lost with her. In a way, I was right. But it's not the location. It's the connection I've found with people who make me feel like she did: warm, accepted, and alight.

CHAPTER TWENTY-SIX

"Come on, I'll walk you over there," Devin says.

I don't decline or ask if they're sure. I'm nervous as hell and not in any position to refuse help. Ms. Powers waves us out of the classroom to catch up on her paperwork in peace.

My initial plan was to drive over to my interview with Finance for the Fam, though it's a short distance from the school. Walking with Devin gives me a few minutes to breathe and shut my brain off after a few intense days.

It's Thursday, and I learned about the interview Monday evening, which gave me three days to prepare. I've been annoying my friends since then, demanding they come up with common interview questions to quiz me with. I made Cory listen to me describe the grant-writing process to make sure I could explain it succinctly. I still don't know if he truly understood or if he wanted to get my clothes off sooner.

Devin has been the most help through all this. They have firsthand experience partnering with Finance for the Fam and shared stories of events they were part of. It gives me a more complete picture of the organization since I have no website to reference. Devin tells me the things they thought Fam did great but also the areas they struggled in.

While we walk to the interview, though, those conversations are gone. Devin discusses the first-grade class they have in art this week. I dropped by and saw the rowdy bunch on Tuesday while my class had their music rotation. The talk of their art projects is enough to get me to stop obsessing about what questions I'll encounter during the interview.

Outside the door, Devin puts their hands on my shoulder. "It's time for my inspirational speech, huh?"

"That'd be nice."

They purse their lips, head tilted upward as if garnering support from a higher power, and then face me again, apparently enlightened.

"Don't fuck it up." They spin me around and give me a small push toward the door. After regaining my balance in my short-heeled boots, I enter.

The woman behind the counter looks up. She has long reddish-brown hair curled at the ends. "Corinne? I'm Aisha." She stands and we shake hands. "Ready to get started? Pedro and Nia are back there already."

She leads me to a small conference room with a table that comfortably fits six chairs. They direct me to sit at the head of the table. Pedro and Nia sit to my left, Aisha on my right. They each have a digital copy of my application, a blank notepad, and a printed list of questions I'd have to crane my neck to see. Nia introduces herself to me, the only board member I had yet to meet. Her short, coiled honey-colored hair and flawless sandy-brown skin make her look ultrachic.

Pedro kicks off the formal introductions, including each person's role. He's in charge of marketing and outreach. Nia follows him since she also helps with outreach and partnerships. It's her responsibility to reach out to companies for sponsorships and donations, such as convincing restaurants and grocery stores to donate food. Aisha is the family liaison. She handles registration and communications as well as the gathering and distribution of resources. Her main goal is to make sure families know they have Finance for the Fam as a resource, which strengthens their relationships within the community.

During their intros, I open my padfolio and start making notes to keep everything straight.

"So the gaping hole," Pedro says, "is the—"

"Financing," I finish.

"Exactly." Nia pushes her gold glasses up to the bridge of her nose. "I worked a lot with Heidi since I sought out funding through sponsorships. But it's too much for me to take on all her duties."

"Same," Pedro says. "I would go to her for marketing, and she'd tell me I was spending too much."

"I read the job responsibilities on the application. It's . . . a lot. No wonder y'all had to take a break," I say.

The table erupts. My eyes widen and my stomach clenches as I hang on to see which way the conversation is going.

"We didn't *have* to take a break," Pedro says.

"We don't have a website right now, dude," Aisha says. "There's a girl who sells Girl Scout cookies in my neighborhood. *She* has a website."

I laugh, marking the first time in my recollection that I've laughed sincerely in an interview.

"It's better to come out with a great, well-put-together event. Not a few haphazard ones with low turnout. We had to press the brakes," Nia says.

"Sure," Pedro says. "Only problem is, when we apply for grants, they want to know our history. What events we've put on in the past year. They're not going to be impressed."

I cautiously cut in, "Well, yes, but no. They give out money all the time for a great plan. We—*you*—can focus on that for applications and use the past events for an extra boost. Like icing on the cake."

"That was Heidi's thought." Nia pulls at a short curl near her ear. "We didn't have any solid plans then."

"Now we do," Aisha says. "Oh. We all collaborate to pitch event ideas, by the way. No one mentioned that as a role because it's all of us."

"Got it," I say, jotting this down too. "Have you found a person to do the website?"

Pedro lets out an exaggerated sigh. By Nia's eye roll and Aisha's massaging of her temples, I realize I've hit on another pressure point.

"We did have a person to do the website," Pedro says, cutting a look at Aisha.

"He was way too expensive," she says.

"A good website is worth the expense. Last thing we want is a website that looks like it's from before the dot-com bubble."

"We are asking a lot from it," Nia says. "We want people to be able to register online, an easier-to-navigate event calendar . . ."

"Virtual event–suggestions box, a feedback form, resources directory," Pedro tacks on.

"I have a friend that does freelance website building," I say, thinking of Elise. "I can give you her info. Even if you don't hire me. She will be fair on cost."

"That would be great," Pedro says. "This time, I'm not waiting for consensus to decide. The website is under my official marketing duties."

"Whatever," Aisha says. "We all have a hat in the ring. My registration is there."

"Plus, I really want to have a tab for partnerships," Nia says. "If any company head happens upon our website, I want them to be able to easily give us money and stuff."

"Makes sense," I say. "The ease of using a website is everything. And with multiple features, it's harder to accomplish. Spend the money; you won't regret it when it's done right. Plus, I could help you get more money." I plug myself since this is an interview. It's feeling more like a conversation, like how it would be if I were part of this team.

As we talk of the various aspects of the nonprofit business, I become more comfortable, interjecting to ask questions or give my two cents.

Occasionally, one of the three board members jots down a note or slashes something off their list of questions.

About forty-five minutes later, they thank me for my time. I blanch as I stand, trying to recall if they asked me any questions during the interview. At one point, I mentioned something about a project budget I made for my previous job in Houston. Aisha asked what my role there had been. That was the sole direct question.

But I can't demand they ask me the interview questions I practiced now as we stand around the table and they start to usher me out. I shake hands and mumble something about hoping to hear from them soon. Then I walk back across the school parking lot to my waiting car. Before driving off I text the group chat, telling them I'm out of the interview with the emoji that looks unsure and kind of queasy.

Cory calls as I'm reversing out of my spot. I answer and spend the twenty-minute drive home detailing as much of the interview as I can remember. It starts off sequential, but soon I'm jumping all over the place as I remember random parts.

"Sounds like you'll get it," Cory says.

"Okay, so you weren't listening to anything I said."

He meets me at my apartment with a duffel bag. Though tomorrow is Friday and we both have work early, we decide if he's going to come by, it should be for the night. Otherwise, we'd only have a few hours before his blasted bedtime alarm went off. We came to this conclusion as if it were the only option—not a big deal, and definitely not something we were trying to avoid lest we set an early habit. With my mom coming, she'd be able to detect any signs of cohabitation. She's going to feel some type of way about my finding a steady boyfriend faster than I've found a steady job.

"Did you get feedback on your article?" I ask him as we're eating leftovers at our usual spot on the kitchen island.

"Nope, still waiting on my mentor. She stays busy but should get it to me by tomorrow."

"Can't I read it now?"

"It's going to change. There's no point."

"I want to see how it develops. What kind of half-ass support is showing up to read the final draft? You used my couch to write a lot of that." As I'm giving my impassioned, persuasive pitch, Cory is shaking his head, unmoved. "If you let me read it now, I'll . . ." I rack my brain for the best thing I could confidently promise him. I grin mischievously as I come up with an idea that would benefit us both. "Okay. I read, and if you survive that, I'll give you complete control tonight."

Cory's reflexive eye widening quickly transforms to a squint. "'Complete control'? You? Yeah right."

"I'm serious. I could do it."

"I'm sure you *think* you can."

Apparently, he's satisfied seeing me try. Something I've picked up on quickly about Cory—his love of control extends to the bedroom. Thing is, I like to lead too. From our first kiss, it's been a contest for power. So far, it's working. We tend to switch on and off and still enjoy the outcome.

Cory pulls up his nine-page article on his tablet, and I take it to the couch to read there. I make myself comfortable, and he stays at the kitchen island, trying to ignore me.

"What's augmented physical activity?" I ask him two pages in.

He turns on his stool. "Starting with a small number of reps or weights and working up to a higher number or intensity. It's one of my favorite approaches. I should probably add a definition to that."

"A short one, maybe." I keep reading, only now I can feel him watching. "Did you want to come sit with me?" I ask hopefully, without turning my gaze from the tablet.

"No, keep going."

Humph. I'll see about that. I only get to the next page before I have another question.

"It's an exercise I use for shoulder and upper-back injuries. All you need is a wall and a towel." Cory stands to demonstrate the exercise, moving his arm as if he's washing the wall in a circular motion. "I explained this in the appendix."

"I know." I grin. "Just wanted to see you do that."

He drops his arm and frowns at me. My smile grows, our lips inverse, and I get back to reading. He leans against the wall to watch me, closer than his post at the kitchen island but not at my goal yet. I read two pages without stopping. Cory starts to pace in the silence.

"So, you're saying all these exercises can be done in the home environment with minimal modifications?"

"Yes! I included the results of five of my clients, each with a different injury to show how it can be applied to a wide range of situations." Cory is fully alive now, moving his arms and stepping toward me until he's right by the couch, looking down at me. I make a show of eyeing him—head to foot, then back up again—and raise a single brow. He plops down onto the couch, never breaking his stream of words. "The reason they requested a home PT visit differed as well. Our company offered home visits to all during this test period without requiring a doctor's referral. One opted in because of lack of childcare, one because they didn't have reliable transportation, and another physically couldn't travel much because of injury. That one was the only one who would have had doctor's orders. Across the board, I observed improved patient outcomes—"

"That answers my question, thanks." I cut him short or else I'd never finish reading. He's already on the couch with me, right where I wanted him. I change positions, lying against him so he can read over my shoulder. Since I still have the nagging feeling of being watched, I doubt he's going through the motion of reading the words he's pored over for the past few months. Bet he knows each word by heart anyway. I make it to the end and skim the appendix section.

"Very informative. It's obvious you worked hard on this." I lift myself up and turn to him, resting my elbow on the back of the couch to idly fiddle with a loose loc of his hair. "Who knows, maybe you'll mess around and change the world of physical therapy as we know it."

He smiles, bright and proud.

"Thank you for letting me read it."

He shakes his head. "Don't thank me. This was a trade, remember?" He leans forward and takes my chin with the tips of his fingers as he kisses me. It's special being able to kiss him like this. Leisurely and without worrying time will run out on us. When I manage to ignore the fear of Met interfering, it's like the concept of time has ceased to exist. I wrap my arms around him, feeling the muscles on his back.

His alarm goes off across the room. I groan. So much for time not existing.

"Guess it's bedtime," I say.

"You wish. That was the first alarm. Plenty of time before I really need to sleep."

Of course, I know that, because it's only eight o'clock, and usually the first alarm results in him leaving to go home. Since we've become a couple, the time it takes for him to successfully get out the door has become longer and longer. Meaning he doesn't actually go to sleep until hours later. *Crap, I don't know what I signed up for.*

"Go start a shower for us while I clean the kitchen," Cory says.

"Sure thing," I say as I kneel on the couch to kiss him again. The asshole pulls his head back and shakes it at me. The raw passion in his gaze softens my wounded pride.

"Shower," he demands. "Take your clothes off, but don't get in without me."

Is this my life right now? I'm staring at my body in the mirror, naked but for my shower cap. I didn't start the shower, because I have a water bill to pay, and it takes all of three seconds to warm up. I've also done my routine breast check for lumps while I'm standing here, waiting around.

There's a quick knock on the door before Cory opens, holding my buzzing phone. "You have a call."

I lift my hands, wave them down my body. "I can take it later. Can we shower now?"

"It's a local number," he says, straining his eyes.

I take it and swipe to answer.

"Hello?"

"Corinne? Sorry for ringing you this late, but it's Aisha. You're on speaker. We're all here."

Pedro and Nia say a jumbled hello.

"No problem. What's up?"

"Well, we decided about a minute after you left. We've been typing up an offer letter for you since and realized we should have a lawyer look over it before we send it to you," Aisha says.

"This means . . ." My heart is eager to accept this as good news, but my brain reels it in under the notion of caution.

"You're part of the team!" Nia says.

"If you want us," Pedro adds.

"We are officially extending an offer to you," Aisha says. "The paperwork will have your salary info, start date, all the good stuff. You can think it over. We're hoping to be able to send it to you by tomorrow. If not, it'll be Monday."

I don't know how I'm still standing, how I have the balance to bounce on my toes right now. Cory waits for my official announcement as he stands in front of me, somehow able to focus on my face and not the jiggle of my nude body. I hang up with the team with the promise to keep an eye on my inbox for the official offer.

"They picked me!" I yell.

Cory wraps me up in a hug and squeezes me tight, the fabric of his clothes a peculiar sensation against my bare skin.

"You picked them," Cory says. "That's the most important part."

"Yeah, yeah." I lightly push him away. "Now, take your clothes off so you can really praise me."

He shakes his head, eyeing me intently as if he's figuring something out. "You really can't do this, can you?"

"I can! Sorry. Okay." I shake my arms out, stretch them like I'm getting ready to run a marathon. Then I smile, though I can feel I've come up short of my intended seductress charm. "Tell me how you want it, zaddy."

Cory's head tilts toward one side, deadpan. "No."

I break out into a fit of giggles. It's impossible to be serious at this point. Cory tries hard, but it's easy to tell when he's fighting a smile. His cheekbones are more pronounced, and his eyes squint in the effort to suppress his joy. When I reach out to touch his abdomen, he gives in, and laughter tumbles out of him.

But only seconds later, he reaches out and traces his fingers from my temple down my jawline. The tenderness of this action sobers me. He kisses me softly against the corner of my mouth, as if not wanting to wade in too deep. Keeping safe on the shore for now.

"Get your fine ass in the shower," he says, his voice clear and low but still reverberating in the confines of the bathroom.

"Happily."

CHAPTER
TWENTY-SEVEN

Lito accepted an internship at Gallaudet University in Washington, DC. He'll research alongside some of the brightest minds in the medical technology field and, as a bonus, be around other Deaf and Hard of Hearing students from around the country. Though it stings a bit my presence couldn't sway him to Chicago, I'm ridiculously proud of my baby brother.

"Why are you looking at me like that?" he signs over the table. We're getting breakfast at a café I discovered near my apartment. Lito arrived yesterday evening, early enough for us to meet up with Tiwanda and Elise for dinner. Cory couldn't make it because he went to spend a long weekend with his mom and sister for Mother's Day. We figured beyond him briefly meeting my mom and Lito, we wouldn't see as much of each other this coming week.

I lift a shoulder. *"You're the most impressive person I know."*

He flashes a cocky smile at me, but then it softens. *"That's only because we lost Joelle."*

We. Joelle meant a lot to him, too, but I never imagined she might be as constant a thought to him as she is for me. Sometimes I get so wrapped up in my own grief I don't consider I'm not the only one suffering. I don't have to go through this alone. I can choose to help and receive help from others. It isn't fair that I've been keeping a final piece of Joelle from Lito.

I tell him about the package Ms. Leyda gave me. To my relief, he isn't upset I wasn't forthcoming about this sooner. Promising to show him everything once we get back to my apartment helps. I detail what I've found out and how the flyer she stuck in the package led me to Finance for the Fam.

He belly laughs at this. *"When you said you 'found' a job, you didn't find it yourself?"*

I scowl at him, but my phone vibrating and flashing on the tabletop distracts me. Lito, the annoying little brother that he is, snatches it up before I can.

"You're getting a call from 'The Other Cory.' If by 'other' you mean 'not you,' is it necessary to specify? I think you'd know if you're calling yourself."

I pluck the phone from his hand and answer.

"I'm not doing that. You can if you want," Cory is saying as he answers the phone, obviously not talking to me. There's music playing in the background with the same bluesy vibe he listens to when he works on his laptop. "Babe? Hey, hold on."

"Oh, she's a babe, huh?" a hearty voice says in the background.

I hear nothing from him until after the click of what I assume is a door.

"All right," Cory says with a huge sigh.

"What was that about?"

"I once told Niqua I hated calling partners 'babe.' But with you, it fits. Of course, she remembers to hold it over me."

"Before that, loser."

"Oh." He sighs again. "Apparently, my mother is having an engagement party Saturday."

"Tomorrow, Saturday? Wait . . . Your mom is engaged? Did you tell me that?"

"I found out yesterday."

Before I can express my surprise, there's an uptick in background noise. I hear Niqua's voice again but can't make out the words this time.

Cory groans. "Fine. Tell her I'm on my way." The door shuts again. "Do you think you can come? I know your family is in town, but can you get away for a bit? It's at four p.m. You can bring them, even."

I lick my lips, suddenly nervous, and glance at Lito. He picks up on my change in demeanor and lifts an eyebrow. I did plan on Cory meeting Mom and Lito, but bringing them to his mom's engagement party seems like premature family merging.

"Yeah, I'll try to get away," I say. "If only for part of it."

"Thank you. I have to go, but I'll text you."

Lito, still skilled at eavesdropping using the combination of his hearing aids and reading my lips, gives me a sly grin.

"Whatever plan you're trying to concoct won't work," he signs with a dismissive fluidity as our waiter approaches with our food.

He's usually right, but I hope I can change that. Mom doesn't know I'm dating anyone. Springing Cory on her along with a proposition to bring her to his mom's engagement party? If she accepted—which she would because she's not one to turn down a party—she'd be there to witness the first time I meet Cory's family. I prefer tackling these meetings separately.

I already planned on us visiting Ms. Leyda and Mr. Walter tomorrow afternoon. My best shot is leaving Mom and Lito there while I swing by the engagement party. It'll be a squeeze with the long drive to get out of the city, but I could make it work.

After breakfast, we have a few hours to chill at the apartment before it's time to pick up Mom from the airport. Without further delay, I retrieve Joelle's gift from its resting place in my nightstand drawer. I hand it over to Lito as he sits at the kitchen counter, checking if all his final grades have been posted. He snaps his laptop closed and clears the area.

Exactly how I did seemingly a long time ago, he carefully slides out the contents and leans over to get a closer look. I replaced everything I'd taken out, including the items I researched already. He should see it like I did, each piece of the puzzle.

I watch him for a moment, noting which items catch his eye. He runs his fingers over the stone of her high school class ring. I hadn't decided what to do with it yet, but the reverence on Lito's face makes it clear. I reach over and close his fingers around it.

"Yours." I press my palm out to him.

He tries to smile at me, but it's way too bitter to qualify. *"I was going to marry her, you know."*

I wrinkle my nose and shake my head. *"She was six years older than you and my best friend."*

"I was going to wait until the age gap was insignificant. When she was about thirty-five."

"Ha! You think she would still be available by then?"

"It wouldn't matter if she wasn't because it wouldn't be the right person."

Even the imagining of this awkward best friend/younger brother coupling makes me ache with the loss of possibility. I leave Lito to continue sorting through the contents alone while I do another quick clean of the bathroom and change the sheets on my bed. Though Mom sent an air mattress, I'm going to insist she take the proper bed. Lito used the air mattress last night, so he can keep that, and I'll move to the couch.

"Oh my God," I hear Lito say aloud, followed by a laugh. I finish tucking in the sheet before going to investigate. When I exit the hallway, he's reopening his laptop. *"Did you see this?"* he asks, holding up the Met button.

I nod, then hold up a finger for him to hang on while I fetch my phone. I pull up the pictures Ms. Leyda sent me.

"They went to the museum in New York."

Lito takes the briefest of glances at my phone. *"Send those to me,"* he signs offhand as he focuses on his laptop. I squint and stick out my head to see what he's about to type in the browser. I suspect he won't be satisfied until he follows the steps himself. He's never been a younger brother satisfied with my hand-me-down lessons.

He faces me, button in hand, and pops off the back part. My eyes bug out. Before I can ask what he's doing, I lose his attention as he looks into his hand. There's something written on the paper inside the button. His sense of urgency and excitement finally reaches me, and I step closer to lean over his shoulder. It's definitely Jo's handwriting.

His hands employed, Lito voices some much-needed clarification. "Remember how me and Jo used to talk about app ideas?" *Duh.* It was a common topic I usually looked away from as they video chatted. "One of her worst ideas was a dating app. She said she would call it Met because once a person met their match, they would delete it." Lito laughs. "Terrible. Told her the dating-app market was oversaturated. She insisted hers would be different because she'd have handpicked matches, not computer picked."

Lito quiets as he enters the username and password for an online drive, the info Joelle wrote on the back of the Met Museum paper. I angle my head to scan the titles of rows of folders. It's not only the Met idea here but also all the app ideas that bubbled out of her when she felt restricted by designing apps to the specifications of her work clients.

Lito gasps and starts to navigate his way over to a folder labeled "Lito's Way," but I nudge his hand aside.

"Met first." My brain is in overdrive, and I need as much information as I can get before it completely fails.

To my dismay, there aren't many files in the folder. I choose the document that holds her general Met-related ideas. One, prefaced as "Far Fetched," catches my eye: a questionnaire required of each person wanting the dating app. Users would have the option to forward invitations for exes to fill out another on their behalf—something like an exit interview. Answers would be kept confidential. Asterisks signify a later thought: *Questionnaires for friends too!*

I can't breathe.

Meanwhile, Lito is having a jolly good time going down memory lane with these notes. He turns his head to me, the joyful look of a fond memory etched on his face. His hands pause on whatever story he was planning to share.

"Cori, what's wrong?"

I bury my hands in my hair, press my fingers against my scalp in an attempt to relieve some of the pressure there. It's not helping. Only admitting what a colossal idiot I've been to ignore all the signs Met—Joelle?—sent me might.

"I made a mistake with Cory."

CHAPTER
TWENTY-EIGHT

Lito sends worried glances at me from the couch he's sharing with Mom. I ignore him and focus on the conversation being carried by Mom and Ms. Leyda. Last night, I told Lito everything that's been going on with the Met app. With Joelle's online drive to back me up, he had no choice but to believe it. If the app had shown up on his phone, he would've made the connection much sooner than I did.

I glance at my phone, checking the time. Since picking up Mom from the airport yesterday, I haven't confessed my plan to ditch her and Lito here to go to the engagement party. I barely want to go myself, to be honest. Maybe Tiwanda is enough of a support system for Cory today. Elise has her first full-cast rehearsal for the play, and I am in no state to be the uncomplicated girlfriend he needs right now.

Mr. Walter returns from the kitchen with the giant bag of Garrett Chicago Mix popcorn we bought before coming over, along with a stack of small paper bowls. He pours out servings for each of us.

"You all staying for dinner?" he asks. "I can order pizza from our favorite place."

"Giordano's," Mom croons at the thought of deep-dish. "We can't stay long, but I do want to go out to dinner before I leave. How's your week look?"

My confusion is reflected in Lito's countenance. As far as I know, we had nothing concrete planned for the rest of the day, thus the potential to get away for a few hours. Lito makes sure Mom isn't looking our direction before signing, *"Told you it's not going to work. Should've been straightforward."*

"'Should've been straightforward,'" I mimic. *"Easy for the preferred child to say."*

He waves my comment away as Mom, Ms. Leyda, and Mr. Walter agree Tuesday is a good day for us to meet up again for dinner.

"Ready to go?" Mom asks me.

I reach up and tug at my ear, racking my brain for a way out of this. "Where?"

"The place you're trying to avoid taking us," Mom says. I whip my head toward Lito, but he only shakes his head, unfazed. Rule number one of deceiving parents is not caving when they express a hunch. Parents get lots of hunches; it's impossible to follow up on all of them. She probably glimpsed me and Lito at a time we thought we were signing inconspicuously. When she takes in the stubborn set of my jaw, Mom decides to reveal her hand. "Do you or do you not have a secret boyfriend waiting on you?"

"He's not a secret," I protest. "Lito knows about him! And apparently you?"

Lito touches his middle fingers to his shoulders, renouncing blame. Ms. Leyda exchanges a look with Mr. Walter before rising to her feet. When she turns away from him to address me and Lito, a small smile rests on Mr. Walter's face. If our family drama initiates the recovery of their relationship, I'm not mad at it.

"Before you head out, let me grab something I found in JoJo's room a few days ago."

"I'll help." Mr. Walter follows her, granting us a moment of privacy, though he wouldn't understand us as we switch to signing.

"I was going to tell you last night, but I got distracted."

Mom purses her lips at me. I can tell she's of split mind, because while I've had frequent spells of being spacey since she arrived, if a person wants to be forthcoming, they find the time to do so. It would be convoluted to explain why I don't want to talk about the boyfriend I really like and why I'm suddenly hesitant to introduce him to my family.

"Now that you're not distracted, is there anything else you want to tell me?"

The most hated question in the history of child-rearing. How am I grown and still having to reckon with this? I blame the rent help. It caused the clock to rewind. *"Come on, Momma. There's a lot I want to tell you, but I don't know which one you want to hear."*

"Start with the job you got a week ago."

My jaw drops to my chest. I haven't even shared the good news with Lito yet. I wanted to tell them together but wasn't in the mood to celebrate last night. Did I leave any paperwork out in my apartment?

"I've been emailing you job postings, wasting my time."

"Who told you?" As soon as I ask, my brain works it out logically. I only told my three local friends. One of whom has the means to contact my mom.

"Tiwanda has been more reliable answering her phone than you the past month."

"Maybe you don't stress her out like you do me." I'm bolder in sign language, but it's still a halting delivery.

Mom's lips turn down like she's happened upon a delightfully inter-esting bit of new information. *"I'm sorry, paying your rent for the first four months of you living here caused you stress?"* It's amazing how I can imagine the sound of her sarcasm through her staccato signing.

"Honestly that would make me stressed too," Lito cuts in with smooth movements, as if detached from the argument. I know better. While

emotion might cause my hands to stammer and Mom's to become more exaggerated, Lito always remains chill as ever. *"But congrats on the job."* Bless him, because his interruption takes the wind out of her sails as she considers this possibility.

She sighs, then relaxes her back against the couch pillow. *"Fair. Tell me about this job."*

"It's a nonprofit called Finance for the Fam. I officially start in two weeks, after you leave." The team is ready to put on a midsize relaunch event at the end of June and wants me to start as soon as possible.

"Nonprofit? That could be a great fit for you."

Her smile seems genuine, but I still check Lito's facial expression to see if he's buying it. His hand is hanging in the air, frozen midway through the motion of shoveling popcorn in his mouth. I decide to dig in case she's hiding her true feelings. Best to get it out and in the open now and not wait for it to ooze poison in the coming days.

"You're not worried about the pay at all?" I ask.

She barks out a laugh. *"Why should I be worried? You're not financing my life with your paycheck. If it's enough for you, then go for it. Or get a part-time job. You'll make it work."*

"I will." Instantly the pressure in my chest recedes. I'd gotten so used to keeping things from my mom, I hadn't realized how it was affecting me. Cory would pester me about mental health and emotions being connected to the physical body and blah blah. Damn, I miss him. It's only been four days, but still. Even with Joelle's posthumous endorsement of Met, the thought of dropping Cory feels counterintuitive.

Ms. Leyda and Mr. Walter return, putting a much-needed pause on our convo. Ms. Leyda sets a thick scrapbook on the coffee table. "Whenever JoJo had a good day, she'd find something to get into. Found all these old pictures we had lying around, lots of them you all are in. One of her friends who does scrapbooking took it from there."

Lito and I lean forward in synchrony to view the picture in the center of the cover. It's a recent one of Jo with her parents, evident by her short, curly hairdo. She's wearing orange, her favorite color. Underneath are scripted words: A LIFE WELL LIVED.

"We can take this with us?" Lito asks. He must be stunned, because he forgot to use his voice for Ms. Leyda. She surmises the meaning.

"Take it. Bring it back at dinner next week."

We say our goodbyes with arrangements in place for reuniting again soon. In the car, I realize we never decided our next steps. Mom knows I have to go support Cory, but what will they do in the meantime? I awkwardly turn in my seat so Lito can see my signs. I use my voice at the same time since neither he nor Mom has a great angle.

"Y'all want to go to the apartment?"

Mom dips her chin a moment, and I've never witnessed anything good follow that movement. "Corinne, if you don't put this car in drive and get us to your boyfriend's mom's engagement party . . . That's right," she adds in response to my stunned expression. "And I know we are welcome there too."

I do what I'm told. I'm going to have to chat with Tiwanda about assuming the status of my communications with my mother. Mom turns around to face forward, but I can feel her stewing from the passenger seat. When I glance in the rearview mirror, Lito shoots me a solidarity grimace before lowering his head to flip through Joelle's scrapbook. When I merge onto the highway, I finally gather the courage to explain.

"I didn't want you to think this was more serious than it is."

She makes a disbelieving noise from deep in her throat. "I'm your mom. Not a child who doesn't understand the concept of temporariness." My face scrunches up in reflex to her statement. "Or whatever it is you kids say nowadays. Situationships. Fuck buddies."

"Momma!"

"Did you say fuck buddies?" Lito asks.

Mom reaches back to slap his leg. "Don't cuss."

I sigh. "Maybe . . . I didn't want myself to think it was more serious than it is."

"Cori, your perception—"

"Is your reality. I know, I know. But I'm not ready for that to be my reality right now."

"Do you know why not?"

Met's meddling is ruining my love life. If I had reservations about committing to Cory with the fourth match still at large before Joelle's connection to the app was confirmed, now I feel downright foolish. At least being able to see our demise coming will allow me the clarity usually reserved for hindsight. I can analyze our relationship missteps in real time. No matter how or when it ends, all signs are likely to point to our origin, the fact that I should've followed my instincts to keep Cory as a friend.

CHAPTER
TWENTY-NINE

Cory's mom lives in a beautiful ranch-style home. It's one expansive story, painted steel blue with gray trim. The landscaping is immaculate, freshly done for spring. The nearest parking spots are all taken since the party started nearly an hour ago. We park across the street, hoping their neighbors will cut us some slack.

"This is the retirement house of my dreams," Mom mutters as we approach the door. She catalogs the exterior architecture as we wait for someone to answer. Lito brings along Joelle's scrapbook like it's a blithe magazine to enjoy when he inevitably gets bored. He eyes my fidgeting hands.

"Ignore the damn app," he signs sharply. *"I told Jo it was a dumb idea. Makes more sense for it not to work."*

I nod and will myself to adopt this stance. Cory's sister is the one to fetch us. I recognize her from his Instagram pictures.

"Come in! I'm Niqua. Cory's running around here somewhere." She hugs each of us in turn, saving me for last. She holds me by the shoulders and looks me over. "I see why Cory is a mess over you." The compliment revives my nerves as I aim to keep her statement figurative.

She takes my arm and leads me toward the chatter mingled with soft music.

The mostly mature crowd is gathered in the living room and kitchen, connected with the open floor plan. At the edge of the living room, there's an exit to a backyard patio enclosed in glass. The sliding doors are open, and people float in and out like jellyfish. We stand on the outskirts of this group of maybe twenty. I scan the faces for Cory but don't find him. I also don't see the person of honor.

"This is a beautiful home," Mom says. "Is this where you grew up?"

"No, I wish," Niqua says. "We lived in the city growing up. Mom and Dad bought this house after me and Cory moved out for college. It was their retirement home. Now it's her retirement home with another man. Go figure. The food is spread out in the kitchen. Help yourselves. I'm gonna go find my mom."

I relay what she said to Lito because the music interferes with his hearing aids. We communicate without words in many ways, and one is the look he gives when he missed what was said and wants it in sign language.

Lito and I make our way toward the food and drinks, but Mom sees something shiny—a dress she loves. She ditches us to address the wearer. A familiar grip catches my arm and I turn, delighted to see Cory. He pulls me into a tight hug.

"I'm glad you're here," he whispers in my ear. The earnestness of his words crawls across my neck and down my spine.

I grab his face and kiss him. Even with strangers around, I can't resist. It's a culmination of missing him and the complicated emotions spurred by Met casting doubt. I make it a short kiss, though, so as not to draw too large an audience. I wish I knew the layout of the house better to pull him into a guest room and properly greet him. When his eyes meet mine after I pull away, I suspect he's thinking the same thing. Then his gaze clears.

"Where's your family?"

"Mom is right there, in the lavender blouse and cream pants." I point her out. She's laughing with the owner of the dress she admired. Her mom sense must tingle, because at that moment, she turns to us. After a quick observation of us, standing with our sides pressed into each other and Cory's arm around me, she lifts her eyebrows appreciatively.

"He's handsome. Nice work for a possible F-buddy," she signs from across the room. *"One sec."* Then she turns back to her new fashion friend. Since the early years of learning sign language, Mom has used it to say embarrassing things to me and Lito. I turn to the kitchen and see Lito laughing, having caught our exchange.

"What did she say?" Cory asks.

"She said she'll be over here to meet you in a second," I tell him. "Lito is right over there, though."

"Oh!" Cory lets go of me, walks up to Lito, and extends an arm. They shake hands. Cory signs, *"I'm Cory. Nice to meet you."*

Lito flicks a look to me, an indulgent smile on his lips. *"Lito,"* he signs back slowly. *"You know sign language?"*

Cory twists his hand back and forth, so-so. *"Learning,"* he signs.

Lito gives him a thumbs-up and looks at me. *"Better than—"* he begins, but I cut him off.

"Don't say it." I threaten him with the daggers in my eyes. Regardless of which ex he planned on comparing Cory to, I don't want to entertain it. Lito laughs and goes back to making a plate.

"You're learning sign language?" I poke Cory in the side.

"That's what I said . . . isn't it?" He's actually unsure if he signed the right thing.

"Yes, but why?"

He picks up a pinwheel sandwich and pops it into his mouth. He answers midchew. "You told me your brother is Deaf, and he prefers communicating through sign language. I've always wanted to learn—figured now is the time."

I'm more pleased by this than I should be, given the outlook I have for our relationship. Once he swallows his food, I give him a peck on the cheek.

"This must be Corinne. Either that or you need your butt whooped, son."

My head follows the voice to a glowing woman dressed in a floor-length blush-pink spring dress.

"She's never whooped me," Cory says, rolling his eyes.

"I'd start."

"Thank you," I say, because I think this is a compliment. His mom willing to defend my honor? "But I am Corinne. Congratulations on your engagement."

Cory's mom reaches out to squeeze my hands. "Call me Lorraine. There's my fiancé, right over there with the pink tie."

I follow her glance over to a man in blue slacks and a heather-gray short-sleeved button-up. The same man I saw the back of at Ricobene's the night of Elise's liberation celebration. His blush-pink tie coordinates with Cory's mom. He looks young—not our age, but not our parents' age either. Cory's eyes darken when I look to him.

"Hold on," Lorraine says. "Let me go save him from talkative-ass Rita. I'll introduce you two."

"Just turned forty," Cory says as soon as his mom is out of earshot.

"Oh. That's not bad," I say. "He looks good."

He shoots me a disapproving look that makes me laugh.

"My mom is fifty-five."

"Yeah, a fifty-five-year-old foxy mama," I tease.

Cory refuses to smile. Lito joins us with a plate of finger foods that I start eating from immediately. He doesn't bat an eye. In fact, he likely put more on his plate knowing I'd take some. It's one of my biggest accomplishments as an older sister: conditioning him to enjoy sharing with me.

Lorraine comes back over with her fiancé in tow. He's super smooth. I can see how she fell for him. I can also see why Cory would be skeptical. I would be, too, if some new man smiled at my mother like a Cheshire cat ready to feast. Cory is pulled away for something before Mom makes it over to meet him. Lito and I find seats in the glass-patio area since it's quieter than the living room. Soon, Tiwanda arrives. I watch as my mom greets her with double the enthusiasm she bestowed upon me yesterday. I start to express this observation to Lito, but he's flipping through the scrapbook, engrossed. Tiwanda makes her rounds. She knows Cory's mom and sister, of course, and a good chunk of his extended family and friends. Finally, she makes it over to us.

One look at my face and she says, "What's wrong with you?"

"Do you know why my mom is here?" I should be the one asking the questions now.

"Because there's a party?"

"No, because *you told her* there was a party. I'm supposed to decide when and where our parents meet."

She winces. "Sorry, cuz. We were talking before her flight, and I told her I'd see her here. I thought you would want this; it's the perfect opportunity."

"It really isn't." My voice goes hoarse.

I haven't had the chance to update Tiwanda and Elise on Met. I'm nervous about their reaction. They already thought I chose irresponsibly, and this new information puts the cherry on top of a shit sundae. That conversation can wait until after the party. "I didn't even get to tell my mom my job news myself."

Tiwanda's eyes widen. "I thought you'd tell her first!"

I give her a tight shake of my head. "No, I told Cory, you, and Elise first. I opened up to you three the most about it. You were the ones I trusted with the information."

Tiwanda blinks rapidly over glossy eyes. I almost feel guilty enough to take back everything I said, though I meant it. "Again, I'm sorry. I'll be more cautious."

"Thank you. I'll also try to be better at letting you know what secrets I'm keeping."

She grins and strikes up a conversation with Lito. Though they are just as much cousins as we are, he knows her less than I initially did. I at least had scattered childhood memories of us running around with a handful of others and playing games in the grassy backyard. He only has the memory of dinner two nights ago. They get on right away, though, chatting about his future internship. Tiwanda doesn't sign, but she speaks clearly and uses natural gestures. Lito seems to be following her well enough to not need my interpretation.

Through the open doors, I catch Cory approach my mom in the living room and sit with her. My first instinct is to run to his aid—or my own, I'm not sure—but Tiwanda reaches across Lito to place a stilling hand on my knee. I stay put, and minutes later, Mom is laughing with him. It makes the partially digested food inch back up my esophagus, so I look away. When I tire of gazing at the vast backyard and the gazebo mostly hidden by shrubbery, I snag the scrapbook from Lito. I decide to work backward from where he paused.

Joelle uncovered childhood photos of us that I don't remember taking. She found a few of us in school uniforms, probably taken with the disposable cameras she was fond of. I linger on one of us in the classroom. We're not the focus of the picture, though. There's a trio of boys who are front and center, making silly faces. Joelle and I are a bit behind them. She's got her arm around me, cheesing directly into the camera. Only my profile is showing as I look at her. Typical. I could never master locating the camera when I was younger.

"I remember braiding your hair in that style," Mom says as she squeezes between me and Lito.

"So?" I prompt. "What do you think of him?"

"I think I'll wait a few weeks before I let you know. That's how we're doing things, right?"

Niqua plops down in the chair to my left, distracting me from Mom's melodramatics. "I'm taking a break before they start the speeches. Stepdaddy Rodney can be long-winded. Oh my God, Mom pulled out the baby pictures already?"

I laugh, though it's not something I would be opposed to.

"No, this one is mine. Well, my friend's."

Niqua squints at me, lips upturned, as if she's waiting for a punch line. "Ma!" She calls to where her mom is accepting a replenished glass of wine from her husband-to-be.

"Is this the young folk's gathering room?" Cory's mom asks as she steps into the patio.

"If it is, I need to run," my mom quips.

Niqua points at the picture. Specifically, at the boy in the middle. His arms are crossed over his chest, and he's looking at the camera like he has this life thing figured out. "Ma, look who it is."

Ms. Lorraine leans down for a better look and harrumphs. "I barely remember how your brother looked before he grew all that hair. What book is this?"

My mind goes blank. While Mom and Ms. Lorraine's trill voices draw conclusions and marvel at the odds, I seek assurance in Tiwanda's and Lito's faces. They both understand the gravity of this discovery.

You gotta be kidding me, Lito half signs, his hands functioning about as well as my trapped voice.

Tiwanda's posture becomes alert as Rodney and Cory walk toward the patio. Rodney has a small paper in his hand. They're ready to start the speeches. Ms. Lorraine and Niqua trip over themselves to tell Cory what they've discovered. Silent from my perch, I watch Cory closely.

He stiffens, and his eyes jump to mine. It isn't surprise there, though. It's distress, possibly from the shock of being caught. That makes no sense. Cory would have told me this if he knew, wouldn't he? After all the griping he did about the app?

"Cor," he begins, the caution in his voice confirming what I feared.

I shake my head as I stand, stumbling to get away. "I need some air."

I realize the easiest way to get distance is the backyard, though what I really want is to get in my car and drive away. The backyard is at a lower level than the house. I take the stairs down, aware everyone in the patio can see me, half of them bemused by my behavior. My only refuge is the sheltered gazebo.

Tiwanda cautiously joins me a minute later. "If I knew, you know I would have accidentally told you," she says. My cheeks jump, but not enough to sustain a smile. I imagine she prevented Cory from following, and I'm grateful. I welcome her to share the bench with a wave of my hand.

"Am I losing it? Should I not be upset right now?"

Tiwanda offers no guidance. I huff and tap my foot on the wooden floor. It's too beautiful a view for my current mood. The colorful arrangement of flowers taunts me. At the core of all this, Cory was dishonest. He knew we'd already met and decided not to share that information with me. Why? He knows about the app. I've been twitchy every time I see someone who looks the slightest bit familiar, worried the other shoe would drop. I've been stressing over the fourth Met match ruining what me and Cory were creating. Joke's on me—Cory was my fourth match all along. Well, technically the second.

"Would you break up with him over this?"

"No," I say immediately. That wasn't on my list of solutions at all. Not very long ago, I was convinced Cory and I would end in heartbreak, yet I was still willing to hang on for the ride. Now, our relationship suddenly has the support of Met—of Joelle. My chest rises and falls irregularly. It's going to take some time for me to process this. I press my fingers against my temples.

"Talk to him before making any conclusions. Gather the data, check the receipts. Make an informed judgment." She frowns. "God, I need to work less."

I nod, agreeing to both working less and talking with Cory.

"I'll send him out. Let me know if you need me," Tiwanda says.

It takes no time at all for Cory to appear at the threshold of the gazebo, scanning me for hints, probably trying to calculate the best approach. I never imagined the man who had the gall to come to my apartment unannounced, fostered a comfortable shared working space, and then nearly kissed me out of my chair would stand before me completely flummoxed. Finally, he grasps at the threads of his confidence and steps in.

CHAPTER THIRTY

I watch Cory fill the spot Tiwanda vacated on the bench. He puts as much space between us as possible to turn and see me fully. It's like we're on opposite ends of the couch in my apartment again but much less comfortable.

He doesn't rush straight into expressing regret. My mom used to tell me and Lito that when people apologize in such situations, they're not truly sorry for the action. They're sorry they got caught. Mom would appreciate his avoidance. I, however, do not. I can tell he's waiting for me to decide the direction of this conversation.

"Why didn't you tell me?" My voice is low, stoic.

He lifts his hands a few inches from their resting position on his lap. "I didn't know." The anger in me deflates as quickly as a pinpricked balloon, leaving a confused heap of sad rubber in its wake. Until Cory adds, "Not for sure."

"So . . . what? You suspected it?"

"You said you didn't care about the app." I don't miss his evasion of the question. I wait for more. He sighs and scoots closer to me, the brushing noise of his pants giving the subtle movement away. "I didn't want you to only consider me because of the app."

"You'd rather me consider you *despite* the app?"

"Yes!" My nostrils flare at the rise of his voice. He apologizes with a dip of his head and continues, "You were willing to go home with a guy because of the app; of course I'd prefer—"

"Back to this shit? If you hadn't noticed, I had two other Met matches and didn't so much as hold hands with either of them. Your logic is flawed."

"It still influenced your decisions."

Something isn't adding up. If Cory had suspicions, why wouldn't he pursue confirmation? He loves research and gathering data to support his hypotheses. No way could he be satisfied with the unknown, not when there were multiple avenues for him to verify.

"We were in the same class together. I've met you before. Why would that be something you don't want to know? Wouldn't it help your case?"

His jaw tenses and he shakes his head, looking up to the ceiling of the gazebo. "It wouldn't be authentic."

"How do I know it didn't influence *your* decisions? Maybe having a hunch that we'd met is the only reason you pursued me." I say this in jest, but as it comes out, I realize it's truly a concern of mine.

"It's not," he says with certainty. I stare at him. His hair is pulled back into a ponytail, and he looks damn handsome. It's the self-assuredness that both drew me to him and pissed me off at our second meeting. "I had feelings for you before I made the connection."

"Which was?"

"The night you told me about Joelle. Tiwanda mentioned your friend passing, but I didn't know her name until then. I recognized it from a friend's posting about her passing. A lot of my old classmates commented with memories, but I didn't remember her myself. When I learned she was your best friend . . ."

"If felt too strange to be mere coincidence?"

His intense focus burns into my eyes as he nods. "I knew there was a chance we might have crossed paths, but how could I prove that?"

"Easily. By being up front with me and pooling our resources. Admit it—you didn't want confirmation." I recall the night he said I'd had "three coincidences," and I assumed Tiwanda or Elise told him about Devin. Really, he'd subconsciously included himself with the Met matches by that point. I stand, snickering as I think of another messed-up aspect of this ordeal. "You know what really gets me? You were like, *'Trust yourself, why are you so focused on an app?'* All the while, you never trusted me."

Cory stands with me because this is who we are, a seesaw of power dynamics. "If I didn't, I would have told you and let the app force us together. I trusted you to choose me without Met."

I scoff. "If that were the case, you wouldn't have withheld information from me."

He looks at the ground, an admission of being trumped. I sit back down, and after a moment he joins me. Hip to hip this time. I want to move, but it's too solid and warm. Too familiar.

Cory turns his hand over, palm up on his lap, and less by choice than instinct, I slide my hand into his, entwining our fingers. His thumb caresses the back of my hand. He brings it to his lips and presses a kiss there. After a minute of silence, he speaks again. "What's next?"

I shrug, causing our shoulders to bump against each other with the movement.

"I guess I have to compare you with my three other suitors to see who my one true love is."

His hand stiffens in mine.

"I'm kidding," I say. He laughs, but it's forced and a poor attempt to distract me from him pulling his hand away. But I notice. That's why I know what he'll say before he opens his mouth.

"Maybe you should take some time. Think about who and what you want."

"I think I've been pretty obvious about that." I try to sound upbeat, though I feel my control on this conversation slipping. The damn seesaw again.

"You wanted me when you thought there was a high chance of it being temporary."

I open my mouth to deny this, but I can't. There's always a chance of a relationship not lasting forever. That's not fair to use against me, but it's true.

"Soul mates don't have to be forever," I say instead.

He frowns at me, a crease forming between his brows. "Mine would be." He stands, about to walk away.

"Wait. Are you ending this?"

"I want to give you the space to really think about it. Go out with other people if you want, whatever you need to do to be sure about me."

"Why are you telling me I'm not sure when I'm here, committed to you, meeting your family?" My throat becomes raw with the force of my words. Tears threaten my eyes, but I press the pads of my fingers to my eyelids to abate the stinging.

"Because . . ." Cory trails off, eyes darting aimlessly in front of him. His head bounces back a bit as if he's been physically hit by a realization. In the moment before he speaks, I have hope he's going to change his mind. "You're right. I don't trust you. I don't trust *this*. I want to but . . . I'm sorry. I need a break." At the sight of my crestfallen face, he takes a step toward where I'm still seated on the bench, his hand outstretched.

I hop up and away from him like a spooked cat. "Nice of you to finally admit it."

I leave him in the gazebo and collect my mom and Lito. On my way out, I mumble something to Tiwanda about texting her later and make my escape amid worried looks from Cory's family. Outside the car, Lito takes the keys from my grip. I slide into the back seat, happy to let him take the wheel. Mom twists around from the passenger seat, her face pulled down in concern as she squeezes my knee. She forgoes interrogating me and faces forward to give me the privacy I need to wallow in.

Tears don't come. I can't settle on a single emotion long enough to elicit that response. My phone buzzes from my bag on the car floor. Elise sent a picture from her rehearsal. It's a selfie with seven other actors squeezed into the frame. I zoom in to get a clearer look at the guy who caught my eye and cackle. It's Anthony. To leave no doubt, Elise follows it up with the message, Mr. #SpitGate himself.

I check the top of the thread, and to my dismay, she used the full-group chat. I never told Cory that specific detail of the hookup, so he'll be drawing his own conclusions about what it means.

I open the Met app. There are no Met Tips, no jokes, nothing to help me figure out which direction I should go now. I'm not disappointed, because I didn't expect there would be. Joelle did all she could, both on Earth and through Met. I still managed to make a mess of it. I exit the app and press my thumb to the icon until it gives me the option to delete. This time, when it asks if I'm sure, I don't hesitate.

CHAPTER THIRTY-ONE

Not much changes immediately—at least not perceptibly, as my mom and brother are still in town. We follow Mom's agenda, visiting her friends and some distant relatives. We enjoy a rite-of-passage deep-dish-pizza dinner with Joelle's parents and go sightseeing downtown. The brightest part of having them here is our nightly dinners in my apartment. Mom does most of the cooking while Lito and I alternate who assists. With all the leftovers, I'll be able to shirk cooking for my entire first week of work, maybe longer if I freeze some meals. Mom and Lito's constant presence leaves little time to obsess over what happened with Cory.

Too soon, it's time for them to leave. I drive them to the airport before the sun rises. It's five thirty, and Lito is asleep in the back seat, though it's only a twenty-five-minute ride to Midway airport. He was out within the first five minutes. Mom yawns, her usual loud *ahh* ending with a satisfied hum. I grin at the familiarity of sharing mornings with her.

"What are you going to do?" she asks.

I turn on the blinker to change lanes, the ticking noise the only sound in the car as I figure out how best to avoid this question.

"I'm going to take Sixty-Third down," I say.

She stares at me, lips pursed.

I sigh. "I don't know, Momma." I spare a cursory glance at the rearview mirror. After refocusing on the road ahead of us, I realize it was probably a subconscious act—checking the rearview of my failed relationship. "There's nothing to do, is there? It's over. I didn't decide that, so it's not something I can change."

"That's the dumbest shit I've ever heard."

I gape at her, taking my eyes off the road for a moment to do so. She looks back at me unabashed.

"I can't force him to trust me."

"You can present a damning case."

I scoff. "Why should I have to convince someone to be with me? Am I supposed to grovel at his doorstep?"

"Honey, no." She turns to me as far as her seat belt will allow. "I met Cory. I saw how you two were together. It's new and obviously still fragile, but that boy isn't going to need any convincing. Some people give trust freely, damn the consequences. I was never that person. My trust was something people had to earn. Some earned it quickly, others took some time."

"Cory wasn't willing to wait for that to happen."

"Maybe you need to extend trust to him and give him the chance to do the same."

"I did. He threw it in my face."

My mom sighs. "All right, be stubborn."

"Fine."

It's better he ends it now before I do something ill advised, like fall in love with him. Mom must be overlooking this silver lining, because she refuses to let it go.

"I'm missing something," she says minutes later, when I begin thinking I'm in the clear. "You two were great, you saw the second-grade picture, then you broke up."

I'm surprised she went this long without realizing the pieces she has don't make a complete picture. I glance at my GPS. Fourteen minutes until our estimated arrival. How long would it take to tell my mom the truth, no matter how outlandish?

Apparently, not long at all. Four minutes later and the whole she-bang is out. My mom listens without interruption, and when I'm done, she still doesn't speak. She rubs her lips together, something she does when deep in thought.

"I know it sounds unlikely," I say.

"Stranger things have happened."

"Do you think Dad is your soul mate?"

She's quiet while she considers. "The instinctive answer would be no since we divorced. But honestly, maybe? I never believed in that stuff. I do know we were deeply in love for some time."

"So you can imagine my hesitation."

"And Cory's," she points out.

I make a dismissive closed-mouth noise. Cory was not just hesitant. He went past that and settled on refusal. Now that she has the full story, Mom lets it go. Guess she finally understands how tangled this situation is. I drop her and Lito off with groggy hugs and safe-travel wishes. When I return to my apartment and climb into the bed that now smells of Mom, I try to ignore how empty it feels.

~

My first day at work is the best I've ever had. I'm pretty sure it's because I've never had a welcome like this—intimate and brimming with sincere excitement.

For my first job out of college, I shared a first day with three other recent grads. We spent the day together, meeting the team and going through HR checkpoints. The team had lunch catered to encourage everyone to come celebrate us and mostly get free food. They gave us welcome gifts of a notepad and pen bearing the company's logo.

At Finance for the Fam, Aisha comes with doughnuts. Pedro is on a health kick and has moved a blender permanently into the kitchen area, so he makes us all smoothies. Then we get to work. They touch on the newest developments, most of which they've been cc'ing me on for the past few weeks. Then I start the process of filling out my first grant application.

"I like us all being here together," Nia says sometime midmorning. She's on her second cup of coffee and is cradling her mug like it's a precious jewel.

"We have flexible working arrangements," Aisha explains. "We're only all together like this once a week. I have a part-time job during the day."

"Me too," Pedro says. "That's why you can usually catch me here at night."

I look at Nia. She toys with her dangling earring. "I don't need much to live off of."

Behind her Pedro exaggeratedly mouths, *"Rich parents."*

"We know there's not monetary wealth in store for this line of work," Aisha says. "If you find a part-time job that fits you, we can schedule around it."

I plan to evaluate how I fare when I pay rent next month from my income for the first time. I've done the calculations on the spreadsheet Tiwanda made me, but there's no accounting for where my discretionary income will fall. If I experience financial stress from one ill-timed car woe or health issue, then I'll need to actively look for a part-time job. Maybe continue subbing or accepting temp jobs.

That's still up in the air, but I accept it. It's unreasonable to expect all facets of my life to be stable for any sustained period. I'm constantly trading off one part for another. For a brief time, I reached a new level of balance. I had a prospective job, a friend group I adored, and an exciting love life. Recovery isn't impossible, but if I am allowed the time, I won't rush past the moments of uncertainty. It's the least I can do, for Joelle.

Tiwanda and Elise wait until the completion of my first week of work to demand a girls' night. The week has gone perfectly. Pedro, Nia, and Aisha made sure someone was always in the office with me while I worked in case I had any questions and to keep me company. Our first event is scheduled for three weeks from now, a couple of weeks after the school year ends.

There's a flurry of activity at the office. Not only are we preparing for the relaunch but we are also finalizing a tentative calendar for future events. Our goal is to have at least two events per month. Every other month, one of those events will be what we've labeled a "medium/large budget event." The money we have in the account now is enough to cover the events for the next six months. If no grants are awarded in a timely manner, we're going to be in deep trouble come fall.

I want a break from my apartment, so we agree to sleep over at Tiwanda's condo. We order food to be delivered and sip wine as I catch them up on my week.

"You seem to really like it," Tiwanda says.

"It's fun being a part of rebuilding something, hopefully making it stronger."

"I'm sure it will be. They have the lessons learned from past mistakes and a fresh perspective with you."

I grin and allow her comment to make me feel syrupy and valued. It's like something Cory would say. I shoo that thought away.

Elise tells us about how play rehearsals are going. We promise to be there opening night. Outside of theater, she's been working with Finance for the Fam for our new website. She's already presented her design and, after incorporating the feedback from the team, thinks it should be finished by the time of the first event. It sucks to not have a website they can register through yet, but Pedro and Nia are developing a comprehensive marketing plan to make up for it.

"How's your job going?" I ask Tiwanda.

She responds by grabbing the open bottle of wine and taking it to the head. We talk about other things instead, like what I did for the rest of the time my family was in town, funny moments from Elise's rehearsals—which she laughs at much more than we do since we had to be there—and soaps Tiwanda made over the past week. She sent my mom and brother home with a couple of bars each.

After we are full and tipsy, we get comfortable in pajamas and with blankets and browse movies to watch. It's the perfect debrief for my workweek.

"Thanks for this. I'm grateful to have you two," I tell them.

Elise pushes my shoulder. "Are you kidding? You never have to thank us for being your friends."

"You don't still hang out with Brian," I point out.

Tiwanda laughs. "Brian was an extension of Cory. You're an extension of us. Your breakup doesn't affect that."

It might be the nicest thing she has ever said to me. Though Tiwanda's my cousin, she's not the type to blindly fall in line with familial ties. If that were the case, we wouldn't be as tight-knit, with our barely counts kinship.

"Plus . . . ," Elise says, glancing at Tiwanda as if expecting she will stop her from continuing, "it's not like this is forever, right? You two are soul mates."

"We're not," I say, deflecting.

"Corinne. The app is powered by your best friend's spirit or some shit! You've met Cory before. If you'd known that from the get-go, what would've happened?"

I shrug and glance at my undisturbed phone on the side table nearby. Despite myself, I've missed the jaunty tone of Met Tip notifications. I downright long for the connection it provided to Joelle, though I didn't realize it quick enough to appreciate it fully. "Something less complicated, that's for sure."

"And less messy," Tiwanda adds.

"Maybe not," says Elise. "You see him . . . where was the first time?"

"Monday happy hour," Tiwanda provides. "When Brian was there, so we never returned. Damn. I really loved that restaurant."

"Right. You see him in Tío Nico's and wonder, *'Do I know him?'* You two riddle out where from, thus confirming it's someone Met promised. You'd still be faced with the same decision you're faced with right now."

"Which is?"

"Are you going to relinquish some control and let it happen?"

"I think you're forgetting it was Cory who broke up with me."

Elise shakes her head. "Cory got scared. And because you're willing to accept this as a finality, I think you are too."

Tiwanda gives me a sad smile in obvious agreement.

"Unless you think Anthony is the one, because I have his digits now in the cast group chat. I can send him a quick text to come over if you want?"

"Oh God, no," I say, laughing. "Maybe it's Devin. They're amazing." I've kept Devin abreast of my job affairs, and they're on the schedule for events we're planning. If I'm honest with myself, though I was attracted to Devin, Cory blocked any chance of our spark of friendship igniting.

Elise presses her lips together and glances at Tiwanda, the portrait of guilt.

"What?" I ask.

"Me and Devin might have gone out."

"And came back in. All night," Tiwanda tattles.

My jaw drops. "Elise!"

She covers her face with her hands. "I know! It happened literally the day before the engagement-party fiasco. You and Cory were happy, I thought Devin was off the table for you and, well . . ."

"On the table for you?" I supplied.

"Ready to be served up like the main dish," Tiwanda instigates.

"I was going to tell you sooner. Sorry!"

"Don't be. You two could be great together," I say. It's true, they'd gotten along so well at game night—more than the usual result of Devin being a people person. "Maybe Met will have a success story after all."

CHAPTER
THIRTY-TWO

The Finance for the Fam doorbell rings, and since I'm the only one in the office on a Friday evening, I walk to the front desk to buzz Devin in. It's policy to keep the door locked if there's only one of us in the office or if it's outside business hours.

"You look nice." Devin has on perfectly tailored navy-blue pants and a printed short-sleeve button-up. I walk closer to peer at the print. "Pineapples?"

"It's an inside joke. Plus, it matches my gift." They place a gift bag on the counter and push aside the tissue paper. I stick my head in the bag and inhale through my nose.

"That's a real pineapple!"

"I know." Devin laughs. "I told Elise I'd show up at her opening night with a bouquet of flowers. She said she'd prefer a bouquet of pineapples instead. She was probably joking, since she was eating a fruit cup at the time, but still."

I stare at Devin.

"What?" they say, a blush creeping onto their face.

"Y'all cute, that's all. I'll be done in about thirty minutes. You can chill in the back office with me."

Devin flips through flyers Pedro designed for upcoming events while I tie up some loose ends. There's correspondence I wanted to follow up with before the weekend, and I need to put finishing touches on a budgeting forecast with the new grant we were awarded. The money isn't in our account yet, but we already have plans depending on it. I'll be glad when we have adequate funds in the bank to not worry about if we'll have to go on hiatus again or cut back on events.

Our relaunch program is tomorrow morning. There are only a few emails in the general inbox with questions about the event, a testament to the clear marketing we've had leading up to this. Plus, our website is officially live! We emailed all the parents who RSVP'd with a link to the website. All the information needed for the event is right there.

"Hey, have you talked to Cory recently?" Devin asks.

I squint at them. They sound nonchalant, but the added "hey" at the beginning gives them away.

"Not since a few weeks ago." He texted me while I was in the office for a charger he left in my apartment. I told him he could let himself in to get it since he still has my key. He asked if I wanted him to leave the key on the counter when he went. If you want, I replied. When I got home from work, the kitchen island was empty except for the usual bowl of fruit. I don't know what to make of that. Possible hope we'll be friends again? He's not the first person I'd call if I were locked out of my apartment. I'd probably call Tiwanda. He's not even the second. I'd rather call Elise to see if she could get the key from Tiwanda before defaulting to Cory. Maybe after tonight, it'll be easier to bear the idea of asking him to come to my aid. "Why?" I ask Devin belatedly.

They smile at me knowingly. "Wondering how awkward tonight is going to be."

"It's not going to be awkward at all. It's a play. We'll all be focused on the stage, watching your super-talented girlfriend."

"Ha, okay, Corinne."

I groan and shut my laptop. I'm not ready to go, but no more pro-crastinating. It's open seating for the family-and-friends section, and Tiwanda expects me and Devin to show up early enough to save her two seats. One is obviously for Cory, but I don't like thinking about that.

Devin drives us in my car because they "can't trust my road aware-ness right now." The theater is about a half hour away. We stop along the way so I can pick up an actual flower bouquet for Elise.

We arrive twenty minutes before the show starts, along with many others, but still manage to snag good center seats in the reserved area for the cast. I put my sweater and purse into the two empty seats beside me as ushers circulate, asking us not to save seats, please.

"This seat for me?"

I don't want to react to the smooth voice I know all too well, despite not hearing it for the past month. The one exception being the time I was in Tiwanda's car, and she accepted a call from him through the Bluetooth. For a panicked moment, I feared it was a reverse of the situ-ation when I called for advice about Anthony. But once Tiwanda told him I was in the car with her, he hastily got off the line.

Cory's locs hang down, framing his face. It's unfair he looks this good in a plain gray T-shirt with an unbuttoned denim shirt over it and a nice pair of black jeans. Then again, I fell for him when most of the outfits I'd seen him in were scrubs.

"I mean for me and Tee," he amends.

"Yeah," I say.

He starts to pick up my purse from the seat nearest to me. I hold out my hand to stop him and end up brushing his in the process. He jerks away from me.

"It'll be easier to save Tiwanda a seat if we sandwich it between us," I say. He nods and hands me my sweater instead, avoiding eye contact as he does. Devin gives me a look, and I'm not sure if it's cautious support or condemnation of that interaction.

In the minutes before the lights go down, Devin and I huddle together to look for Elise's name and bio in the program, then gush over the set. It's decorated to look like a neighborhood street corner in Chicago.

The seat between us doesn't make it any easier to ignore Cory. I want to casually tell him I read his published article printout, the one Tiwanda suspiciously left on my coffee table when she came over last weekend. I've read it twice more since. It's a well-written, informative piece of work. And I couldn't help wishing Cory were there for me to ask unnecessary questions, questions that could lead to . . .

Nope, that part I wouldn't tell him. But now that he's here, scrolling slowly on his phone like he's reading a news article, I can't bring myself to offer even the first part.

As the lights start to fade, and a voice over the loudspeaker asks us to silence our phones and refrain from taking photographs, Tiwanda arrives. She shuffles down the row, excusing herself as the backs of her thighs brush knees and as she probably steps on a few toes. "Scoot over," she stage-whispers to Cory after he tries and fails to make himself small enough for her to comfortably squeeze past. I move my purse to my lap, and he bounces over, a waft of his scent making my throat constrict as he leans over to me.

"I can make her switch with me during intermission," he says apologetically.

"It's fine, whatever," I whisper back as the announcements end and a single light illuminates a circle on the stage. He straightens and tries to get settled in his new seat, arms bumping into me before he draws them in tight. He's going to have a lot of tension if he stays like that the entire play, but that's not my concern.

The play starts with the main character rapping to introduce every-one in the neighborhood, which draws me in right away. Elise sang songs from the play ad nauseum for the past few weeks, but I didn't imagine it would be like this. I'm totally focused on the stage and don't spare a thought to Cory sitting beside me. That is, until he, too, is only paying attention to the stage and loosens his shoulders. Now he presses solidly against me. I tense for a moment myself, then sigh and release it. Neither of us explodes. Life continues.

Anthony's character is introduced. He sings a few lines and sounds better than I remember. I exchange a look with Devin because to do that with Tiwanda would require leaning over Cory. He shifts beside me, undoubtedly recognizing him.

Then Elise's character enters the stage. She's beautiful in her costume, and her vocals have us rapt. Her introduction turns into a scene change, and then she sings a solo. Devin grips my forearm throughout the number; they're more nervous than Elise, who handles each note with ease.

As the song ends and the audience applauds, Tiwanda leans over Cory and mouths, *"Wow."* All three of us nod.

The entire first act is similarly stunning. It's like the cast was made to harmonize with one another. There's a mix of fast-paced rapping and ballads. The dialogue is chock-full of comedic moments. Anthony's character, a pushover in every sense of the word, asserts he's going to start taking charge in all aspects of his life. His wife then pauses and gives him *a look*. I laugh and turn to Cory, who reciprocates the action. We don't rush to end the moment once we realize this isn't what we do anymore.

Intermission comes, and Cory stands and excuses himself. After saying hello to Elise's aunt and some of her other friends, Tiwanda takes Cory's place, and we rave about Elise's performance. At the end of the fifteen minutes, Cory returns with bottles of water, a couple of boxes of popcorn, and a few choices of candy. He settles in Tiwanda's vacated seat and passes things down, including my favorite, Twizzlers. I snag those for myself and share a popcorn with Devin, feeling a tinge disappointed to be separated from Cory again.

When the play ends, we're all wiping tears from our eyes. Well, I can't speak for Cory, since I can't see him on the other side of Tiwanda. But if I know him as well as I thought I did, then, yeah, he's teary-eyed too. Once the theater clears a bit, the cast comes out to say hello to their family and friends. We crowd around Elise and shower her with love, praise, and gifts. When she reaches in the gift bag Devin handed her, then quickly retreats once pricked, she pretty much mauls Devin right there in front of us.

Anthony doesn't have any family from home here, but he's happy to see me. He sweeps me up in a hug that I pray Cory doesn't notice. We're not together, but I don't want him to take this interaction as some twisted sort of proof he was right. I say hello to Anthony's friends from the improv troupe, then rejoin Elise and company.

"The cast is going out to celebrate," Elise is saying. "You all are coming, right?"

Cory and I look at each other. I hurry forward before he can speak. "I have to wake up early, but we'll celebrate again later."

Elise accepts this and wraps her arms around me. I give quick departing hugs to Devin and Tiwanda. I'll see them all tomorrow when they volunteer for the relaunch. When I get to Cory, I dither. His gaze flicks to me, then away repeatedly, giving me the option to skip him. I step backward and say bye to the entire group again with a quick wave, and then I walk away.

That wasn't too bad. Not awkward at all.

In the safe confines of Bessie, I start the engine and let my eyes close as my head falls back on the headrest. I need a moment to breathe before getting on the road. Maybe a silent drive home will help me sort through all the thoughts coursing through my brain.

A knock on the driver's-side window makes me jump out of my skin. My engine vrooms as my foot comes down on the accelerator, but I'm still in park. This is fortunate because I probably would have rolled over Cory's foot if I'd switched gears. I lower my window and stick my head out as Cory stoops to meet me halfway. We nearly touch noses. I lean back.

"What are you doing?" I ask him.

"Sorry for scaring you," he says, not at all answering my question. I raise my eyebrows at him, though he probably can't see me with the dim lighting of the parking area. "I needed to talk to you."

"Okay," I say, irked. He had the past two hours to talk. When I took my leave, he stood there, reticent.

"Okay," he parrots. He straightens as he gathers his poise but then realizes he must continue bending down if he wants me to hear him.

"Do you want to sit?" I wave to the seat beside me.

His relieved sigh makes me suspicious he views this offering as some feat. "That would be great."

I unlock the door.

CHAPTER
THIRTY-THREE

Cory sinks into my passenger seat. The moment his door closes, the inside lights turn off. I start to turn them back on but decide against it. Maybe it'll be easier to do this if I can't see him. I switch my headlights off, too, as I notice people walk by. They're momentarily bathed in the light of my unmoving car, probably wondering if they can cross or if I'm going to run them over.

"I wasn't going to bother you tonight," Cory starts. It might be the third-worst start of a sentence uttered in the English language, ever. Right after "No offense, but . . ." and "I think we can all agree that . . ."

"But Tiwanda threatened me the moment you left," he finishes.

"Figures. We can both tell her we had a good chat, then."

"No, I mean"—Cory turns in his seat—"I wanted to speak with you. But I know you have an important day tomorrow. I don't want to distract you with this."

A small chuckle escapes me because he's been a distraction for a while. Might as well let him know. "Cory, you're always a distraction."

"Why's that?"

I shake my head, annoyed. "What did you need to tell me, Cory?"

"Mostly that I miss you."

He says this factually, and I stop breathing for a moment. I can't meet his eyes because it would reveal how much of an understatement that would be on my behalf.

"All right," I say instead.

"We've been apart now for more time than we were together. Officially together. It doesn't make sense that I'm still like this."

"Like what?" I press.

"Stuck, Cor. On pause. Ever since you left my mom's house, I feel like I haven't moved forward."

"What are you talking about? Your article was published. It was amazing."

"You read it? Again?"

"I was basically a coauthor, so. Had to make sure you implemented my critique." I defiantly refuse to return his gaze, but from my peripheral, it's clear that doesn't brush off this being a big deal. I mean . . . obviously, I still care about him. Guys can be dense.

"Elise and Tee wanted to go out and celebrate when it was published. You know they're big on that." It's true. I didn't realize I needed such a championing group after losing Joelle, but I desperately did.

"You should be proud."

"I am, but . . . I didn't see the point of celebrating without you."

This causes me to turn my head to face him. His eyes catch mine, glossy and intent.

"I'm sorry for pushing you away."

I shake my head. "You don't have to apologize for that. You told me how you felt. That's fair."

"Well, then, I'm sorry for not telling you we'd probably met."

I tilt my head from side to side. "Okay, you can apologize for that one."

He laughs, and I instinctively smile at the sight. Damn. Will his joy ever *not* positively affect me? I could probably see him laughing with another partner and still feel warm at the smile on his face. I frown at that thought. No, then, perhaps not.

"What's wrong?" Cory asks, his laughter cut short.

"I was thinking of you dating someone else."

His lips turn down now too. He looks at his lap, then back up to me. "Can't picture it," he says. His voice is tight, like he had to force out those words.

I lick my lips and swallow the lump in my throat. "Maybe one day." I bite the corner of my lip and look away, hoping that might be true for me too. What a joke, meeting your soul mate only to learn you're not meant to be with him. Cory reaches out to touch my arm, willing my attention back to him. He's closer now as he leans across the armrest. He can probably smell the faint strawberry scent of Twizzlers on my breath.

"That's the thing," he says. "I don't want to."

I need to turn away from him. It doesn't matter that he misses me. He damn well should—I'm fantastic! We were great together. In lots of ways. How easily we molded ourselves to be what the other needed. How great of a friend he was to me before we committed to being more. How we responded to each other's passion, both in careers and in bed.

I groan as I close the distance between us, disappointed in myself but not enough to deter this. Cory's hands move to cradle my face and hold me in place faster than I can get to his. I grip on to his shirt instead. Perhaps sensing my discomfort, he shifts his hands down to loosely bracket my neck, his thumbs on my jaw. Compromise. He wastes no time slipping his tongue into my mouth, making me whimper and press my legs together to keep from climbing into his lap.

As our mouths get reacquainted, I loosen my grip on his shirt and use my hands for better purposes. They roam his chest and abdomen, reveling in the defined muscles beneath the soft fabric of his shirt. It's easy for me to find the hem and slide underneath. This elicits a low groan from him as my fingers meet his warm skin. The sound sends electricity through my veins. Though I'd only intended to satisfy my impulse to get closer to him, hold on to the bare skin of his sides, I find myself changing course. It's like I'm wired to seek those sounds from him. I want more. My hands move to his belt, and I start to undo it. I slide it through the loop and am working on undoing the buckle when we are doused in light.

I see it through my closed eyelids, but it still causes me to jump back and release my grip on Cory's belt. I duck my head away from the blinding headlights, thinking we've been caught, but no. It's a car exiting the parking lot. The light leaves as quickly as it came.

I fall back into my seat, brushing my fingers over my tender lips. Cory reaches over and places his hand on my thigh. This slip in judgment will make me feel a hundred times worse than before. What am I supposed to do with this? We both miss each other—so what? It doesn't change the fact that he doesn't trust being with me. I push his hand away.

"We can't do this, Cory. You ended it, and I've been . . . okay." I sigh and press the heels of my hands against my eyelids. I shake my head and drop my hands back to my lap. "You were right. You shouldn't have bothered me tonight. Full stop."

"I love you," he blurts.

My heart stills for a beat before logic kicks in. This is the same guy who spent a week after breaking up with Brian moping under the assumption they had been in love.

"You don't love me, Cory. If you did, you wouldn't have been able to discard me so easily. Not while I stood there practically begging you to keep me. That was the decision you made—not to trust me because you didn't have complete control with Met involved." His eyes roam my face like he's puzzling something out. Maybe he's in the process of understanding I'm right. I can't wait for him to get to this conclusion. Knowing Cory, he'd need to develop a thesis and gather evidence to support it first.

"I need to get home," I tell him.

It takes him a moment to respond, and I imagine him sifting through options in his brain. In the end, all he says is, "Good luck tomorrow."

CHAP

THIRTY

Pedro is freaking out, certain we for
massaging her temples as she takes
parent who wants to register their
to coming early. We only have a fe
might have to turn folks away if too m
That's another stressor on Pedro. He
if we send people away.

It's not true, because we have a p
our Come Again plan. Any family
brochure for the parent and a goody
of those for the children attending
today.

I'm setting up with Nia in the
the South Side. It's the perfect space
and are working to find our site for
is positioned near the entrance. Alon
we're using four rooms.

Our team has planned the event
shop. Families will have the opportu

upon check-in. Each session is fun
to complete educational activities
a competition planned. Above all,
rces. We hope the subjects touched
goals.

ble on one side of the lobby, starting
nola bars, pastries, juice, and water.
ch switch, and the event ends with

ng at it alone since seven a.m. The
with presenters scheduled to arrive
irty, and the event kicks off at ten.
ome speech planned, which gives late-

ff the phone. "I have all the volunteer
s they arrive, I'll handle that. Nia and
sign-in later. If there are any problems
over. Pedro will be the main contact for
hands full with that. We good?"

lking to," Nia says.
lling in. I see Tiwanda through the glass
me is Elise to hurry up. She's probably
nd. Tiwanda drops her arms and stomps
and leave the lobby for the main room
n chairs. We need to place a small branded

she enters the main room. "This is a
opposite of hungover. If I didn't witness
performed her ass off last night. It's cool
thanks to the website collaboration.

Devin trails Elise. Our first art event with Devin will happen next month. My guess is they'll be volunteering in general today, but I have no idea, since Aisha handled the volunteer sign-ups and duties. We tend to divide work by assigning each responsibility a main person and support person. If I'm neither of those, I only have a general idea of what's going on. Basically, I know whatever is shared during our weekly meeting. I hug both Elise and Devin and tell them they can start helping place the goodies on each chair.

Finally, Tiwanda comes in, slipping her volunteer tag around her neck. I move to meet her and stop in my tracks as Cory follows her in. I force myself to keep walking. This is my event, my territory. Cory is the one trespassing.

"What are you doing here?" I ask.

"Nice to see you too," Tiwanda says.

I apologize and give her a quick hug, then turn back to Cory. He picks up the volunteer badge hanging on his neck. I knead my knuckles into my forehead, my brain not comprehending.

"I signed up to volunteer," Cory assists.

"Why? When?"

"A few weeks ago, same time as Tee and Elise."

How was I okay not knowing who all was going to be here? How naive of me. Tiwanda looks slightly apologetic, but I can tell she would stand by her meddling if I called her on it. I make the decision to appeal to Cory. He looks out of his comfort zone anyway. He'll probably bail if I give him an out.

"You don't have to stay. We got way more volunteers than we expected." Mostly because each member of the board recruited our friends to help. Then a few of those friends brought younger siblings who needed volunteer hours. "What are you assigned? Aisha can get someone to cover your duty, I'm sure."

Cory opens his mouth, then closes it and clenches his teeth. The muscles of his jaw flex as he does. "I'm doing the Brain Breaks. I listed physical therapy as a special skill on my volunteer questionnaire, so Aisha asked me if I'd do some light but fun exercises."

"That, um,"—I waver—"sounds great. Yeah. Okay."

Pedro sticks his head into the room. "Corinne, the sign-language interpreters are here."

"I need to get them set up," I tell Tiwanda and Cory.

I follow Pedro back out to the lobby, my brain whirring. We can skirt around each other for the rest of the event. Fine. Brain Breaks happen in the lobby, where I'll be for break times, too, but I'll be focused on making sure the snack table is orderly and stocked. This will all be fine.

Ultimately, it is not fine. But Cory sure is. I can't stop staring at him across the lobby easily managing the large group of children who decided to partake. He's turned it into a team competition. There's an interpreter beside him, signing his directions. The kids are yelling and laughing with him as their parents spectate or roam around, chatting with other parents, moving through the snack line, and stopping at our resource table. I'm so riveted by the Brain Break, a man had to ask twice if we had more granola bars before I realized he was talking to me.

The event is going great. Parents have been coming up to me and the rest of the crew asking about future events all morning. After this break ends, we have our third and last rotation before lunch.

"You all right over here?" Tiwanda asks as she bumps her side into mine. I scowl at her from the corner of my eye.

"Why?" I ask.

"Because you two are both childish, and I'm annoyed. I miss hanging out with all of us. Together."

"We can do that. We went to the play yesterday, and that went . . ." I picture me and Cory in my car. A flash of his hands around my neck and our mouths hungry for each other. I clear my throat. "Fine."

"Mhmm. Also, Cory is no fun to be around like this."

I've avoided asking Tiwanda and Elise about Cory because I don't want to put them more in the middle than they already are. But now,

Tiwanda has brought it up. Before I can fish for more information, my wristband vibrates, and I lift it to check the message coming through. It's a one-minute warning from Pedro. Cory's group is now moving toward us to get drinks. Cory starts to follow, but Aisha cuts him off. She speaks to him energetically, placing her hand on his bicep for a few seconds longer than I like.

"Easy, tiger," Tiwanda says.

I wipe my face free of tension. Finance for the Fam was the best place for me to not think about Cory for a while. I stayed busy, and my coworkers didn't know I was going through a breakup. Even so, they unwittingly helped me move past it. I'm not upset at Aisha for noticing how attractive Cory is. It's not her fault she doesn't know he's mine. Or was. Whatever.

Cory and Aisha finish talking, and he walks over to us with a happy swagger in his step.

"How'd it go?" I ask.

"Great. I love these kids. This is the perfect job for you, Cor."

Wow, he *loves* to throw that word around. I lift a nonchalant shoulder. "I know."

He nods at me, brown eyes glittering like we're sharing some deeper-level communication.

Pedro announces it's time to begin the final rotation and asks everyone to move to their designated rooms. During this forty-minute session, I'll be packing away the extra snacks to use for our next event and getting everything set up for lunch. The caterer should be here any moment.

"All right, I'm out," Cory announces. "Where's Elise?"

"She and Devin were helping Room Two set up," Tiwanda says.

"You're leaving?" I ask. It's a mistake, because he brightens at that. This is why I can't be cordial. I want to add an insincere *I'm only asking because it would bring me joy if you were.*

"Aisha said I was free to go since that was the last Brain Break. Nothing really left for me to do except wait for lunch. Unless you needed something?"

"Oh, no. We're all set. Thanks for volunteering, though," I say with a tight smile. As I hurry off to get the food bins from the closet, I realize those weren't empty words. I'm genuinely grateful for Cory volunteering. The kids loved him, that's for sure. Each Brain Break drew a larger crowd. More than that, it felt right to have him here. The past month of working, I've shared nothing with him about it, for obvious reasons. Cory was along for the ride with the discovery of this job and the interview process, and he was there when I got the offer call. I didn't linger on it before, but as much as I found comfort in keeping busy, something felt off about not sharing this with him, not telling him when we finalized the event plans or found the perfect venue. Maybe he felt that void, too, and that's why he volunteered in the first place. Today, he finally got to see the result of all he missed in the past month. A terrified part of me hates to admit it, but Cory being here made the event perfect.

CHAPTER THIRTY-FIVE

After all the families have gone home with smiles, financial knowledge, and resources; after the volunteers have left, and we've packed up and cleaned the venue to the best of our ability, the Finance for the Fam crew returns to the office.

We have supplies to take back, all spread out among the three of us with cars. We put the perishables in the fridge; Nia will donate them to our partner homeless shelter on Monday. The snacks that can hold for a while—granola bars, fruit snacks, etc.—are stored in plastic bins for the next event. Aisha is a stickler for organization, which requires us to take our time putting away the resources and miscellaneous supplies.

When everything is stowed and there is nothing left to do, we huddle together by the front desk for an epic celebratory group hug. Aisha is laughing, Pedro is tearing up, Nia is saying how proud she is of us, and I'm thanking them for letting me be part of this. They say wonderful things like, "Don't be a dumbass," and "Corinne, we couldn't have pulled this off without you." That gets me teary-eyed too.

I don't want to go home to my empty apartment after I leave the crew. I call Tiwanda and Elise to see what they're doing. Tiwanda doesn't answer. Elise is at Devin's apartment. Mom answers, eager to hear how everything went. I recap the day as I drive home. I don't omit a single detail, not even Cory's involvement. Photos of the event should be up on the website within a few days to help her visualize it better.

"That's really something, Cori," she tells me as I open the door to my apartment building. "I'm proud of you. Bet Joelle would be too."

I smile. "She's the reason I found this job." I pause to check my mailbox. Anything to delay shutting myself in my apartment for the rest of the day. "My life here so far has been . . . weird."

"To put it mildly," Mom says, chuckling. "What you got going on for the rest of the day?"

"Resting. It'll take me the weekend to recover." With each step up the stairs, I try to reframe my perspective from one of loneliness to relaxation. On the halfway landing I stop short, my eyes trained to the bent figure outside my door. Immediately, I recognize it's Cory, so panic doesn't come. He hurries to straighten. My eyes flick between his face and whatever he's left on the floor.

"I'm sorry I let myself in the building. I didn't want to leave this outside." His arm slightly swings in the direction of his offering. I take a few more steps up, and he shifts enough for me to see it's a manila envelope. I start to ask what's inside, but my mom's voice in my ear causes me to jump.

"Everything all right?" she asks.

"Yeah." I signal to Cory that I'm on a call with a tap on my earpiece.

"Are you going to ask him how he was able to get into the building?"

"He has a key," I mumble.

My mom exhales a stream of words. I'm assuming it's mostly her bemoaning my decision to give him this level of access. I tune out the specifics as Cory distracts me with rare fidgeting. After a bout of internal deliberation, he stoops to pick up the envelope and holds it out to me.

"Momma, I have to go."

I can feel her speculative silence on the other end of the line.

"Handle your business," she says and hangs up.

I meet him at the top of the stairs to accept the nondescript parcel. It's flat except for a small bump at the bottom. I give it a slight shake. The jangling sound of metal, along with the size being on par with a set of keys, makes the panic that didn't show up earlier begin to trickle through my veins. So, we've finally reached a true ending. A line drawn on how our relationship will go from here on out. Apparently, we can't remain friends that double as keepers of spare keys. My mom will be relieved at this update.

"I wrote that for you," Cory says. He regains his confidence under my reproachful gaze.

How thoughtful—he's included a return note along with the keys, I suppose. "Should I read it now?" I start to undo the hooks to open the flap. He places a hand over mine, halting my progress.

"You can read it by yourself. I'm gonna step outside." He holds still for a stretched moment, his eyes unblinking as they connect with mine. Then he pulls away from me and turns to leave. I watch his back descend the staircase, my lips twitching as I recall how he hates watching me read the things he's written. I knew it applied to physical therapy–related articles but not informal notes.

Unlocking the door, I slip into my apartment and toss my bag in the lounge chair. At the kitchen island, I waste no time exploring the contents of the envelope. The keys slide out of the downturned opening. As expected, but it still makes my chest ache. I pull out the accompanying papers. It's a few typed pages long.

Evaluating the sentiment of love: Retrieving and interpreting high quality evidence
Abstract: I messed up and hurt both of us in the process. The way I handled things leaves room for doubt regarding my love for you. Thus, this presentation of my very scientific findings. Participants involved in this study were Corinne Evans and Courtland Mayes.

Method of data gathering largely involved retrospective analysis of past events. This resulted in proving what I'd suspected—I'm in love with you. The data also leaned heavily towards you feeling the same for me, but as it is a one-sided analysis, this was deemed inconclusive pending further data.

I reach my arm behind me to make sure the stool is there in time to correct the direction of my fall onto it. I don't know if I want to laugh, speed-read the rest, or start over from the beginning. To head off getting stuck in a loop of the abstract, I press forward.

Method: Data gathered was collected from March to June of this year. Though not an exhaustive list, I chose markers that, combined, form a wide scope of the relationship we've built. One built, I seek to prove, upon love. Without further ado:

1. I was more content struggling to work in your apartment with you sitting across from me than anyplace else. Even when I had no appointments left for the day and sensibly could have gone home, I found reasons to be with you instead.
2. My first foray into sharing the weight of your world was when you told me about Joelle and the package left behind. That moment is significant for another reason, but it's also the moment I knew I cared for you, deeply.
3. The first time we ate dinner together, and I shared my favorite childhood dessert with you, I imagined having a routine with you.

4. I witnessed you get offered your job in the bathroom, wearing nothing but your birthday suit. I knew then I wanted to be present for all these big moments.

5. Talking about my dad with you felt so easy, nothing like the slight constriction of my airways that happens when I've discussed him with anyone else.

6. We managed to make hair maintenance, a job in and of itself, slightly erotic.

7. My mom and sister both liked you, which has a meager 18.75% probability.

8. Without seeing you regularly, conversing and laughing with you, making love to you . . . I've been, in Tiwanda's words, "a pitiful, pissy mess."

9. I was reluctant to include this, as Met's involvement was the root of opposition on my behalf. However, for scientific purposes, it's necessary. Met is on our side. Its involvement doesn't cast suspicion on the authenticity of our relationship, as previously believed. It affirms it.

My eyes travel back up the list, scanning each "data point" again. When it's laid out like this, it's near impossible to refute the evidence, no matter how shoddy Cory's scientific process might be. As I reread, I find myself adding my own points to supplement his, providing the missing side of this study. They include memories of my early responses to him, like when he popped up and corrected my exercise form. The underdog win we were cheated out of at Elise's Amazing Race to Liberation makes my list because it proves we work well together. Cory's vulnerability encouraged me to be more forthright, like the morning we solidified our status as a couple. Suddenly, me loving Cory doesn't seem inconclusive.

> **Results Summary:** I might have met you two decades ago, but I only got to know you recently. Together, we experienced the moments listed above and many others. This is what comes to mind when I tell you I love you. This is how I know I mean it.
>
> **Conclusion:** You gave me these keys as friends. I'm offering them back to you because I don't know where our relationship stands now. At first, I felt comfort in the fact that I still held them. As if it were a sign the door to what we had could be reopened. But that's for you to decide. I promise if you do choose to regrant me that access, to your life and your heart, I'll never voluntarily walk away from this again. Loving you scared me, made me feel out of control. Still does. But that bit of fear doesn't compare to the rightness of being with you. And it's got nothing on the misery of being without you.

I rest the papers on the countertop and reach for my cell phone, hesitantly pulling up the contact for The Other Cory. Should I call and declare my love? Or maybe text him a formal *Your study has been accepted for publication in the journal of my heart?* I inwardly berate myself for that idea and abandon my phone altogether, snatching up his keys instead. It took me no more than a few minutes to read this, so there's a chance he hasn't left yet.

The landing outside my door is empty, and the only person in the stairwell is my neighbor entering his unit on the first floor. I'm scanning the line of cars through the glass door as I push it open but don't see his SUV. On Saturdays, the street is packed with the cars of people enjoying not having to leave for their weekday jobs. It took perfect arrival timing for me to get a spot out front. Cory could have parked a block away. I step onto the porch, allowing the door's weight to settle against my side. My hope deflates as I realize it would probably be fruitless to pick a direction to travel at random.

"Hey." Cory's voice comes from my left. I startle, so focused on the curbside cars ahead of me, I didn't spare a glance at the corner of the porch where he stands. I let the door close so I can face him without the glass barrier.

"Hey." I lift my chin in greeting, adopting a cool poise. "I had a chance to read your latest article."

He takes a step toward me, and with that movement I'm certain he already knows where this is headed. If my coming after him didn't clue him in, then it must be clearly written in my eager eyes, or how I can't stop the upper half of my body from swaying toward him.

"Yeah? Any feedback?"

"You mentioned the limitations with one-sided data, but I think I can help. That way, my feelings won't be ruled inconclusive."

One of his eyebrows quirks up. I take his hand, put the keys on his palm, and fold his fingers around them. He wraps his free arm around me, pulling me flush against him. Giddy, I laugh into his chest, then tilt my head back. Our lips brush, breaths mingling in anticipation of every exciting thing that lies ahead of us. With sound mind to prevent us from going too far in view of my neighborhood, I step back from him and grasp his hand. I pull him back inside my apartment, back into my life, never intending to let go.

～

My phone chirps from the nightstand, the sharp noise jolting me from my uncomfortable slumber. I have a crick in my neck from lying on Cory's chest. The lamp bathes his profile in amber light. We fell asleep after two in the morning, midconversation. There was a lot to catch each other up on. Our connection has notably changed. Before, we built a foundation upon quicksand. Now, we've found solid ground. This new confidence we have in each other will impact all aspects of our relationship. It's still every bit as exciting as our first attempt. I roll away from him gently to avoid waking him. His arms fall aside, allowing me to reach my phone. The awaiting notification makes my eyes bulge. I swipe to open the app I deleted weeks ago. True to form, it didn't ask my permission to revisit my phone.

Met Tip: . . .

The three dots dawdle, my teeth clenching harder with each passing second. Finally, more words appear.

Following Met Tips could've gotten you here sooner.

I glare at the non-tip and the winking emoji that follows. My mouth falls open as a gust of air escapes my lungs. Sure, there were some missteps, but I figured it out! The Met Tip disappears and is replaced with another message.

Kidding. Good teamwork. I carried us for a while there, but you got it from here.

Cathartic tears spring to my eyes and leak out onto my pillow before I can catch them. Cory turns on his side and reaches an arm out to rest over me, his breathing still deep and sedated. My chest shudders on an elongated inhale. Met might be gone for good after this, but Icelle can never be extinguished.

Thank Met by leaving a rating!

The outline of five stars pops up. A hushed laugh escapes me as I indulgently select five stars. They swoosh around the screen in a shimmering victory lap.

Share Met with a friend?

My eyebrows furrow as the option to Choose from contacts appears at the bottom. I scroll through names and phone numbers I've collected over the years. Some are family, some are friends, others are brief acquaintances I have little memory of. None feel like the right choice until I get farther down the list.

I abruptly stop scrolling and tap Tiwanda's name.

A mischievous grin spreads across my face as I press the confirmation box.

Share Met.

ACKNOWLEDGMENTS

This being my debut, it's impossible not to look back and see a throng of people who had a part in making this dream happen. I hope I'm able to convey how much your support means to me.

First off, all the praise for my agent, Samantha Fabien. I still remember the hopeful feeling I had when reading your MSWL for the first time. Every conversation I've had with you since makes me feel even more hopeful and excited about my writing career. Grateful to have had the LDLA team backing me, along with my #TeamSamantha sibs! Thank you, Alicia Clancy, for seeing the heart of my book so clearly and treating it with care. Working with you and the APub team has been more than I could have imagined.

Joclyn, you are one of my favorite humans and I'm 100 percent sure my mom orchestrated me having you as a best friend. Thank you for inspiring me in so many ways. Keisha, most of the fast-forward part of this journey happened during the wildest pandemic summer with you, Trey, and Joc in Virginia. Long live "Three Sisters and a Baby!" I'm glad they compared our heights in fifth grade. Cathryn, I'm always my goofiest self around you. Thank you for not only believing but also sharing in my vision to become an author. Let's get our girl group going next. Diana, top earner of DM sirens, your Twitter wildin' is second only to your support. My second favorite Guevara—Bri, you're a real one.

My first CP and writing friend, Gaby—we took the leap to put our writing out there at the same time, leading us to meet each other. I love seeing us reach new levels with our writing each year since. Thank you, Casey Harris-Parks, for the plot session that shaped this book and brought it so much closer to my vision. MadCap is one of my favorite memories, and I'm so glad I met you there. Thank you to the amazing Randy Ribay for teaching me how to revise and sharing writing wisdom I apply with every new project.

The Lit Squad! You all bring me so much happiness and laughter. I'm in awe of the talent and passion in our group. I love how we lift each other up with aggressive positivity. True Grit Writers! Thank you, Jessica Conoley, for bringing us all together and teaching us so much. Thank you, Natasha: your positive response to this book during #RevPit readied me to query. Literary Queens, thank you for the constant shenanigans and the late-night Zoom calls that helped me meet my deadlines.

Domonique, you were one of the first people I told I wanted to write books. Thanks for being a great source of comedy. Thank you, Keirra, Asia, Alexandria, and Brianna. My degree from Ohio State might be futile, but the friendships I formed with you all are worth it.

Shout-out to the San Antonio College ITP community! You will always be my interpreting home. Madi, thank you for lending your artistic talent to my website and making me laugh until I cry countless times. Thanks to the rest of our internship crew: Desiree, Linda Rose, Pamela, and Rupal. You all not only supported me with my interpreting endeavors but with this too. Jessica Franks, for all our art and writing chats. Alicia Uecker, my fellow signer/writer, thank you for your encouragement and bright spirit. Also, thank you to my Chicago interpreting fam, especially Nate and Kaylyn for always checking on my writer life.

This book is largely about carrying loved ones who have passed with us, so I would be remiss not to give thanks to Mom, Grandma, and Auntie Budgie for guiding me. I'm fortunate to have a family that fills the gaps of these losses with love and encouragement. Grandmother, I know you're my dedication, but thank you for all the hours spent on opposite ends of the couch. I know you'll promote my books even more than you did my Girl Scout cookies two decades ago. My fellow grandkids, we may jostle each other in the unofficial grandkid ranking, but you all are like siblings. William, my brother, I'm beyond fortunate to have you as a partner in childhood. You're the only man's initials I'll ever have tatted on me. Ashleigh, thank you for clowning me by often asking, "Is this the same book you were writing before?" It never was. Thank you, Brendyn, for trolling me with your obstinate belief in my first-ever somewhat-completed book from seven years ago. D'Aun, thanks for always sharing my love of stories.

My source of strength is my aunts and uncles. Thanks for the countless hours you spent with me at the kitchen table while I wrote, Auntie Mella. Back in high school, I wanted to downgrade Pre-AP Spanish, and you wouldn't let me. Thank you for teaching me to not quit on myself. Auntie Rejara, you set examples of patience and consideration constantly. Thanks for advising me on all things Chicago. Rayya, where would I be without you hyping me up and challenging me to think outside the box? Thank you, Auntie Janet, for the singing, humor, and openness I get from you. Uncle Eric, for so many enlightening chats and good vibes. Uncle Theo, the impact you've had by being the father figure in my life is immeasurable. Much love to Uncle Mike, Farid, Dad, and Uncle Stanley. My godmother and namesake, Michelle, thank you for the support. Thank you, cousins Monzie, Dionne, Misty, Rosemary, and Juan. I want to party with you all for the rest of my life.

ABOUT THE AUTHOR

Photo © 2020 Joclyn Torain

Camille Baker earned a bachelor's degree in finance from The Ohio State University. There, she took sign language classes for fun and wrote stories during business classes that didn't hold her interest. After graduating, she completed the interpreter training program at San Antonio College. Camille now resides, interprets, and writes in South Chicago. For more information visit www.camillebaker.com.